The Tainted Wars

Awakening

W. J. Grupe Jr

Twin Pines Publishing

ISBN (Paperback) 9781952662027
ISBN (Paperback) 9781952662010
ISBN (Ebook) 9781952662003

For Marie.
Without your love and support this book, and all the ones to follow, would never be possible.

The Tainted Wars

Awakening

W. J. Grupe Jr.

Chapter One

M Y LIFE CHANGED IN a small town with a small church while attending my cousin's wedding. Or was it my second cousin? Second cousin once removed? Whatever. I was getting out of my rented Bronco and into the oppressive heat of an August morning. If that wasn't bad enough, I was crammed into a suit that brought back memories of my old Army Ranger dress uniform. I was hot, uncomfortable, and in upstate New York.

The only time a true Manhattanite wants to head upstate is when they are picking apples or pumpkins. Something needs to be picked besides noses. The only thing I was looking forward to was the hotel. We were staying at the Susquehanna Hotel and I was determined to find the hat company before I left. I love Abbot and Costello. Jackie did too, but I doubted she still would after this trip.

"Why the hell did you have to rent this monstrosity?" Jackie asked as she lowered herself down from the high perch.

She was trying desperately to climb down without giving the world a crotch shot. She was wearing what she referred to as an LBD—short for 'little black dress.' She looked stunning in it, though claustrophobic.

"That's what you get for telling me on the way that the wedding you've invited me to is actually my cousin's."

"The look on your face was priceless."

Jackie Townsend had long black tresses, an hourglass figure, and hazel eyes. She's still the most beautiful woman I'd ever seen, and I've been in love with her since the fourth grade.

"I hope there are some horny single women. If I don't hook up soon, somebody's gonna get hurt," she said.

Oh, and did I mention she's gay?

Jackie hit the blacktop of the parking lot like a gymnast sticking a landing and grinned.

"Where is the bridge?" I asked.

Her smile disappeared. "This again?"

"I'm sorry, but if you are going to name a place Chenango Bridge, there needs to be a bridge."

"We drove over it when we got off the highway," Jackie replied. "That was no bridge, that was a road on stilts. A bridge has massive cables and those structures that look like bowlegged women straddling the road."

"Those are suspension bridges. The bow-legged women, a description that highlights way too many personal issues, are called towers. This one was a beam bridge. Why are they women, anyway?"

"Because if they were men, their dangly bits would mess with traffic."

Jackie shook her head. "Idiot."

"For God's sake, this town--"

"Hamlet."

"What about Hamlet? I am talking about the bridge."

"No, you were talking about the town. It's not a town, it's a hamlet."

"Fine, the hamlet, or whatever, was named after the bridge," I said.

"And if that was the only bridge, then it was the most anticlimactic namesake ever."

"What did you want, the Golden Gate Bridge in two square miles? Now shut up about it before you embarrass me," Jackie said as we approached the doors to the church.

"How can I embarrass you? They're my family and you barely know them. Hell, I barely know them. They only invited me because they were confident I'd say no, but would still get credit for asking. I still don't know why you did this."

"Because you suck at relationships and you need to start by building some with family. Now shut up!"

The last was growled through clenched teeth as we approached the parents of the bride, who were greeting guests as they came in—Jackie with her usual bright smile and me with anything but.

The father of the bride glanced up and unsuccessfully suppressed a scowl.

"Christian." He made the name seem like an accusation as he extended a hand. "Been a long time."

"Chaz, not long enough, right? So, you married one of them off? How many goats did it take?"

"Hilarious, and it's Charles if you please," he retorted.

He was dressed like a nineteenth century aristocrat, complete with ascot the color of his wife's dress. He even had a top hat. I couldn't constrain my outward chuckle. The only thing he was missing was a monocle.

"I was surprised when I received your acceptance response."

I was going to say, I'm sure you were, but Jackie's elbow prevented most of it from getting out.

"We would not have missed it for the world. I'm Jackie, Christian's friend, and I apologize for his lousy sense of humor. He thinks he's funny no matter how much I try to convince him of the contrary."

Charles' smile returned and he shook Jackie's extended hand. "Well, hopefully you will be able to dissuade him one day. May I present my wife, Tricia," he said, motioning to the woman on his right, who was absolutely beaming.

"I think I remember you," Tricia mused. "You used to come with Christian occasionally when he and his family came up to visit."

"Yes! I can't believe you remember that."

"Your visits were a treat for me. I used to hate those weeks. Christian used to follow us around, causing no end of trouble. When you came with him, he had someone else to torture."

I thought back to those times when Mom used to drag us to their enormous house on Lake George. It had been handed down over three generations. Because of it, they had this image of themselves as part of the upper crust of society. It was far from the truth. The origin of their upper middle-class fortune came from manure. They've expanded into other areas since then, and—don't get me wrong—I have nothing against cow dung. But it's not what you stand on while looking down on people. I mentally detached myself from the rest of the conversation as I ruminated further on the lack of the bridge.

The church seemed even smaller on the inside, with room for maybe six people across on each side. I was surprised by how bright it was. The churches I remembered from my youth all seemed to be made from the same forest of dark trees, which had the innate ability to suck out the light and joy from the place. Then again, I was seven at the time.

We were ushered to our seats, or pews, or whatever, and the ceremony began shortly thereafter. Samantha and Matt—Jackie had to remind me of their names—appeared to be as happy as a couple could be. The two of them lit a central candle from their individual ones, which in turn were lit by their parents. I had to admit it was touching. It lulled me off into a comfortable state which was cut short by another elbow to the ribs.

"I was just resting my eyes." I said, while rubbing my side. "Okay, Grandpa. Tell that to your snoring."

I glanced around to see at what point we were in the mass. Ah, religious snack time. I recognized communion from my youth when Mom was still alive, and was amazed at how vividly I could recall it. I was dressed very much as I was now (without the accompanying claustrophobic feeling), standing next to my mother as she explained the meaning behind everything going on. How the priest washed away his sins with holy water before initiating the ceremony. How the small drop of holy water in the cup of wine represented Christ's first miracle. All the little details that she would relate nearly every Sunday, as though she hadn't just done it the week before.

I remembered the reverence in her voice as she spoke in a near whisper to avoid disturbing the people around us. The two voices merged in my head. The priest's traditional litany, and my mother's whisper fleshing out what was unsaid. It had always put me in a semi-hypnotic state.

Now, unbidden, her voice came back to me. It laced itself with the Episcopalian priest as he, like the Roman Catholic priest of my past, brought the ceremony to its climax. This time, however, something was different. The priests I remembered sounded almost bored with repeating these same words for the ninth time that weekend, whereas Father Mike held more of the love and reverence that my mother had so many years ago. The two monologues flowed together into a liturgy, and I found myself locked between the past and the present. All other sounds and activity disappeared for me. There was only the external source of Father Mike and my mother's internal voice.

"While they were eating, Jesus took bread and blessed it."

We always give thanks to the Lord, for He provides for all our needs.

"He broke the bread, gave it to his disciples and said, take this all of you and eat it. This is my body which will be given up for you."

He gave up everything for us. His very body was sacrificed for our souls.

"Do this in memory of me."

The altar server picked up a set of brass bells and gave it a shake three times, with a slight pause in between each.

CHIME!

God, be praised for your gift.

CHIME!

Jesus, be praised for your sacrifice.

CHIME!

Holy Spirit, be with us always.

"When supper was ended, He took the cup..." Father Mike continued.

The cup Jesus used was much simpler but cherished none the less, for it came from Him.

"... again, He gave you thanks and praise."

Thanks to the Almighty for all that we have, all that we see, and all whom we love. For only through His will are they possible.

"He gave the cup to His disciples and said, take this all of you and drink from it. This is the cup of My blood—the blood of the new and everlasting covenant."

We are that Covenant, the defenders of His faith.

"It will be shed for you and for all men so that sins may be forgiven."

We are all flawed. We are all sinners, but the Father loves us, regardless.

"Do this in memory of me."

CHIME!

God, be praised for your gift.
CHIME!
Jesus, be honored for your sacrifice.
 CHIME!
Holy Spirit, be with us always.

Something clicked in me and my breath caught. Light flooded my vision, and my hands shook slightly as Father Mike continued in a more conversational tone.

"If you are of another faith and wish to take part in communion, you are welcome."

This was different from the church from my past; there was no welcoming in the church I remembered. My mind drifted above the congregation, beyond the mass. I was in a fog, one that separated me but augmented the experience.

"If you haven't been to mass this year, you are welcome. If you have not been to mass in many years, you are welcome. If you have never received before, you are welcome."

The sense of belonging touched me in a way I could not describe, nor ignore. It pulled at me, called to me. I took a deep breath, trying to clear my head. The incense filled my senses, somehow increasing what I was feeling. Connections to the past I'd lost years, even decades ago, came flooding back. They pounded on me like the waves against an old dock. I stood as the pew ahead finished filing out—a Pavlovian response.

I followed the person in front of me, still in a trance-like state. My hands automatically folded in prayer, an act remembered from a life long forgotten. My conscious mind barely acknowledged the confused whispers coming from Jackie behind me. No one else shared in Jackie's bewilderment. To them, I was just another lemming following the dinner bell. I passed my cousin, whose dark look and mumbled words rippled through the surrounding people. My disconnection from the church was well known in my family. Father Mike's invitation didn't align with their beliefs. But even my dour cousin could not penetrate the aura that spurred me forward.

I reached the priest and looked into his eyes, but it was my mother's eyes that stared back at me—a shocking blue, which her full image coalesced around.

She stood there in her blue and white dress, the color making her eyes all the more luminescent. Her blonde hair fell in tresses past her shoulder. Her smile gleamed with happiness. She held out the host to me.

"The body of Christ."

"Amen," came my response, as though it was the most natural thing—like saying thank you.

My mother placed the wafer in my upturned, cupped hands. A warmth flowed from my palm through my arm. The hairs all over my body stood up and I could feel waves of power rippling them as if I was standing in a wind tunnel. I imagined this is what it would be like to hold a piece of plutonium in your hand. Putting the host on my tongue, it dissolved, sinking quickly into my bloodstream. There was a flood of heat and my eyes dilated, causing the light in the church to become blinding. A shock, like one receives when touching an exposed outlet, shot through me. My back arched and my muscles tighten. My teeth chattered, and my feet came free of the floor.

I hovered as my mother looked down on me, the blurred form of the crucifix silhouetted behind her and framed in a blazing light.

"Welcome home my son. It has been a long time," she said. Her voice was no longer distant but full, as if she stood there in the flesh. She smiled again, then disappeared. Reality slammed back into place. My mother was replaced by Father Mike. The congregation came back into focus. My body, which hovered no more than a quarter of an inch off the floor, dropped onto muscles that were not ready to handle their weight. I fell to my hands and knees and everything went dim. My ears felt as if someone had stuffed them with cotton, blocking out everything except for a throbbing, high-pitched tone.

When the ringing stopped, and my vision cleared, I looked up at the priest. He gave a slight nod, put his hand on my head, and said very quietly so only I could hear, "Lord, welcome your new Knight of the Cloth and guide him on his path."

With that, he made the sign of the cross on my forehead, then slap me with a resounding crack that set me back on my ass.

Chapter Two

THE TRANSITION INTO SEPTEMBER brought with it the long overdue shift in weather. My days were dedicated to keeping old furnaces running well past their useful years or installing new units where the old ones had finally given up the ghost. But I was mostly dealing with cold, unhappy customers that weren't keen to pay the exorbitant fees needed to keep their houses at a nice, comfy temperature.

"No, Mr. Johnson, there is no union discount on central air units. Yes, Mrs. Harris, I completely agree that the maintenance fees are too high, but that is corporate policy and there is nothing I can do about it."

That last was a lie, I am corporate. I started the company quite accidentally after I got out of the army and started helping some older people in my apartment building. I had only one policy. The work covered is directly proportional to a client's age and politeness. I made most of my money from twenty-something asshats.

"Hey, Chris, almost done?" asked Ms. Popov.

With her accent, my name sounded more like *Kreese*. I don't go by Chris or *Kreese*, but I was brought up with the idea that the customer is always right. Not to mention I tried correcting her the first two hundred times, then eventually gave up.

"Just finishing up."

"You stay after, have drink."

It was a statement, not a question. This was a dance we did every time she called me to come service her—and I meant to say it that way. I had no idea if she would follow through on any of the multiple double entendres she threw at me. Some of them couldn't even be labeled as such, more of a non-tendre. She's actually very attractive for a woman in her seventies. In her prime, I doubt any man said no to her.

"You know I would love to, Ms. Popov, but I have other clients I need to take care of."

"Call me Nadia. Screw other clients. You stay here and take care of me."

See what I mean, non-tendre.

I packed up my tools and extracted myself from Ms. Popov's apartment—and her grasp—but not before she shoved a tip in my pocket. She's elderly and on a budget, so it was a Lincoln. Oh, and it was my front pocket. I guess my continued, honest interest in her life is what encouraged her to shove small bills in my pants.

I walked back to the truck five dollars richer, smiling at the paint job as I opened the back double doors and hung my tools. I named the heating and cooling business Miser Brothers. One half of the truck was painted red and orange to look like the land of the Heat Miser; the other half depicted the land of his brother, the Snow Miser. On both the hood and back doors, the two brothers were at constant war—one shooting flames from his finger, the other an ice storm. Truth be told, I named the business that because I thought the idea for the truck would be awesome. I was right and smiled at it every time. It never got old. Unfortunately, the name also had people constantly asking where my brother was. Oh, and if you've never seen *The Year Without a Santa Claus*, I'm not sure we can talk anymore.

I slammed the door closed and was startled by a man standing behind it. "Geez, you scared the crap out of me!"

"My apologies, Mr. Bateleur. I didn't mean to startle you."

The mystery man was dressed in the typical uniform of a Hasidic Jew, so I immediately ruled out Jehovah's witness trying to show me the way.

"I'm sorry, have we met?" I asked. "Not before now," he replied.

"So, how do you know my name?"

"It is a somewhat complicated story, for which I would like to discuss if you have the time."

He had a subtle accent that placed him in England in his youth. I thought all these guys were supposed to sound like characters from *Fiddler on the Roof.*

"Sorry, Mr..."

"Hager."

"Mr. Hager, but I am really busy; and, unless you can breathe life into the twelve-year-old furnace at my next call, I am afraid I can't spare the time for a complicated story," I said, making my way back to the driver's door. This guy was obviously a salesman and I had little tolerance for them.

"Mr. Bateleur, this is actually very important," Mr. Hager said, following me.

"Are you here to tell me that someone is in the Long Island Jewish Hospital?"

"Heavens, no!" He exclaimed.

"Did I win something?"

"Well, not quite."

"Do I owe someone money?"

"How about the bum you stole your clothes from?"

I hopped in the driver's seat and started the car, ignoring his burn. "Then I'm sorry, Mr. Hager, you will just need to make an appointment with the main office."

I slammed the transmission into drive and pulled away from the curb until something caught my ear and made me stomp on the brakes, screeching to a stop. I stuck my head out the window. "What did you say?"

"I said your mother sent me."

"Really Mr. Bateleur, if I would just be allowed to explain—"

"I told you, not until I have coffee."

"For a man who claimed not to have time to talk before, you seem to have found enough of it to walk to the nearest coffee shop," Mr. Hager complained.

"There are certain things you simply don't do unless you have either a beer, scotch, or coffee in your hand. Normally the top of that list is breaking up, but break ups have just been trumped—damn, I need to stop using that phrase—they've just been beat out by whatever this is."

I accepted the white cup of black coffee with my name written on it and walked over to the nearest empty table. Mr. Hager sat down across from me, folded his hands on the table and waited patiently while I ritualistically inhaled the aroma of my coffee, then took a hesitant sip. I closed my eyes for a second as I reveled in the rich, earthy flavor. After a deep sigh, I glanced across at him and said, "Okay, what is this crap about my mother sending you?"

"I did not mean that in the literal sense."

"No shit." It was not a question. Mr. Hager cringed.

"Please, Mr. Bateleur, the language."

"Sorry. Habit," I said, honestly apologetic. This was obviously a very religious man. Although I rarely bought into that stuff (despite the hallucination I experienced back in the church), my mother taught me to be respectful of those who did. My mind went back to that afternoon in the church, an experience which no amount of alcohol had been able to erase. I shook my head to clear it.

"Apology accepted," Mr. Hager said, then continued as if he had not interrupted. "She, in fact, requested that I contact you once your initiation was completed through your First Communion."

"I never received my First Communion," I said. "Precisely. Until now—or should I say August."

"Wait, how can you know about that? Were you there? Have you been following me?"

"Please, Mr. Bateleur, I have far more important things to concern myself with than following you around to see if you would ever enter a place of worship again."

"Then how did you know?"

"Father Mike notified me."

"Of course, how can I be so stupid?"

"I have wondered the same myself as of late."

"What?!"

"Mr. Bateleur, if you will allow me to continue without interruption, we will get through this much more quickly. Then you can deny all of it and I can be on my way."

I looked at the stern-faced man, whose white beard would make Santa jealous. Another quip came to mind, but for some reason, I swallowed it with some more coffee.

Mr. Hager inclined his head slightly and continued. "Your mother belonged to a quasi-religious sect that is unknown to the general population. It is made up of people of many belief structures, whose common connection is their desire to defend those unable to defend themselves. Membership is passed down from parent to child and initiated at specific coming of age rituals. Yours was your First Communion. However, as you pointed out, your father did not continue your religious education after your mother passed. Subsequently, your initiation did not occur until you took communion at your cousin's wedding."

"I am very confused."

"Of that, I have no doubt. Suffice to say, you are now a member of The Covenant of Bishops with all rights, privileges, and requirements that are associated with it."

Mr. Hager stood up, reached into his inside jacket pocket, withdrew a business card, and dropped it onto the table.

"I am afraid that is all the time *I* have right now, since you wasted most of it supporting your coffee habit. If you wish to discuss this further, please contact me."

With that, he turned to leave. I picked up the card and examined it. It was completely white with a gold chess piece centered on the front: a bishop. I turned it over to find that the rest of the card was blank.

"Hey, how am I supposed to get in touch with you?"

I looked up but saw only the door closing. Jumping up and grabbing my coffee, I followed Mr. Hager out into the street, but he was nowhere to be seen. What the hell? How could I possibly lose this guy in the middle of Little Italy

Chapter Three

"N ooooo"
"Aw, what the hell, man?"
"You suck! Find another job!"
"How the hell did he walk another one?"

Those were the mellow versions of the mass insults being thrown around at the bar. I added my own, then took a pull from my beer. This is one of those times I wondered, again, why I was a Mets fan. People crowded around the big projection screen, or one of the other twenty TVs in the place. Baseball, pizza, burgers, ribs, and beer. What else could one ask for?

"I told you he was brought up too fast. His slider is magical but inconsistent," Jackie said.

I looked over at her, completely enthralled. Her black hair was pulled into a ponytail and stuck out of the back of a Mets cap. Apart from Jackie being a senior executive at a marketing firm and highly intelligent, she was also a Mets fanatic. She picked up her phone.

"Shit, I have to go."

"That thing you mentioned?"

"It's a marketing luncheon with Macy's. Why don't you come?"

"Yeah, I don't think so."

"What are you going to do, go back to your apartment and read?"

"Anything wrong with that?"

"Because of extra innings, I don't have time to explain them all. You need to get out of the house."

I looked around, feigning confusion.

"I mean on a date with someone besides your gay best friend."

"Yeah, yeah. I get out of the house with other people."

"Really? When was the last time?"

I opened my mouth to answer, only to realize that I couldn't remember.

"Point, Jackie," she said in a self-congratulatory way. "I'm not a loner."

"No argument, but you have to admit you don't tolerate people all that well."

I shrugged and grunted in response. "What about Beth?"

"Who?"

She pointed in the direction of the bar.

"The bartender?"

"Yeah. We have been coming here for years, and she flirted with you for the first two. Then she finally gave up."

"Have you ever heard the expression 'don't crap where you eat'?"

"Why not? She and I hooked up awhile back and she never spit in my beer."

"That you know of. Wait, hold up. You had sex with Beth?"

"Keep your voice down, you moron."

I repeated the question in a whisper. Then added, "I didn't know she was gay."

"She's not."

"But you said—"

"You really need to get with the times. It was what it was. No more, no less. Not everything needs a label."

"Okay, fine. Is there a point to this besides that I'm stuck in the past?"

"Yes. Up to now she was Beth, the bartender. You put her in a little box, she was the one that poured your drinks. Safely tucked into her spot in your life. The only way she can be more is for you to open yourself up to the possibility. To accept that people can be more than one thing to you, and to allow yourself to make a connection."

"Any reason you are trying to get me to hook up with the bartender?"

She cuffed me on the side of the head.

"Not hook up, you ass. And it's Beth, remember. I want you to expand your circle of friends. Real friends, not acquaintances."

"I don't tolerate people very well."

"That's because you don't give them a chance."

She stood up and downed the rest of her beer. Then she kissed me on the cheek and made her way to the door, calling back, "Text me what happens."

"Of course," I replied. Then I wondered if she meant Beth or the game.

She exchanged a few words with the bartender—Beth—and they both laughed. I assumed it was at my expense. Then Jackie bounced out of the bar, riding her unending reservoir of energy. If the luncheon was like most of her other functions, she would be gone the rest of the day. I tossed back the last of my beer and ordered another from a passing waitress—this one was new, so it's not my fault for not knowing her name, sign or sexual preference.

A few minutes later, she returned with my next draft. I prefer to pay for each drink as they arrive. It lets me get up and walk out without waiting for the convenience of the bar staff. I counted out the bills and was about to place it on her small round tray when I considered taking Jackie's advice. My whole body flushed and a bead of sweat rolled down my spine. What the hell.

"I'm sorry, what was your name again?"

Her expression changed, probably assuming a clunky pickup line was coming for the fifteenth time today. She pasted on a fake smile and said, "Ali."

Okay, now what? "Ali, right," awkward pause. "Thanks." I placed the money on the tray.

She hesitated another second, then walked away looking confused. I glanced back at the bar. Beth was smiling and shaking her head. Baby steps, I thought to myself.

I grabbed a handful of peanuts, throwing them into my mouth one at a time. Sipping at my beer, I tried to refocus on the game. A figure caught my eye out the window and I nearly choked on a nut.

That could not have been who I thought it was. I carried my barely touched beer up to the bar.

"Hey Beth."

She looked surprised at my use of her name. "Hey Christian, everything okay?"

She didn't shorten my name to Chris as everyone seems to want to do. Why hadn't I noticed before?

"Yeah, I just thought I saw someone that I need to talk to. Can you keep this on ice for me? I'll be right back."

"Sure," she said with a smile. "No problem."

She took the beer behind the bar, and I headed for the door. That had to be Mr. Hager—how many people dressed like him were walking around this neighborhood? I mean, sure, there are probably a few, but none that I had ever seen. I exited through the glass door, turned right, and started scanning the crowd. Sure enough, I caught sight of the top of his black hat about a block up.

I wasn't even sure why I was following him. After all, he was probably just some crazy old man that claimed to have known my mother and be part of a secret religious organization—one which included both a Hasidic Jew and a Roman Catholic. Yeah, that made sense. Or he was stalking me for undetermined reasons. Father Mike may have contacted him for some reason after my incident. But how did he know that it was the first time I received Communion? Han referred to Obi-Wan as a crazy old man once, and he was one of the most powerful Jedi that ever lived. I wasn't sure if that idiom applied, but it solidified my resolve, and I pushed harder through the Sunday evening Manhattan crowd.

My quarry took a quick right into an alley up ahead, disappearing from view. It took me less than a minute before I reached the spot and turned to follow. The alley, however, was empty except for a dumpster and some trash cans, each strategically placed next to doors that served as supplemental entrances to several establishments.

"Ok, where did he go?" I said to no one in particular.

It didn't seem plausible that he could have walked to the other end before I got there. But, just to be sure, I jogged the length anyway. I poked my head out, stood on tiptoe, and checked all directions for any bobbing black hats. Nothing.

Making my way back, I got lost in thought trying to determine where Mr. Hager might have gone. When I finally picked my head up, I was staring at a figure dressed in a black sari. She was slight of build, and shorter than me. She stood unmoving, head tilted down, hands clasped behind her back. Her hair was buzzed on the sides but full on top, and stirred slightly in the breeze. She looked to be of Indian descent, but I doubted my ethnic identification expertise. The figure said nothing, though seemed aware of my presence.

"Excuse me, did you see a crazy old guy come through here?" I asked. The figure twitched her head at that, finding it noteworthy, but did not immediately respond. I got the uncanny feeling that she was scanning the area without looking around. She looked to be something out of a comic book. In short, she was creepy.

"No, I did not see Mr. Hager come in here. If I did, you would have found him lying in a pool of his own blood."

Definitely creepy, with a good helping of disturbing emotional issues.

"Okay, that's a little dramatic don't you think? What did he do, screw up your boyfriend's bris?"

"Do you think you're funny?" she asked with a slight hiss in her voice. Was she seriously going for a full-on manga persona?

"Actually, yes. Although some of my ex-girlfriends tended to disagree. But, hey, what do they know?"

"Where is the old man?" She definitely hissed this time.

"Uh, remember, I asked you?" I said with that 'you're a moron,' tone to my voice, the one Jackie hated. "Listen, if you don't know where he is and I don't know where he is, then we're probably not really useful to each other. So not that this conversation hasn't been a little slice of heaven, but I need to be going."

I was just about to check a door when the woman blurred. That was the only way to describe what I saw before I was flat on my back. She had one knee on my chest, and something sharp was at my throat. I didn't remember falling. I could feel what I assumed was a knife pulling at my skin and knew that if I moved, it would draw blood.

"I will ask you once again. If I don't like your answer, you will not like the consequences," she said.

My mind raced, but I just couldn't stop thinking about Daffy Duck saying 'consequences, schmonsequences.' Why did stress always make me think of *Looney Toons?*

"Where is Amram Hager?"

This hiss went up a few octaves, more akin to a scream from someone with asthma. My Ranger training was spurring me to rip off her arm and throttle her with it, but the chances of throwing her off before she cut my throat seemed slim. She didn't appear that large, but she felt like an elephant sitting on my chest. Like she was made of lead. I was thinking this would not end well when another blur came into view and hit the woman, sending her sprawling into the dumpster and creating a massive dent in the steel side.

The blur solidified into Mr. Hager. "I'm right here, little one."

He offered his hand to me. I accepted, rubbing my throat as I climbed to my feet.

"Thanks," I said, "both for the hand and the rescue."

"Well, you do have some manners after all. You are quite welcome. Now please get back before you get hurt." Mr. Hager replied.

"Hey, I had her right where I wanted her."

"Yes, I am sure her knife was very concerned about your throat staining its surface."

Before I could come back with a crushing reply, I heard a rustling where the crazy anime woman landed. She didn't groan, grunt, huff, or even curse. She just stood up, took the 'I am a badass' stance and brushed dirt off her sari. I had to admit, it looked cool.

"So, old man, is this your new protégé?" She was back to her hiss of a voice.

"Hardly, he is supposed to be fixing my air conditioner," Mr. Hager said dismissively. "You know how hard it is to find good help these days."

"Hey!" I retorted.

"Oh, shut up, fool." She flipped a hand upwards as though shooing a fly. Something hit me, and I found myself on my back once again. I was feeling a little picked on. Not a feeling I was used to and I was getting a little pissed.

I lifted my head up in time to see the two standing off. Had I not known firsthand what she was capable of, the scene would have been comical. Mr. Hager standing well over six feet with the hat, staring down a woman whose height probably capped out at around five-two. That, however, is where the comedic aspect ended. Despite her size, the woman practically crackled with contained rage. The ordinarily congenial, although insulting, Mr. Hager also had an aura of danger about him I would have associated with a fellow Ranger in the midst of a fire fight.

She slowly reached into the folds of her clothes and produced another knife, sporting a wide grin.

"Still out of synch with your environment, I see," Hager said in the voice of a teacher chiding a student. His words turned her smile into a sneer that could have snapped nails.

She launched into an attack, blurring straight at Hager. He fell back and flicked his hands, batting away her advance. I was having a hard time even following the fight from my comfy hiding place—that is flat on my back, surrounded by garbage on the dirty alley floor. I figured, why bother getting up if I was just going to get knocked down again? Aw crap, now I'll never get that song out of my head.

Three more blurs and three more parries. Mr. Hager, his long coat billowing behind him, flowed into a double palm strike that threw her back a few steps before she regained her footing. Growling again, she blurred straight at him. This time, the tall man pivoted, redirecting her momentum into the wall behind him—but not before one of her knives cut a long line across his stomach, slicing several layers of fabric but nothing else.

"You're getting slow, old man," she hissed as she climbed back to her feet.

"Yes, quite. My wardrobe shutters at your speed."

"Prepare to bleed," she growled and flipped the knives dramatically. Her next move was interrupted as something fell from the sky. It was a woman, and it was more like she floated. As she descended, her long, straight black hair flowed around her freely as though she was underwater. A middle-aged Chinese woman landed lightly next to Hager as though she were on strings. She was wearing a muted yellow, modern version of a Chinese suit, with frog buttons and all.

It was stitched with red flowers down one side of her tunic, across her abdomen, and then down the opposite leg.

It was now two against one, and Hager's attacker was clearly not happy with the new odds.

"So, you need backup from the chatterbox," she said.

This elicited a string of what I assume were Mandarin curses, based on the expression on the faces of both Hager and the violent Indian woman. In response to being insulted, she put both knives away, turned and grabbed the dented dumpster, then launched it straight at yours truly. *Tub Thumping* played in my mind as I watched the massive steel box hurtle toward me.

The new arrival blurred toward me and shielded me with her body while Mr. Hager leaped up and collided with the airborne dumpster. He deflected it just enough so that it only hit a glancing blow on the woman protecting me. Still, it must have felt akin to being clipped by a fast-moving car.

I looked up into the woman's eyes as she stood over me, her bosom uncomfortably close to my face.

"Uh, thanks."

"You are very welcome," she said with a wink and only a hint of an accent.

"Misses?" I didn't want to refer to her as chatterbox after she literally put herself in harm's way for me.

"Yuan," she said. "But please call me Soon-Li."

"Soon-Li," I repeated.

"Now that introductions have been made," Mr. Hager added as he approached, "we should be going."

"You are going to just walk away after that? What about..." But the attacker was gone. "Wait, where did she go?"

"She made her escape while we were busy saving your life again," Hager said. "Now we will never find out what she was doing in this part of town. If you hadn't blundered in announcing our presence, we could have followed her discreetly to whatever her goal was."

"How can you follow anyone discreetly dressed like that?"

"I was hidden from her sight. But she will be more cautious next time," he said while looking around the area. A long string of Mandarin came pouring out of Soon-Li again. He replied, "Yes, that's possible, but we will never know for sure. We should leave before she returns with others. I suggest you do the same, Mr. Bateleur."

"At least tell me who she is," I asked.

"Kali. She is extremely dangerous, so if you come across her again, my suggestion would be to run and find people. She will not want to draw attention to herself and her abilities."

"Speaking of which..." I struggled for the words to encompass what had just occurred. I could only wave my arms and say, "What the hell?"

"Hell is actually not far off, but you would not comprehend beyond that, even if I had the time or inclination to enlighten you," Mr. Hager chided.

"But you said I was a member of some cult."

"It is not a cult, and apparently I was wrong."

"What's that supposed to mean?"

"It means that you have not chosen us and, until you do, there is nothing I can do for you," Hager said, exasperated.

"How do I do that? What does that even mean?" I asked.

"How is simple, follow your faith. You will understand my advice when you do."

Mr. Hager turned and walked out of the alley. Soon-Li turned to me and grabbed both my hands, looking deep into my eyes.

"It was so nice to see you again, Christian. Please follow Hager's advice and seek us out. It has been too long, and you need to come home."

Soon-Li's eyes glistened, and she blinked several times as she turned to follow him, leaving me standing among the strewn garbage from the dumpster. I was too shocked to follow them, and I had a feeling that the attempt would have been fruitless. Walking back to the bar, those two statements kept repeating over and over in my head: 'follow your faith' and 'come home.' I cleaned up in the washroom and finished my beer. Then followed it up with several more.

Chapter Four

CLICK.

'If you act now, you can have the grand sucker three-thousand for three easy payments of—'

Click.

'The only way you can stay on the island is to eat this stink bug.'

Click.

'John, how can you do this to me? And with my own mother!'

Sunday afternoon TV sucks. Thank God for sports.

I switched back to the game. While between channels, the screen went black, becoming a large ineffective mirror. A small white rectangle appeared dead center before the next commercial came on. I turned in my recliner. The reflection had come from the white card propped up on the small table by the door. Getting up, I retrieved it and brought it back to for further examination. I wasn't sure what I was looking for. I had puzzled over it many times in the weeks since my run-in with the dumpster destroyers. The only thing of note was that it was made of soft plastic instead of the standard card stock.

What the hell was this card supposed to tell me? What was it that guy said? Follow your faith? What was that supposed to mean? I didn't have faith in many things, except maybe the home team and the pastrami on rye from *Eisenberg's*.

My mind wandered back to the wedding months ago, and the image of my mother. I could still call it up in all its clarity, though I did my best to forget it. My mother, long dead, smiling at me. Her hair was longer than I'd remembered. Her blue eyes were clear and bright. I hadn't known her eye color. None of the pictures I had were close enough to tell. I squeezed my eyes shut trying to clear my mind, and looked up at the TV. Still commercials, of course—this one was trying to get you to believe that the oil-based product they were selling tasted just like butter. The following ad depicted some guy balancing hard financial times, fighting with his spouse, and being yelled at by his boss. After a trip to church, though, everything was looking up, and he returned with a smile on his face.

"*Even when times are at their darkest, when you follow your faith, you walk an enlightened path.*"

I jerked my attention to the screen. The game came on. Scooping up the remote, I rewound the live TV a few seconds to hear the soft-spoken woman repeat the cheesy line. I glanced at the card and considered the idea, which I was already acknowledging as stupid. Ah, what the hell? This game was pretty much over, anyway. I clicked the power button and headed for the shower. If I was going to church, I wasn't doing so wearing sweatpants. Mom would reach out from the grave and smack me upside my head. A half hours later, I stood in front of Saint Peters, staring up at the marble steps and columns, which highlighted the Roman part of the church's heritage. I skipped the full suit this time and selected a nice dress shirt and pants. My mother would forgive the slight, seeing as there would not be a mass going on at this hour. I didn't know what was making me hesitate. Shaking my head at my foolishness, I walked to the stairs. As my foot touched the first step, I felt the hairs on the back of my neck rise. I rubbed them into silence and continued upwards. There wasn't an active mass, but I wasn't alone either. A few people were milling about, lighting candles, and the confessional was open. Dipping my fingers in the holy water, I made the sign of the cross. The action was so ingrained that I hadn't even realized I was doing it until it was done. The place the water had touched my skin seemed unusually cold and I rubbed at my forehead. Meandering down the center aisle, I chose a pew at random, and sat.

The hardwood bench was uncomfortable but not excessively so and smooth under my touch—thanks to decades of reverent attendees (or their less respectful, more antsy children). The warm color of the wood pulled at my memories. An image was brought to mind of a much younger version of myself pushing a little smuggled matchbox car across the grain. I smiled at the thought. Stained glass windows flanked me on either side and the sun's rays streamed in, lending a majesty to the atmosphere that fluorescent lighting could never hope to replicate. The marble altar stood upon the raised chancel, draped with its stole of ivory.

"You are a little late for mass."

I was startled by the Irish accent coming from behind me. It was an old priest with red, graying hair parted to the side. He had a full beard with a distinctive mustache that fell just short of waxed handlebars.

"Father Murphy?"

"So, you still have some bit of sense left in that stubborn head of yours?"

"Oh my God."

Father Murphy's face turned dark.

"Oh, sorry Father."

"Apparently not that much sense. Where have you been, lad?"

"Uh, around."

"Obviously not around the church," the priest said.

"Yes, well..." My usual defenses—cursing, degrading, or making fun at someone else's expense—didn't seem viable options in this conversation.

"As much as I like verbally abusing you, I will leave off. It's good to see you, Christian."

I breathed a sigh of relief and smiled at my old teacher. "It's good to see you too, Father."

I scooted down a bit, making room. The priest took the wordlessly offered seat and reached out his hand, which I gratefully accepted. I marveled at how this man popped up when least expected. Be it at a carnival, at the grocery store, or a chance meeting right on the streets of Manhattan, Father Murphy would appear out of nowhere every couple of years. Sometimes he would even call and invite himself for dinner. It usually coincided with a new love interest entering the picture, almost like he knew. When my mother was alive, he was practically one of the family. After she passed, he would drop by the house to see how I was and attempt to change my father's mind about religious education.

Later, once my father tired of Father Murphy's "interference," the chance meetings started. I hadn't realized he had been stationed at this church when I entered. It was simply the closest to where I lived according to Google Maps.

"What are you doing here?" I asked.

"I transferred here a few years ago. They needed the help and experience, and I was glad to assist."

"Hmm."

"What are you doing here? All of my coaxing has not persuaded you to enter a church for decades. Now you're not only here, but on a Sunday, without an event or service to attend, and in the middle of a ball game."

"Yeah, but did you see how many games out we are? It would take a miracle to put us in the running."

The priest's only response was a look.

I sighed. "To be honest with you, Father, I have no idea. The strangest things have been happening lately and it is difficult to grasp, much less explain."

"Like you said, we're not in the running. I'm up for a good story."

"Okay, fine, but I need your word that you won't call the guys with the straightjackets when I'm done."

"You have my word. I'll wait at least fifteen minutes before I make the call."

I looked sideways at the old priest, who smiled. I started with the wedding, then talked about Mr. Hager and finally the fight in the alley. Father Murphy didn't say a word as I told the wild story, nor did he look at me like I was insane. He just played with the crucifix that hung around his neck. The action drew my attention. It was rather small and gold, but that was not what I found odd. The nails that held Jesus to the cross were tiny diamonds. I thought priests took a vow of poverty. One more question for another time.

"Well, ready to call the paddy wagon?"

"Not quite yet. So, tell me, why did you come here?"

"Mr. Hager said to follow my faith and, strangely enough, so did a commercial."

"So, you came to church because of a commercial?"

"I came here for answers."

"To what questions?"

"You heard the story."

"Yes, fantastic. Sounds like it would make a good book. I will give you two pieces of advice. Then I will leave you to your communal. The sluggard craves and gets nothing, but the desires of the diligent are fully satisfied."

"What does that mean?"

Father Murphy sighed.

"Do you remember when you were six?"

"No, not really."

"There was one thing you wanted more than anything."

"Seriously? How the... How would I remember that?"

"Think, Christian." He put equal emphasis on both words. It pulled me out of my negative attitude.

"Alright. Six, huh? That would be nineteen ninety-six."

The act of attempting to answer the question called up the memory.

"Yeah, okay. I used to go to that comic book store all the time. The one on the corner before they turned it into a Starbucks."

It only took another few seconds before I had the answer. "Darryl Strawberry. His rookie card. They had it in a frame with an autographed paper. It was the best thing I had ever seen."

"But your mom wouldn't get it for you."

"No." I was lost in the memory, giving a blow-by-blow as I watched the movie being played against the back of my eyes. "She told me that if I wanted it, I would have to work for it."

I met the priest's gaze. "That was when I started helping around the church."

He nodded. "Your mother gave me the money for the card with instructions to dole it out to you, little by little."

"Really? I never knew. It makes sense now that I think about it."

"The point is, you needed to put in effort. You had skin in the game."

"So, what does that have to do with this?"

"God helps those that help themselves."

I smiled at him. "What is the other life-changing piece of information?"

"It's a quote from Einstein: 'If I had an hour to solve a problem, I'd spend fifty-five minutes thinking about the problem and five minutes thinking about the solution.'"

With that, the priest stood up and walked towards the door.

I sat there more confused than before, unable to think of anything. "But what am I looking for?" I called after him.

"That is the right question. And don't lose faith—we're only six games out."

I was alone once again, my mind bouncing around like a beer pong ball that has gone astray of its target. I shook my head and rubbed my face.

Alright, let's get logical. What are my questions? One, how did Mr. Hager and that other woman do the things they did? No, that's a little too far along. More like question four than one. Okay, what else? What the heck happened to me during that wedding? No, still too complicated. I need more information for that. How did they find me? Well, I guess Google is as good of an answer as any for that. How do all these things tie together? That's a good one, but still not enough information about individual parts. What can I answer now? How about why would someone give me a business card with no info on it?

I pulled the card out of my back pocket and looked at it again, turning it over. A thought came to me. I pulled out my phone and used it to zoom into the bishop symbol. Nothing. What was I expecting to find, a micro-message laser etched into the shape of a chess piece? I dropped my hands to my lap in frustration. The face of the phone caught the light streaming in through the stained-glass window. It reflected a small beam onto the white surface. I was reminded of when I would sit near the window in school. I liked to use the reflected light from my watch to annoy the teacher. Hey, you had to make math fun somehow. Where the small dot of light hit the card, I noticed a discoloration. No, that's wrong, more like a burst of color. I turned it to get a better look, taking it unconsciously out of its path. It once again revealed only plain white.

Feeling a renewed confidence I aimed the beam intentionally at the card. Where it touched, I saw not simply discoloration but a filigree design surrounding the bishop. I looked from it to the window and back again, then leaped up and moved closer, holding the card directly into the light. The full design became visible. It sparkled in the light, which seemed to give it life. But it was only ornamentation, no additional information.

What the...?

I was about to let out a vile curse in a completely inappropriate place when the 'duh' moment hit me. I flipped it over. There, surrounded by more filigree, was an address.

Chapter Five

GOOD OLD GOOGLE MAPS. I stood in front of an old, nondescript building that I had passed many times before. It seemed to be perpetually under construction or renovation, making its main decor that of twentieth-century scaffolding made from metal pipes and painted plywood. It was peppered with ads stapled next to block lettering that requested passersby to "Place No Bills."

I was admittedly disappointed. I'm not sure what I was hoping for. Well, that's not true. I knew exactly what I was expecting. I pictured a fancy gothic building that called up images of Notre Dame with a smartly dressed doorman that called me by name. What I was not hoping for, nor expecting, was this shithole. I couldn't even see the front of the building thanks to the safety netting. Compared to the buildings on either side, it was tiny, under ten floors. The only thing notable was the complete lack of homeless squatters in the makeshift shelter the scaffolding provided.

I crossed the street, shaking my head slightly. The traffic on this block was lighter than others, so I didn't have to wait for a stream of cars. In place of a glass door that would usually welcome potential customers sat a portal of solid metal with a centered doorknob.

"That must be a bitch to replace," I said to no one.

I tried the knob, nothing. It didn't give the normal jiggle with resistance to indicate a locked entry, nor did it rotate freely. I stared at the blocked entryway and tried to think. After a moment, an idea popped into my head. I stood up straighter, then slowly and deliberately made the sign of the cross and held my breath.

"Okay, fine. Stupid idea."

I inspected the door, looking for alternate handles, hidden latches, panels, a doorbell. Hell, even a rope attached to a bell somewhere. There was nothing of the sort. Then I looked at the doorknob again. It was far more intricate than I first realized, although faded through time and wear. At some point it may have been used as an actual knob instead of just decoration. There were symbols surrounded by more filigree, a few of which I recognized—namely a Jewish star, a crucifix, and a chess piece. In the center, where the keyhole should be, was a clear crystal about the size of a nickel.

I tried all the secret entry methods I could think of. Pushing, pulling, turning, tapping out "Amazing Grace", then "The Battle Hymn Of The Republic". Okay, that last one was a stretch, but I was running out of ideas. I took a step back, shifted my weight to one side and took on a standing version of the thinking man; though I doubted this would provide me, as Mr. Gambini so beautifully put it in *My Cousin Vinny*, "great spontaneous knowledge." Absently, I tapped the little white card against my chin.

"I'm missing something."

Tap, tap, tap.

"I know I am."

Tap, tap, tap.

"I feel like it is staring me in the face."

I continued talking to myself, getting strange glances from the few passersby that made their way through. I kept tapping the business card until it irritated my skin.

"What moron would make a business card out of plastic? It looks like a hotel key..."

I looked from the card with the bishop, to the small crystal with the bishop, and back again.

"Stupid, stupid, stupid!"

Stepping up to the door again, I placed the card against the crystal. There was a distinct buzzing sound, followed by a click, and the door swung in a few inches. I took a deep breath, pushed the door open further and stepped inside.

The door closed behind me. What I thought was a single click from the noisy street turned out to be an entire set of electronic locks. Can you say overkill? The room inside was bright and airy though not spacious, a typical foyer with the standard furniture. A loud cheer sounded from behind the double doors opposite the street entry. I hesitated for a moment but then thought, *well, he gave me a key.*

I was still hesitant to burst in on a bunch of strangers in their... home, I guess. I walked up to the doors and gently pulled one open.

I thought I was confused before. The room was furnished with several comfortable-looking couches, as well as a few easy chairs. At opposite ends of the large room was a fireplace and a large flat screen television framed by two bookcases. A group of people who resembled a small subsection of the United Nations were watching the end of the ballgame I had left.

I recognized Soon-Li—the woman that protected me from the flying dumpster in the alley. The other two, engrossed in the game's outcome, were not familiar to me. All three had their attention on the screen and had not noticed my entrance.

"Well, it's about time," came a familiar snooty voice. I looked towards the source and found Mr. Hager staring at me from around the side of an armchair facing the fireplace. "I wasn't sure you would ever put two and two together."

The sound from the T.V. suddenly stopped. I turned to find the three other occupants staring at me and felt self-conscious, like walking into the high school faculty lounge as a student. Soon-Li was the first one to move. She maneuvered around the furniture and pulled me into a crushing bear hug.

"Welcome home, Christian."

"Uh, thanks," was the only reply I could extract.

"Your mother would be so proud."

I pulled back from the hug and looked into her eyes. "You knew my mother too?"

"Yes, Angela and I were good friends from childhood," Soon-Li said. "If you want, when there is time, we can sit, and I'll tell you about her."

I hadn't heard someone mention her by name in years. She was always referred to as 'your mom.' I had forgotten how beautiful it was. "Yeah, I would like that," I said through a lump that had developed in my throat.

Soon-Li smiled, took my hand as though we were old friends and brought me into the circle.

"Everyone, this is Christian Bateleur, son of Angela Bateleur."

That simple statement seemed to send a shock through the small group. Their looks of welcome shifted to that of surprise, and something else. Soon-Li, however, didn't pause long enough for me to sort out what.

"Christian, this is John McCaw."

The uncertainty that had painted John's face just a second before was gone.

"Good to meet you," John said with a subtle southern drawl, extending his hand. He was shorter than me by a few inches and his shoulder length dreadlocks swayed slightly as we shook. I could feel the strength radiating from him, both physically and in a deeper sense. He had black thick-rimmed glasses that matched his dark skin.

"You too."

I managed to keep the 'uh' out of my reply and pull together a smile, although I had a feeling that it looked a little confused. Soon-Li directed me away from John and placed me in front of a woman of Indian descent. Her skin was dark caramel, and she gave off an inner luminance. Her eyes were teardrops, framed by high cheekbones and slanted eyebrows. She had a prominent nose and lips. Her beauty was the equal to—though vastly different from—Jackie's, whom I have always thought to be the most gorgeous woman on the planet.

"This is Tira," Soon-Li said.

She reached out her hand to me. The back was covered with an intricate henna design that stopped at her last knuckle, giving the impression that she was wearing a delicate set of fingerless gloves. When I shook it, I felt a connection—a spark, but one that didn't resonate from my hand. If anyone asked me at the time, I don't think I could have put the feeling into words, but it was there.

It took me a second, or a couple of seconds, to realize Soon-Li was looking at me expectantly.

"It's very nice to meet you," we both said in stereo.

Apparently, I was not the only one somewhat thrown by the introduction.

"So, you decided to remove your head from your nether regions." This, of course, came from Mr. Hager. "I believe we are overdue for a chat."

He walked off carrying the book he had been reading. Soon-Li motioned for me to follow. I went to do so, only to realize that I was still holding on to Tira's hand. She realized it as well and we both released, looking sheepish. I followed Mr. Hager up to the fourth floor. Despite my regular exercise regimen, I was slightly out of breath. My guide breathed normally. Show off.

The hallway looked as though it belonged in an office building in the fifties. Both sides were lined with doors. The top half of each was translucent glass, with gold lettering identifying whose office it was. He led me to the last door at the end of the hall. The gold lettering declared it to be the office of *Amram Hager Covenant Head*.

"I guess you are the head honcho," I said.

Mr. Hager looked at me. "I currently have the honor of leading the Covenant, if that's what you mean."

With that, he opened the door to his office and walked in. The furnishings were a direct contrast to what I'd seen of his personality. They were warm and inviting. Cushioned chairs, rich wood, and bookshelves lined with a large variety of volumes—all of which appeared to be decades old. I didn't recognize the paintings on display. I am far from an art history expert but have been to enough museums to acknowledge their age. One was of a mother and baby, sitting on an outcropping under a small tree and surrounded by a host of people, mostly men and a few women. The child was reaching out to one man, who was prostrate. In the background were what appeared to be Roman ruins. The pigmentation, though muted with age, still captured the emotions. It was the colors that threw me, though I wasn't sure why. Kind of like when you watch *Miracle on 34th Street* and it's not in the original black and white.

"Please have a seat. Will you require coffee to support this discussion? I am afraid I don't have anything stronger to offer you."

"No, thanks. I'm good."

I chose a chair that was part of a bistro set off to the side, deciding not to give Mr. Hager the option of looking at me from across his desk, a principal with a student.

"Very well."

"So why all the cloak and dagger stuff? Is this your initiation rite? Seems a bit cruel to do to a bunch of eight-year-olds."

Hager gave me a questioning look.

"You said when we first met that my initiation should have occurred during my first communion."

He nodded once and said, "actually no, it isn't."

"Isn't cruel?"

"Isn't a ritual. It's actually the first occasion we've done it. As I said at our first meeting, membership is passed down from parent to child."

"So why make me go through it?" I asked.

"Frankly, I didn't trust you. I wanted to see how committed you were, wanted to see if you would just forget about everything and go back to your life. Ignore the opportunity and responsibility. I needed to know if you would return to your faith."

"Faith," I said with contempt. Faith had failed me throughout my life. I had faith that my father would recover from his depression. Faith that my squad would survive the nightmare of being stranded in the middle of the desert, surrounded by hostiles. When I was little, my mother had filled my well with the vast ocean of her faith. I turned to that font often in my youth, as I was taught. God will protect you. The Lord will guide you. You are never given more than you can handle. When you continually bang your head against a low beam, eventually you learn to duck. That well was now dry.

"Yes, faith, Mr. Bateleur. That is what this entire organization is founded on—what drives us and what gives us our abilities. Faith in ourselves, faith in our friends and, yes, faith in our God."

"Our God? When did you start worshiping Shiva or Buddha?" Mr.

Hager raised an eyebrow at me.

"Perhaps you are more knowledgeable than I give you credit for."

Actually, I had pulled those from *The Temple of Doom* and hours watching old Kung Fu movies, but I wasn't about to tell him that.

"I like to think of it as one God with many faces and many ways to worship," he continued. "But, at the core of any religion, you will find faith. You, Mr. Bateleur, have lost it. You have lost faith in God and, most of all, lost it in yourself."

"Ha," I blurted out. "I'm the only one I can count on." Mr. Hager stared me down, unblinking. "Really? Is that why you choose the profession you are in?"

"You have a problem with my business?"

Mr. Hager narrowed his eyes at me. Then he seemed to come to a decision. He stood and went over to his desk where he opened a drawer, removed a file and laid it on the surface. He glanced through it, selected a piece of paper, and closed the file, leaving it on the desk as he returned.

"There you are," he said, handing the paper over. It was an I.Q. scoresheet. Mine from high school.

"So?" My mouth was getting dry.

"What score did you get?"

"I don't know. I don't pay attention to those things."

"As a matter of fact, you do. It was shortly after this test that your grades declined sharply. You lost all interest in going to college and ultimately entered the military."

"I'm not sure what you're getting at. How did you get a copy of this?"

"Tell me the score."

"What is that going to prove?"

"Tell me the score."

"This is a waste of time."

Mr. Hager met my eyes. He didn't get angry or raise his voice. He merely said calmly, "The score if you please, Mr. Bateleur?"

"One Thirty-Seven," I said without looking down at the paper.

"One Thirty-Seven. Only a few points below genius level, if I am not mistaken. People of your intelligence level are studying particle physics or quantum mechanics, not installing air conditioners."

"I do heaters as well."

"And we return to the humor. My point is that you took one look at that score, knew the paths that it implied, and you did not have enough faith in yourself to even try. In fact, you went out of your way to sabotage yourself rather than face potential failure."

Was that really what I had done? I didn't remember any decision that led me here. I did recall feeling that the score had to be a mistake. It was my sophomore year. I tried to think back to what classes had been like before that. The images that came to mind were of exams with near perfect marks. Flashes of frustration over what I could have gotten wrong. That feeling was inevitably followed by a blasé consideration that maybe next time, I would try studying.

I mentally growled at myself, pushing the memory away. I looked back at the waiting Mr. Hager. He didn't look smug, just calm.

"Again, I say, so?" I expected a reaction but got none. "What do you want from me, anyway?"

"I want nothing from you, Mr. Bateleur. It is what I am offering you."

"What are you offering?"

"Challenge. Challenge and meaning."

"Sounds like an infomercial."

"Do us both a favor and make your next question an intelligent one, please. Don't let the short downtime you witnessed give you the impression that we are like the Knights of Columbus. For all the good work that organization provides, this is not a place to share a pint and complain about your spouse."

"Okay, so who are the bishops?"

"Ah, good. I knew you had it in you." Mr. Hager did not appear to revel in my frown and continued. "Our lineage can be traced back before Moses. Unfortunately, records before that become somewhat fuzzy. Suffice to say, for as long as there has been religion, there have been the Bishops. Our sole purpose is the protection of humankind from those that would seek to do it harm."

"Who would want to harm us besides ourselves?"

"The Tainted."

"Sounds like a good name for a band," I scoffed.

"You are not the first person to say so."

"Really? Maybe this place isn't as stuffy as I thought."

Mr. Hager sniffed at that. "For every action, there is a reaction. For every God of love, there is a God of war and for every good—"

"There is evil."

"Precisely. The Tainted are that evil."

"Where do they come from?"

"Procreation, same as us."

"That's not what I meant."

"Yes, I know. Like us, they become tainted through their faith. Their faith rests in chaos, destruction, conquest, and perversion."

"So, they are like the dark side."

"Mr. Bateleur, this is neither a movie nor a joke. The Tainted have killed millions of people over the centuries. They have caused pain and strife for entire continents, and been the puppet masters behind some of the bloodiest wars that the world has seen. They are not an allegorical representation of evil—they are evil. As we worship God, they worship Satan. In fact, some of us believe the Bishops were created because of the Tainted."

"How is that?" I asked.

Hager sighed deeply. "That is a story for another time."

"So, the war for the heavens is being fought on Earth?"

"Once again, you watch too many movies. The heavens do not concern themselves with mortals. This is a war for humanity; a war that has raged nearly since the beginning of time. A secret war that will likely go on until the Earth stops spinning."

"Then why fight? If there can be no winner, no end to the struggle, why bother?"

"Because the alternative is too horrible to consider."

Mr. Hager gazed deeper into my eyes and withdrew the answer to an unspoken question. At almost that exact moment, there was a light knock on the door and Tira entered.

"Am I interrupting?"

"No, I believe Mr. Bateleur was just about to refuse our family politely or, more likely, not so politely."

"What?" she exclaimed.

"Whoa, I didn't say anything."

"You didn't have to. It was clear that my words had as little effect on you as a bad movie. You have no interest in fighting this war, no interest in regaining your faith, and you have no interest in us."

"Listen, you really need to stop putting words in my mouth."

"Oh, so you will be joining us?" Hager asked, arching an eyebrow.

"I didn't say that, either."

"Precisely."

With that, Mr. Hager stood up and walked out. After giving me a look I couldn't interpret, Tira followed close behind, leaving me alone.

I sat there and stewed for a few minutes. How dare he call me out like that? I was just trying to figure out what was going on. I wasn't looking to join a cult or sign up for yet another war. Still, something about what he had said struck a nerve. I couldn't pinpoint what it was, but it sparked something in me. It almost made me consider the offer. Almost.

Hey, I have issues, I will be the first to admit them. I sometimes drink too much, and I spend way too much time watching movies. Sometimes both at the same time. I prefer to be alone most of the time. I just don't understand people, and after thirty plus years I've discovered, they don't get me either. But my biggest pet peeve is this concept of faith.

You hear it all the time from people that don't want to face reality. They just act and have "faith" that everything will be alright. Shouldn't we do something about those bills piling up? No! Have faith and they will get paid. What about that tumor? Should we see a doctor? Bah! Who needs medicine when I have faith? I know you're worried Christian, but your mother will get back from her trip safe and sound. Have faith.

I withdrew the white card, placed it on the table, and left.

Chapter Six

I WOKE TO THE alarm and tapped it into silence with a groan. Panic shot through me as I looked at the time: eight o'clock. The first appointments of the day were always scheduled for eight-thirty. I would have to take the quickest shower of my life to be on time. After a few seconds, my brain kicked into gear and I remembered it was Sunday. Then why the Hell was my alarm going off at all? Oh yeah, church.

I had spoken to Father Murphy after my meeting at the Bishop Club—the name I had chosen for the strange cult building hidden in plain sight. He had somehow talked me into attending nine o'clock mass. I selected that time because the one at seven-thirty was too friggin' early and, if I waited until ten-thirty, the chances of me attending would drop dramatically.

"Why am I doing this again?" I asked myself out loud.

The answer, however, required way too much introspection and I was not about to do that before coffee. Groaning again I rolled out of bed. In the shower, I shoved my head under the stream of hot water for a good five minutes trying to drown my desire for more sleep. Thoroughly scrubbed, I selected clothes that were somewhere between casual and formal. My first week at mass had revealed that few people wore suits anymore. I got dressed, feeling confident that my mother agree it was a good trade off for regular attendance.

Mass was okay. I still stumbled over some prayers since they had, apparently, changed several years ago. I assumed the Roman Catholic Church did it just to shake things up. Give a jolt to those who have been sleep-praying for too many years.

The other weekly habit I had picked up was going to brunch at a local diner with Father Murphy. I couldn't say that I eagerly anticipated services, but I looked forward to brunch. Between the two I felt, what? The only word I could use that didn't sound like a commercial by the Latter-Day Saints was *better*.

The diner was old-fashioned, with stainless steel everywhere, including the exterior. Decorations had shifted this week from Halloween to Thanksgiving. The seating was primarily bench booths with thick, plastic-covered cushions fastened with domed stainless-steel nails. On the wall opposite the front door, a half oval bar framed the entrance to the kitchen. Booths lined the large windows and created the center seating area in the middle of the long room. These diners always made me think of a Winnebago on steroids. The two of us were in a booth on the kitchen side of the central aisle.

"What did you think of my homily?"

I did say I looked forward to the brunches, right? "Was that from the bullfrog profit?"

Father Murphy stopped chewing his eggs Benedict and stared at me with an unamused look. I chose not to look too deeply into his choice of breakfast. He swallowed and asked, "how long have you been holding that one in?"

"Ever since the woman said, 'a reading from the Prophet Jeremiah.' I wasn't sure I could fit it into a conversation. I appreciate the assist."

He continued to stare.

"Okay, sorry. Homily, based on the Gospel according to Mark, where Jesus heals the blind man Barfholomew."

"Bartimaeus, not John Candy's character from *Spaceballs*."

"Yeah, him. It was very enlightening."

"Why?"

Ah, crap. If I had known there was going to be a test, I would have tried harder not to doze off. I searched for a thread of a memory that I could weave into a tapestry of bullshit he might actually believe. I delayed by shoving an extra-large slice of waffle in my mouth.

"Blindness is a metaphor," I said after I swallowed. "It is really the illusion that we each paint for ourselves about our own realities.

We ignore our shortcomings instead of meeting them head on. We blame others for problems instead of taking responsibility, and we call ourselves good Christians while visiting porn sites when no one is watching."

The priest stopped chewing again. Then he made a circular motion with his fork, so I continued.

"Jesus curing the blindness was really giving him the clarity to look at all of his flaws and accept himself as he was. By doing so, he gained enlightenment and put himself on the path of God. Hence him following Jesus."

Father Murphy took his time, swallowed the next bite and followed it with a swig of coffee. I followed suit with mine.

"Interesting."

"Yes, I thought it was, too." It seemed like I may have dodged that bullet.

"No, what is interesting is that none of what you said was in my homily."

"Oh." Shit.

"It is also interesting how you remembered what the Gospel was about."

"Uh-huh," was what I said. What I was thinking was *danger! Danger Will Robinson!*

"Then you translated the homily into something that highlights your current dilemma."

I took another sip of coffee, choosing not to respond.

Father Murphy smiled into his then let me off the hook. "How's Jackie?"

"Great," I said.

"Is she ever going to join us?"

"Probably not. She usually likes to spend the first few hours of every day working."

"She seems to have everything together."

"Yeah, she likes to shove that in my face."

"Why is that? You're a successful businessman with your own company."

"Yeah, but she's a corporate lawyer. I work on ACs."

"Have you been back to the house?"

Despite the vagueness of the statement, I knew what house he meant. "No."

The priest sipped his coffee.

"No comment?" I asked.

"What comment should I give?"

"Not going to try to talk me into joining?"

"Why would I do that?"

"Because you think it is the right thing to do. Because it is a family tradition, passed down through generations tracing back to the days of the pharaohs. Because it was what my mother had planned."

"You forgot the 'with great power' speech." Father Murphy punctuated his statement with another sip of coffee, then continued. "You realize I didn't make any of those clearly well-thought-out arguments. You have done some deep thinking on this."

"How can I not? I told you what these people can do. I also told you that each one is a devout religious nut. That's not me."

"What, in the thirty seconds you spent with them, makes you think they are all—as you so snidely put it—devout religious nuts?"

"Sorry, no offense intended."

"How could I possibly be offended by that heartfelt comment?"

I winced visibly and the priest nodded.

"Here is what I don't understand," he continued. "You are so concerned about being connected to a religious organization that you are overlooking the fact that your mother was, based on your description, a real-life superhero."

That stopped me. I hadn't thought of it that way. I didn't connect her with the supernatural aspects. The religious points aligned with the picture in my head, so it fit cleanly into my personal narrative. Thinking that my mother had abilities that would place her securely in the Hall of Justice didn't sit right, no matter how I turned the inkblot. I guess the two things you don't acknowledge your parents doing are having sex and leaping tall buildings. I banished those thoughts. Things were complex enough without trying to live up to Wonder Woman.

"What I meant was they..." I struggled for the words.

"Have faith?" Father Murphy offered.

I nodded.

"And you don't, is that it?"

I didn't reply.

"Listen, Christian, you have been coming to mass for the past couple of weeks, but did you pay attention to what was around you?"

I still remained silent.

"Do me a favor, describe the church."

"What?"

"You confided your I.Q. score, so please don't play dumb."

I shrugged. "It's a large building with wooden benches, an altar, a large crucifix, and many stained-glass windows."

"That's it?"

"Would you like more details?" I asked.

"Please."

I sighed dramatically and pulled up an image in my mind. "At the back of the church, there is a balcony where the organ sits, and the choir occasionally sings from. Below the balcony, on the right side, is the crying room. To the left of the altar is the lectern. To the right, the pulpit." I looked at the Father expectantly but received no sign he was satisfied, so continued. "The stations of the cross are set up around the outside of the pews. On the right side, near the exit, is the confessional."

"Ah, there we are. It took you long enough to get around to it."

I regarded him, confused.

"The confessional. Used for what exactly?"

"To confess sins."

"Yes, of course. Whose sins?"

"Well, everybody's."

"Exactly." Father Murphy leaned forward and stared right into my eyes. "Everyone's sins, because everyone is flawed."

"Even priests?" I baited.

"Sometimes especially priests." For a second, his eyes took on a distant look and he rubbed his crucifix, which was currently under his clothes. He pulled himself back quickly, leaving me to wonder if I imagined it. "My point is that no one is perfect, and everyone loses faith. Do you remember what Jesus said on the cross near the time of his death?"

I shook my head.

"My God, why have you abandoned me?"

Father Murphy held eye contact for several seconds, letting his words sink in.

"There has to be a catch." I said.

"Christian, I know you've had it rough. But there is not always an ulterior motive."

We remained quiet until the waitress came over with the check. I glanced at it, placed cash on the table, and we both headed for the door. I was rearranging my money when I noticed a man entering dressed in a gray hoodie and dark sunglasses. He saw me, pulled an automatic pistol out of the pouch of the sweatshirt, and aimed it at me.

Chapter Seven

A FORCE CRASHED INTO me, taking me to the floor, as a shot rang out. The momentum carried me behind a set of booths and out of the range of fire. Father Murphy had tackled me, saving my life.

"Are you hurt?" the priest grunted.

"No," I replied.

"Good," he said.

With that, he pulled a flask out of his pocket, opened it, and dumped it on my head.

The first shock was what you might expect given the circumstances. The second was more extreme, like touching a nine-volt battery to your tongue, but all over.

The surrounding scene changed. Or rather, my perspective changed, like when Dorothy first opens her front door to Oz. Everything became clearer and in more stark contrast. The crumbs of food under the table were as noticeable as black rocks on a white, sandy beach. Fine cracks in the ceiling stood out like magic marker on white paper.

It was not only my vision that had been enhanced; all of my other senses had as well. I could feel the individual threads that made up my clothes. The jumble of yelling patrons separated and became distinct. I felt that if I concentrated, I could focus and listen to each individual conversation around me. I could smell everyone's breakfast and identify each. Just above me were pancakes with strawberry syrup. Next to that was a slightly burned English muffin with orange marmalade, followed by a western omelet.

All my senses built a picture of my surroundings. In all the commotion, one image was clearest. The shooter was getting closer. I could hear his heavy, booted footfalls; feel the air as it was pushed around the corner by the approaching figure. Father Murphy's weight rolled off me just as the hooded figure rounded the corner and found his target.

I locked eyes with the attacker despite his dark glasses. Water still dripped from my newly wet hair. My whole body screamed that I needed to move. Grab the gun before he can fire again. I pushed off the floor and into action; my only thought was to make sure no one could get hurt, especially Father Murphy.

Everything around me slowed. People scrambled to get out of the path of the gunman, but did so in slow motion. A cup of coffee that had been hit during their retreat floated in the air, the contents hovering above in an arc of displacement. The only thing unaffected by this strange phenomenon was me. I leaped up and ran at my attacker. I cleared the few feet between us and grabbed his slowly rising gun arm, lifting it towards the ceiling.

Everything around me returned to normal. People finished their retreat. The coffee cup spilled its contents across the table and onto the omelet. The hooded man's expression registered shock as his target suddenly stood in front of him, holding his forearm in the air. At this distance, I could see through the sunglasses into the man's eyes. They narrowed into resolve.

I put all of my strength into keeping that gun pointed up and held fast as the assailant struggled with little effect. I held him in place as easily as when roughhousing with the village children in Afghanistan. His other hand reached behind him and came out with a butterfly knife, which he deftly opened with a few flicks of his wrist. I moved as fast as I could to catch that hand as well, losing my iron grip on the other.

My heart pounded in my ears and my mouth went dry. He closed in with both weapons. Close combat training was clear, disarm, then incapacitate. But I was out of hands, so I kicked. My foot connected square in his chest, launching him backward over the booth behind him and into the plate-glass window. It shattered upon impact. He landed motionless on the sidewalk amongst a shower of glass. I stood open-mouthed as I realized I held both the gun and knife. My breath came in gulps while a sheen of sweat coated my back and dripped down my spine. Or that could have been the water Father Murphy dumped on my head.

As I stood there, bewildered, people around me recovered as well. Realizing what happened, they began applauding. Strangers came up and patted me on the back, or just hooted the typical supportive one-liners.

"You da man!"

"Thank God you were here!"

A smile just lightened my face when a different tone of voice cut through the revelry.

"Oh my God, he's bleeding. Someone call 911!"

I turned towards the voice. Several people surrounded a supine figure on the floor, lying in a pool of blood. I rushed forward to see who it was, but the feeling of dread that settled into my chest told me I already knew. Pushing through the crowd, I kneeled down beside Father Murphy. I checked for a pulse—it was weak and thready, but still there. Peeling up his shirt, I found the wound on his side and ripped off my shirt to act as a bandage, putting pressure to stem the flow of blood.

"Did anyone call for help!?"

My voice cracked as I yelled out to the onlookers.

"I am on with them now," said a man holding a phone to his ear. I took a deep breath and swallowed the lump in my throat.

"Tell them we have a single GSW with extensive bleeding. We need an ambulance, fast."

With the amount of blood and the position of the wound, I wasn't sure if they would get there in time. He was shot in the side, so the bullet had gone across his body, doing an extensive amount of damage to a great number of organs.

"No, you don't, Father. You can't leave me now."

No response.

"Do you hear me?" I growled.

No response.

"I said you are *not going anywhere.*"

I placed a hand on his bare shoulder—a counterweight to my pressure on the wound—and immediately felt a warm sensation. It started in my chest and radiated out of my palm. Father Murphy's back arched and, gasping a ragged breath, opened his eyes a crack. He looked into mine as though searching for something. He must have found it because a small, pained smile pulled at the corners of his mouth. He rattled out a single, barely audible word, "Bishop."

He closed his eyes again, his breathing labored. I thought he had a punctured lung. But it felt like he might have a chance after all. Whatever had changed seemed to have given him a little strength back—maybe enough to get him to a hospital.

"Tough son of a bitch," I muttered.

Father Murphy nodded ever so slightly. I called for plastic wrap and tape as the sounds of sirens approached. As I worked, Father Murphy lay there, barely clinging to life, with a smile on his face.

Chapter Eight

THE HEART MONITOR BEEPED rhythmically, though slower than it should have. Father Murphy's breathing was shallow and raspy. Not much more could be expected after a bullet had torn through his lung. That he was breathing on his own was a miracle. He wasn't conscious, nor was he expected to be. Maybe not ever.

"Did you want me to come down and sit with you?" Jackie asked over the phone.

"No, that's not necessary. I know you had plans with your friends. They will be disappointed if you don't show."

"Bullshit, I'm coming down."

"Thank you, really. I appreciate the offer, but they're probably going to kick me out soon, anyway. Go have fun. We'll talk later."

"Are you sure?" Jackie persisted.

"Positive."

"Okay. Wish me luck."

"You're hot and rich. Somehow, I think you'll manage."

"Later slacker."

Jackie hung up and I clicked the phone off putting it away. I reached out and grabbed Father Murphy's forearm, just above the IV. He had become more than my priest in the past few weeks. More than an occasional spiritual guide. He was a friend and a better father figure than my actual one.

My father had tried in the beginning. No, that wasn't fair. He tried the most at the beginning, using our shared grief as a bond. But while my pain had ebbed after a while, his did not. Daniel Bateleur was a software engineer that had married up. He was devoted to my mother to a fault. His talent at coding developed into a high-paying job running the emerging technologies department. The only thing he was more passionate about was her. Our house smelled like a funeral home with the constant stream of fresh flowers. When he was home, he was constantly by her side, trying desperately to address her every whim. It was not a simple thing, since my mother wanted little. She was happy with the flowers but never asked for them. She had a deep belief in earning your way, so had no interest in being showered with gifts.

When she died, it devastated him. My father and I had a bizarre relationship. There was no fighting and no drunken arguments; no abuse or neglect. Just sadness. He became more and more distant. He committed suicide shortly after I moved out. As though having completed his parental duty, he could no longer be parted from my mother.

All throughout this time, Father Murphy found ways to be near me. When my father fell short, he picked up the slack. He came to every game of my short little league career. My even shorter stint in soccer. My three trombone recitals when I realized I was better at watching sports than playing them. Now sitting with him in the hospital room, watching the monitors and his labored breathing, I thought maybe we were a little closer than I had admitted to myself.

"How is he?"

I looked up to find Mr. Hager. He stood just inside the door, looking forlorn, his wide-brimmed hat held in his hands. I responded with a snort.

"What are you doing here?"

"I came to look in on my friend."

"So, I am your friend now?"

"I was not referring to you, Mr. Bateleur."

I was taken aback and could only respond with a look of confusion.

"Yes, I have known Francis for many years and have counted him one of my dearest and undoubtedly oldest friends."

It took me a moment to realize that he was referring to Father

Murphy. I had all but forgotten his first name.

"I didn't realize," I said. Then, after a slight hesitation, "Sorry."

"As am I."

I wasn't sure what he was apologizing for, but I was not in the mood to press the question.

"He is doing okay, considering."

"That is thanks to you, from what I hear."

"Heh, I'm good, but not that good."

"How do you mean, exactly?" he asked.

I looked up and gathered my thoughts for a few seconds.

"I have seen wounds far less deadly kill a man, no matter what I did."

"Maybe it was a miracle."

I frowned then asked, "How did you hear he was hurt?"

"The news."

I gave him a quizzical look.

"This may be the city that has seen everything, but a shooting with an injured priest is still noteworthy."

"They mentioned him by name?" I asked.

"No. I went down to the scene to see if any help was needed and Jeff, the manager of the diner, told me. May I?"

"Yeah, sure, pull up a chair."

He did so, pulling up the only other chair in the room.

"How did you get by the police barricades?"

"We have contacts."

"Huh." I wondered if he would ever answer a direct question with something other than vague statements.

We sat there for a while in silence, with only the monitors providing background noise. A nurse wandered in and breezed past us— checking vitals, changing the saline drip, and jotting notes. As she crossed, I caught a faint hint of lavender soap; it's that clean smell that accompanies someone who has just showered. I hypothesized a recent shift change. She finished her ministrations and left as quietly as she appeared. The only sound was the squeak of her sneakers on the highly polished tile floor. I finally broke the silence.

"How did you two meet?"

"Through you."

I stared at the older man, looking for some sign he was making a joke, but found none.

"Care to elaborate?"

"Your baptism," Mr. Hager answered simply. "Father Murphy presided over the ceremony and I... was there too."

"You were at my baptism?"

"I just said as much, didn't I?"

I grunted a response. After a second or two, I asked, "can I ask you something?"

"I believe you just did."

I chose to ignore that. "During the struggle for the gun, I had some strange sensations,"

"Based on the description the manager gave me, I don't doubt it."

"Before it all started, Father Murphy poured a flask of..."

"Hold that thought." Mr. Hager interrupted.

"But..."

He held a hand up for silence. His expression made me think that he was trying to remember Babe Ruth's rookie batting average.

"Continue," he said.

His voice sounded different, almost as if the acoustics of the room had changed.

"Okay." I dragged the word out. "Where was I? Oh yeah, so just after he dragged me to the floor, he dumps a flask of water on my head. What was *that* about?"

"That, Mr. Bateleur, was to save your life."

"What is that supposed to mean? How is getting me wet supposed to help?"

"Describe what you felt during your struggle. And I need you to be very specific about your thoughts and motivations at each point."

I thought for a second.

"Well, for one, my senses were going nuts." I explained the details I could recall.

"What were you thinking at that point?"

"Well, just before he dumped the water on my head, I was trying to figure out where the shooter was."

"Okay, then what?"

"When the guy came around the booths, I was on the ground. I knew he was going to shoot at any moment, so I tried to get to him as fast as I could."

I ran through the rest of the interaction while describing what I was doing, thinking, and feeling. Mr. Hager sat in silence for a few moments. Then he said quietly, "Impressive."

"What is?"

He thought a moment more.

"Your actions are unprecedented. In almost every other instance for the past thousand years, every Bishop has been trained from youth. This is not a movie in which the hero is prophesied in an obscure poem. No bastard children were spirited out of a castle to head up a future revolution.

"There are forty Bishop families. Only two are blessed in each family—the parent and the first-born child. When the child reaches the age of ascension, they go through a coming-of-age ceremony. It is different for each religion—as each religion has different ways to worship. But we know who they are—all of them. We know when they will inherit their powers.

"Once done, they are inducted into the Covenant. They are taught from a reasonably early age about what we are and why we exist, and their training begins. It takes weeks, sometimes months, to even touch their blessing. Months more to use one of them. To do what you did, instinctively, would have taken years of practice and training."

I stared at him, trying to grasp the breadth of what he was saying. I couldn't.

"I don't even know what I did."

"We will need to speak of this later."

I noticed a bead of sweat fall from under a lock of his hair. His face changed. He sighed, rolling his neck slightly.

"How come?"

"Because this is not the place to discuss such things, and I cannot hold the barrier any longer."

The strange echo to his voice was gone again. "The what?"

"Again, later."

"But why can't..."

"Please, Mr. Bateleur."

The sincerity made me stop. "Okay, later."

We sat there in silence for a while, sending good thoughts and feelings to our friend lying between us.

"I hear you have returned to church."

"I guess you can say that. I have been attending recently."

"That's good to hear."

"How so?"

"Religion is often taught as an obligation. We are supposed to be attending service to pay God back for the gift of our life, or as an entrance fee for the hereafter."

Mr. Hager shook his head then continued.

"I prefer to think of it as a lifeline. A set of rituals provided to ground us. A place to go when the world becomes too much. One where you will always be forgiven, and you will always feel at home."

"I had never thought of it that way."

"Nor had I, once."

"What changed?"

He motioned towards Father Murphy.

"Really." It was not a question.

"It was a turning point for me. A crossroads he helped me navigate."

"I know what you mean. He was less of a priest to me throughout the years, more of a bartender."

"He does like his scotch."

I laughed, partially from the surprise of a joke coming from Mr. Hager.

"What I meant was he was always there to listen to my tales of woe. Mostly about my latest failure with women."

He nodded.

"But you're right. He does like his scotch."

It was his turn to chuckle. It was an odd sound coming from this stoic man. I liked it.

We talked like this for a while, finding a subject we agreed upon: the high quality of character our friend embodied. Eventually, a nurse came in and announced that we needed to leave and let her patient get some rest.

I couldn't resist saying, "yes, come, Mr. Hager, we are very rude disturbing our friend's coma."

He smirked. As we got up to leave, he pulled out a cell phone and made a quick call as we made our way toward the elevator.

"I am assuming you need a ride since you came in with the ambulance." He said when he hung up.

"Thanks, but I can just take the subway."

"It is no trouble; I have a car coming."

"Are you sure?"

"Certainly."

"Okay, thanks."

Honestly, I wasn't sure if I really wanted to continue this small gathering outside the hospital room. I was afraid it may have been the catalyst that kept him civil. But not accepting the ride might put a crack in the bridge that Father Murphy had built. I wasn't sure why I cared.

In the lobby, Mr. Hager stopped well short of the door, apparently waiting. I was not sure how he would know when the car arrived. We made small talk while we waited. I felt my fears coming true. His phone rang. He brought it immediately to his ear.

"Are we set?" He must have received the response he was hoping for because he replied, "Okay, good."

Mr. Hager hung up again and looked at me. "We need to do this quickly."

"What? Why?"

"I promise I will explain once we are past this. For now, please, just listen."

Again, there was something in his voice that made me want to do as requested. I nodded.

"There is a black SUV parked outside. Keep your head down, walk straight for it, and jump in the back. The door will open before you get there. Don't run, but don't dawdle. We are trying to keep a low profile. We get in and go. Clear?"

"No, but let's get it done."

"Good enough."

We walked towards the door and it slid open. I caught sight of the vehicle and moved toward it, head down as instructed. Mr. Hager followed like a shadow a few paces behind. The car door opened at our approach, the interior lights illuminating the empty seats.

The attack came without warning—a blur coming from the side. There was nothing I could do. Just before it collided with me, I was hit from the back. The momentum carried me head-first into the waiting car. I ducked, barely avoiding a concussion.

I felt the wind whip by as the figure blew through the space that I occupied only a second before. Tumbling into the backseat, I curled into a ball to protect myself, and ended up plastered against the other door. Before I could right myself, I heard the door close. There was the screech of tires and I was pushed against the backrest as the car accelerated. I righted myself and found Mr. Hager buckled in beside me with his hat resting on his lap. I recognized the man driving as John McCaw.

"What the hell was that?!"

"That was one of the Tainted," answered Mr. Hager.

"Did you see which one it was, I couldn't get a good look?" John called back.

"Nor I. I was just trying to distract them long enough to allow us to flee."

"At least we know it wasn't Baldemar."

"Who is Baldemar and how do we know it wasn't him?" I asked. Hager sighed deeply and fiddled with the brim of his hat.

"Who, is a conversation for another day. However if it were he, we would likely all be dead."

The silence felt like a living, breathing thing.

"Are we clear?" I asked, no longer able to tolerate it.

"Yeah," John said. "That attempt was about as public as they will get. A broken neck or back—even a stabbing or shooting—can be explained away. A car chase, or what people will assume is a car chase, would create a little more attention than they would like. They know from experience the problems that would cause."

"What was it doing here?" I asked.

"Looking to finish the job they started in the diner," suggested John.

"I thought it was just a random shooter," I said.

"Hardly," Mr. Hager interjected. "He only fired once at his intended target. He didn't attempt another until he was in a better position."

I thought about that for a minute. Could it be possible? It seemed obvious now that I looked at it from that angle. Why would anyone be after Father Murphy, especially one of these Tainted things? Then another thought occurred to me.

"He wasn't going after Father Murphy, was he?"

"No. They figured out who you are, or rather what you are, and have decided to end your family line before you learn to use your abilities."

I considered this, but it led into areas I didn't want to dwell on. I did, however, follow the logic down several other paths. One led to a startling conclusion.

"I don't have a choice anymore, do I?"

Mr. Hager looked over at me again.

"The Tainted know who I am. I cannot simply go back to my life unless I want to be plagued by supernatural mercenaries, and their hired thugs. I am being forced to become a Bishop."

"So it would seem." Mr. Hager replied.

I considered the implications. I would have to move from my apartment. In this digital age, it was too easy to find someone. I couldn't service my clients personally for a while, or maybe ever. Would I need to move out of the city? Would Jackie be safe, or would she be tortured for just knowing me? And what about—a thought came to me that made me physically ill. A consideration that scratched at my very being, the core of who I was. What would happen to my Mets season tickets?

"Aw, shit!"

Chapter Nine

JOHN AND I SAT in the common room. We chose the high-backed chairs near the fireplace, staring into the flames. Few things in life can transport me to a quiet place of reflection more than the sound, smell, and dance of fire.

John sat across a small, round table with a beer in hand. I needed something a little stronger, opting for a glass of single malt scotch. Twirling the large, round ice cube around and around, I was comforted by the 'clink' against the glass. I savored the amber liquid, rolling it around my tongue before swallowing.

Mr. Hager had gone straight to his office, but Soon-Li sat with us awhile. She offered her sympathies over Father Murphy's injuries, as well as an official welcome to the Covenant. She had reviewed the security footage and couldn't believe we had survived. I must be truly blessed, she had said. At this moment, I didn't share her optimistic view. She kissed me on the cheek before leaving.

I glanced over at my remaining drinking companion, who was lost in his own contemplation. John acknowledged and returned that look, apparently taking it as an invitation.

"How's the scotch?" he asked in his slow drawl.

"It doesn't suck."

John smiled, taking another swig from his beer. I had a feeling that I would get along with this guy. While we were getting the drinks I had grabbed a glass for my scotch and asked him if he wanted one. He had looked at me like I was crazy, then glanced at the bottle in his hand saying, "It's already in a glass."

He seemed out of place here; too laid back, and not preachy or

sanctimonious, as I feared he might be. Granted, I hadn't spoken exten-
sively with anyone besides Mr. Hager, but that was the image I had of
these people. John, though, seemed a kindred spirit. I felt a connection to
him I rarely found in other people—one of the main reasons I had few
real friends. You need to work on friendships. They take time and energy
and are supposed to be a two-way street, though never are. If neglected,
they will fizzle out as quickly as the fire in front of me. Friendships that
spark to life quickly and require no maintenance are rare. Jackie was
the only one who fell on that side of the line. Possibly, until now.

"How did you get involved in this?" I asked.

"Same as everyone here. Born into it."

"Oh yeah, right. It's just that you seem, I don't know, normal."

John blurted out a belly laugh that was nearly a spit take. "Because
I don't dress in a cassock and quote scripture?"

"Well, actually, yeah."

John chuckled again and took another pull from the bottle.

"I was named after John the Baptist. My father was not only a
Bishop but also a practicing deacon. He would have taken his vows,
but he was too dedicated to the Covenant and knew that he needed
to father children. He could quote sections of the Bible that most
people have never heard of, and even studied the gospels that were
not included in the King George version."

John took another sip.

"See, that's what I'm talking about."

John continued as if I hadn't spoken, "But he loves his baseball,
curses like a drunken sailor, and he is the one who taught me about
beer. Christian, having faith is not about being pious. It's about believing in something bigger than yourself. It doesn't need to be about a
higher power. Having faith is putting your trust in something and
allowing yourself to be guided."

I was silent for a few seconds. Then I looked up, my face deadpan,
and said, "That was a little pious."

The bottle in John's hand stopped halfway to his lips as he looked
back at me. After a second, he smiled and held his bottle out in salute.

"Fuck you."

I clinked my glass against the bottle. "Amen!"

We both laughed, taking a sip when we finally caught our breath. "Thanks, I needed that." I said.

"I know this is not the type of club you're used to, but I can assure you we're not a cult."

"Said every cult ever."

John chuckled. "Yeah, okay. But I can tell you this: we will never tell you what to believe. If you haven't noticed, we represent many religions. When you finally get to look around, you will notice several areas for prayer. Being a Bishop, despite the name, does not require you to believe in anything specific. You don't need to attend services or to adhere to strict religious restrictions. You believe what you want, the way you want. The important thing is that you have faith in something and use that faith to benefit others."

"To protect and serve?"

"Something like that."

An intercom beeped on the wall and Mr. Hager's voice came on. "Mr. Bateleur?"

John pointed out the exact location. I approached the intercom and pushed the button marked speak.

"Yes, oh-mighty voice on the wall? How may I serve you?"

"Humorous. Would you please come up to my office when you are done with your convalescing?"

"I will do so with great haste," I replied in a mock English accent.

"That would be most appreciated."

I shook my head and emptied the glass in one shot. John was grinning at the repartee.

"You can take the stairs in the kitchen."

"Thanks," I responded, lifting my glass. I made my way to the large kitchen behind the common room and placed my now empty glass in the dishwasher. It was a very modern kitchen that looked like it could support a small restaurant, with many of the appliances being of the industrial variety. On the left wall was an old-fashioned dumbwaiter. On the back wall were double doors leading to a dining room that could serve thirty with ease. I found the spiral staircase in the back right corner.

It was one of those retro metal ones that led to a hole in the floor. A faint glow came from above. I didn't remember seeing a spiral staircase on my last visit and had no idea where it led. I remembered his office was three floors up, so I started climbing. The natural tendency, when entering the next level of a house, is to expect a room with a similar layout to the one you just vacated. The area I stepped into was a little disorientating.

At first, based on the furniture, I thought I was entering a second common room with a higher ceiling. Then I saw the books. I stopped halfway up the stairs, my legs still in the kitchen and my head and chest in what could only be the library. Either that, or a really fancy scotch bar. It was expansive, extending up three levels. Books lined every wall on both levels and were separated by a balcony that ran its circumference. I stood there, hovering between the two rooms, until I could rein in my awe enough to finish the climb.

Well-padded chairs created various reading areas, from little nooks to larger spaces where several people could work together. But it was the books that held my gaze. I turned slowly, taking it all in. It was like looking at a section of the New York Public Library that had been removed whole and placed into the house. A voice came from the middle of the room.

"Are you lost?"

I looked over to see Tira, who was sitting a chair with a book on her lap and her feet curled up under her.

"Hey. No. It's just... this place is amazing. I have never seen so many books outside of a library."

"This is a library."

"I meant a public one."

"Yeah, this one is pretty impressive," she said with the makings of a smile.

She took a second to take in what was an everyday sight to her; a chance to see it with fresh eyes again.

"Are you looking for anything specific?"

"Actually, I was on my way to Mr. Hager's office."

"Oh, sure. Just take the spiral up to the top level and follow the walkway to the door on the opposite wall. That will take you out into the office hallway."

"Thanks. What are you reading?"

"Some research on the creation and dispatching of demons."

"Just a little light reading, huh?" My smile quickly vanished. "Wait, you're serious? Demons actually exist? People can be possessed?"

"You watch too much TV." Tira flipped her hand dismissively.

"Okay, teach me."

"I don't have time to teach you everything you need to know about demons. And don't you have to go meet Amram?"

"Come on. You can't just throw demons on the table and not give a little commentary. Just give me the highlights."

She looked at me as though gauging my worth, then she slowly closed the book.

"Fine. First, they don't hop from one person to another via black smoke."

"You watch that show too?"

She ignored me and continued leaning in a little.

"What is black is their souls. It takes months of torture to weaken them, then years of having them commit unspeakable acts." Tira's eyes narrowed. "The circumstances have to be just right to support a being of such vast evil and massive power."

"Holy crap."

She leaned back in a more casual way.

"You're not kidding. But the super strength is accurate. Even with our blessing, going up against one is like Arnold Schwarzenegger going up against a rhinoceros. It would be an interesting fight to watch, but the ending would be inevitable."

"That bad?"

She opened the book again, devoting her attention back to it. "They are tough to kill and impossible to remove. Once a soul has been corrupted to the degree necessary to support a demon, there can be no redemption."

"What about the adage that says it is never too late to repent?"

She looked up from the book just enough to meet my eyes. "Whoever said that never met a demon."

That didn't sit well with me. I wasn't sure why but the feeling stuck in my craw. I made a mental note to do some research of my own.

"What about the black eyes?"

"Nope, their eyes are fine."

"So how do you know they're a demon?"

Tira sighed dramatically and looked up again from her book. "Like I said, the *eyes* are fine, but the whole person gives off a sense of wrongness. Most people replace the wrongness with some physical manifestation—that is, if they look closely enough and don't just keep their eyes averted. The longer they look, the more wrong the feeling gets."

"Wrong?"

"That is the only way the books describe it. No one I know has ever seen one. They are actually very rare."

"Huh."

Tira adjusted her positioning and redirected her full attention to her pages. I thought about asking some follow-up questions, then decided against it. Ignoring the multitude of books beckoning me to explore, I followed Tira's directions and exited the library. I stepped into the now familiar hallway and knocked on the closed door.

"Come in."

Mr. Hager sat at the bistro table, reading a book and sipping tea. I sat down opposite him and poured some into the waiting cup in front of me.

"Get lost on the way up?" he asked, turning the page.

"Came up through the library. I was discussing demons with Tira."

He looked past his eyebrows at me. Then after a second said, "well she would be our resident expert."

He went back to his book. People do a lot of reading here. Maybe it won't be so bad after all, as long as I can watch the game too.

"So, what did you want to talk to me about?" I picked up the cup and saucer to take a sip.

"Nothing. I just wanted to return something to you."

I stopped with the cup halfway to my lips. Under the saucer was the white key card.

Chapter Ten

I WOKE WITH A start. There were a few seconds of disorientation as I tried to figure out where I was. What bed was I in? Where was the wall? I reached for my TV remote but found only air where my shelf should have been. Blinking a few times, I ran a hand over my face and hair as it slowly came back to me. I was in a room at the Covenant house.

My room, if you could believe that. It had a small attached bathroom, which was basically just a toilet, sink, and shower stall. The room itself was equally barren: bed, nightstand, small desk, dresser, and closet. The last two pieces were mostly empty, except for some extra clothes they had bought for me before my arrival. Being an eternal rebel, I wanted to rage against the linear path laid out before me. I felt like Mario but without the ability to go back, only forward. Forced to either rescue Princess Peach or be stomped on by Bowser.

Mr. Hager told me I could decorate as I liked, so I had that going for me; although I still couldn't attempt a visit to my apartment to collect my things, since it was probably being watched. He informed me they would take me shopping for the necessities. My response of 'thanks Dad' had not gone over well.

I got up and made my way to the bathroom. After taking care of my morning requirements, I cranked the shower up to near scalding level and stood under the stream for a good ten minutes. By the time I finished, I felt rejuvenated. I was smiling when I pulled on my only set of clothes. They were the right size and looked exactly like some pieces in my wardrobe which creeped me out a little. I made my way down to the kitchen where I found Tira cooking herself breakfast.

"Good Morning," I said. "I see you are an early riser too."

She looked up and said, rather coolly, "Good morning. I am making an omelet. Would you like one?"

"That would be great, thanks. Can I help? Fry up some bacon, maybe?"

"I don't eat meat. If you want some, I believe there's some in the fridge."

"No, not necessary. What can I do to help?"

"The coffee is brewing, but we will need cups and plates."

She pointed to each, and I got to work, trying to make myself useful. After a few minutes, I caught the rhythm. Once the place settings were arranged at the large kitchen table, I cleaned up behind her as she worked.

"Not bad," she said, "Looks like you are not completely useless in the kitchen."

Since I apparently could not open my mouth without saying something stupid, I decided to just smile and say, "You too."

We ate our omelets in silence. It tasted great, despite the lack of meat, and I said so—leaving out the last part.

"Thanks, I'm glad you liked it. I didn't peg you as an early riser."

"I enjoy the mornings. One of my favorite things to do is sit outside on a crisp morning with a piping hot cup of coffee and watch the city wake up."

"Where, like Times Square?"

"No, somewhere more laid back, like Jackson Park. Do you know it?" Tira shook her head.

"It's beautiful. A tiny park in the triangle where Greenwich connects to Eighth. A window of green among all the brick and cement, with a big black fountain in the middle. Green enough to provide some fresh air, small enough to not let you forget you are in the best city on earth. A place where you get to see shops opening. Parents struggling to keep up with their older child as they run for the bus stop, dragging their younger child behind them. The zombie walk of those who didn't really wake up until eleven. The impatient business people trying to maneuver around crowds, more interested in what's on their phones than where they're going. And the guy setting up his sign and cup, letting people know it's his birthday for the fourth day in a row. Mornings are new beginnings; the promise, or hope, that whatever happened yesterday is over."

I pulled myself out of my revelry and saw that Tira was watching me with a strange expression on her face.

"Sorry," I said flatly.

"Why?"

"I don't know. Seems a bit deep for the morning."

Mr. Hager walked in. "Good morning," he said as he went to the cabinet for a mug and poured himself some coffee. "I see you are not without a few good habits, Mr. Bateleur."

I gave him a questioning look.

"I didn't think you would be up before noon."

"What, does everyone think that I'm a slacker?" I asked no one in particular.

"Yes," they both answered in unison.

I sighed, shaking my head. Maybe I could hide out at Charles' lake house until this died down. At least there I had the repartee high ground. I turned to Tira.

"Thanks for breakfast. Since you cooked, I will take care of the dishes," I replied.

"Great, thanks," she said and left the kitchen, coffee in hand.

I got to work on clearing the table. Mr. Hager, in the meantime, grabbed half a grapefruit from the refrigerator, along with a spoon, and began to eat. When I finished, I refreshed my coffee and sat down across from him.

"So, what is on the agenda for today?"

"We will complete your tour," he said between bites.

"I thought John did that last night."

This place was bigger than it looked from the outside and was mostly empty. Besides the common area, there were several floors of offices several more of mini-apartments like the one I was assigned. There were also larger suites which had multiple bedrooms and a small common area. I asked Hager why I couldn't have one of those instead of the smaller one I now occupied.

"You can," he said. "As soon as you get married."

I guess I needed to up my game.

The top floor held several places of worship aligning with different religions. They weren't large, but they all had stained glass skylights, which added a sense of awe.

"Mr. McCaw showed you the skin and organs. I will show you the heart."

"I didn't know there were more floors."

"Not up, there aren't."

"Cool, do we slide down poles to get there?"

Mr. Hager scowled at that but didn't take the bait. "Have you spoken with Ms. Townsend?"

"Yeah, last night."

"What did you tell her?"

"What can I tell her? How do you explain this?"

"So, you made up a story?"

"No. We have one constant, we don't lie. Plus she can spot a lie a mile away." I said.

"While admirable, it seems a serious commitment for a friend. Seems more appropriate for a spouse."

"Jackie is more than a friend, she's family."

"I know many families where lying is the norm. Did you never plan her a surprise party?"

"That's different."

"How so?"

"I'm not trying to deceive her. I'm doing something for her. Something that will make her happy."

"And how is this different?" I looked at him, confused.

"This has weight, it has meaning. Just because something is difficult doesn't mean it should be avoided."

Mr. Hager nodded.

"So, what did you tell her?"

"I told her I met someone who was also close to Father Murphy. That there was a chance that the shooter was after me, and I was holding out at your place until it could be sorted out. I suggested that she avoid my place so she didn't get caught up in whatever this was."

"And?"

"She was worried, of course. I told her I would find a time to meet up with her and explain more, that this was larger than a phone conversation."

I really hated this. Jackie and I shared everything. I just wasn't sure how to tell her about this, and it was driving me crazy.

Mr. Hager finished his breakfast and placed his dishes in the dishwasher. I followed suit with my cup.

"Sufficiently caffeinated?"

"Yup, lead on Obi-Wan."

He narrowed his eyes but made his way over to the other side of the kitchen in silence. He stood next to the dumbwaiter and raised his hand as though he was half-heartedly asking a question in a class. Although he touched nothing, there were several loud clicks. Then a section of the wall split in two and swung outward. It didn't separate evenly. The seam followed whatever lines had naturally formed on the wall, making the two doors resemble a complex jigsaw puzzle. Inside was a cramped, empty room. Mr. Hager waved his arm in an 'after you' motion.

I hesitantly stepped in while my silent tour guide followed and pulled the doors closed behind us. A second set of doors slid shut, and we began to move.

"Elevator, huh?"

"Nothing gets by your keen sense of deduction."

I couldn't tell how far we descended, since I had no idea how fast the Wonkavator was traveling. There were no indicator lights or digital countdowns to guide me. The doors opened on a short, wide corridor that led to one massive metal door. Once again, Mr. Hager raised his hand to no one. A panel opened in the middle of the door, revealing two pads and an adjustable dual iris scanner. He placed one hand on each pad and brought his eye to the scanner. Another resonant set of clicks followed, sounding more like a *thunk* this time, and the door swung silently outward.

"Fingerprint and iris scanning? Seems kind of old-fashioned. My cell phone has facial recognition."

"It's actually a fingerprint, palm print, vein pattern, iris, and eye capillary pattern. It also measures the distance between the eyes. Facial recognition can be fooled. Now, if you wouldn't mind, please stand as I did. I wish to add you to the database."

I hesitated for a second, then did as requested.

"Eve, add a new Bishop."

A whir emanated from the system, and the adjustable eye scanner shifted slightly.

"Scan complete. Bishop Christian Bateleur added." The female voice had no hint of computerization.

"How did it know who I was?"

"Your keycard is specific to you. I presume you have it on you. If you didn't, you would not have come this far without me authorizing an override command. It is one of the safeguards. No one without a key gets to the basement."

"How does it know I have it with me?"

"We have scanners all over. They always know where the approved guest cards are and if they are with their owner. Eve, where is Mr. Bateleur's key card?"

"In his back-right pocket," the disembodied voice said.

"The chip in the keycard is matched to you so that no one else can use it," Mr. Hager explained.

"You said guest card. Am I still only a guest?"

"Until the ceremony tonight."

"Ceremony?" I asked, a little hesitantly. The thought of going through a ritual like that of a college fraternity did not sit well. We had a few unauthorized versions in the army. I was not a fan.

"More tradition than anything else. The acceptance of your gifts; an oath to use them with integrity and honor for the good of mankind."

"Then I get an official card?"

"Then you get a subcutaneous chip that can't be lost or stolen. It is injected into your forearm." Mr. Hager said.

"Ah, hence the arm raising."

"Correct. Shall we?"

"One more question: if you have a chip planted in your forearm, why the additional security?"

I expected to be getting on Mr. Hager's nerves, but the questions did not seem to bother him. Here's my problem—I am naturally curious, which got me in trouble as a kid. I would ask too many questions, which annoyed the adults, my teachers, and most other authority figures. The habit did not go over well in the army. At times, they didn't know if they should promote me or hand me my walking papers. To compound my irritating nature, I am, for the most part, an introvert. I spend much of my time alone, so I am not always aware of when I go too far.

"If an intruder had access to a chip, they may fool the sensors and pass themselves off as a Bishop. But only rightful members can get through that security."

"How would someone get access to a chip?"

Mr. Hager gave me a pointed look that told me more than I wanted to know. Then he motioned us through the door, which shut itself and locked behind us.

We entered another corridor. This one was very long, running perpendicular to the one we just left.

"This is our headquarters, as it were. To the left, you will find R&D and technical analysis labs. The door in front of us is our strategy room. To the right are exercise and training rooms, as well as the garage."

"Wait, hold up, garage? Down here?"

"You've never heard of an underground parking garage?"

I had no suitable response, so remained quiet.

"None of the doors are locked, save one, which I will show you later. Feel free to explore any area on your own time. For now, we need to start your training." Hager headed right.

"Don't I need to wait for the ceremony before training?"

"As I indicated, it is more of a tradition than anything else, and we are pressed for time."

We passed a door on the left with no description and no further commentary. Apparently, the brief tour was over. A little further down was another lone door, and I could just make out a final one at the very end.

"Any thought to marking the doors?" I asked.

"Why? Do you feel the need to do so in your own home?"

"Touché."

We turned down a short corridor which had a door on either side, and double swinging doors at the far end.

"You can change in there," Mr. Hager said, pointing to the door on his left. "You will find a locker containing the appropriate garments. I will meet you in the training area, which you can access through the south door in the locker room."

I nodded and repressed the myriad of questions that bounced around my head.

Which locker should I use? Where do I find workout clothes? Are you sure you have my size? How the hell do I figure out which way south is underground? I presumed such questions would only be met with sarcasm and avoidance. For the little time I had known this man, I felt he was a big believer in the figure it out for yourself method of teaching. This should be interesting.

Most of my questions were answered by a short perusal of the locker room. This was less like a gym changing room and more like the setup you would find being used by a major league baseball team. The one exception was that each person's area included a little changing room with its own swinging door. It would aid modesty but not hinder conversation. A gold-plated plaque was mounted on each door, etched with the owner's name. I was pleasantly surprised to find mine was not labeled with a piece of masking tape as I had imagined, but was installed as if I had been a member of this strange little club for years. I was about to go in and look for clothes when the name on the next door caught my eye. *Angela Bateleur.*

I wasn't sure why my mother's stall was still here. I wanted to investigate but resisted. This was not the time. I preferred to be alone for it, not rushed by my impatient teacher. With conscious effort, I pushed down the curiosity and opened my door. The workout clothes I found were not Nike or Under Armour. The pants were roomy without being overly baggy, and the jacket-like top had an open front that wrapped around, tying on both sides. I changed quickly and found the south door. It was the only other door.

I was not prepared for the vastness of the training room. It was as if a friend brought me into his basement to show me the stadium that he just installed, complete with a running track surrounding faux buildings, and an obstacle course. I didn't have time to soak in the scenery.

"Ready to work?"

Mr. Hager sat off to the side on a bench. "As ready as I'll ever be."

He didn't guide me over to the obstacle course, as I had hoped. Nor did he start with the numerous heavy-looking punching bags, or with one of the other intriguing sections. We went, instead, to the corner, where a fountain stood. It was completely out of place in a chamber that screamed of sweat and blood and competition. Religious figures from various periods had been carved throughout its three levels. On top, where the water emerged, was a depiction of every deity you could conceive of. They all sprouted from the same central point, yet none dominated. Water flowed down to the reservoir, which was about the size of a kiddy pool, though perhaps a little deeper. There were a few benches lined up, concentric to the font.

Mr. Hager sat on one bench and closed his eyes. I followed suit but didn't pray. Although I had been going to church regularly for a while, I was by no means devout. I did, however, do some self-reflecting.

The irony of my situation wasn't lost on me. I was sitting in the underground haven of a small band of—for lack of a better term—superheroes, whose powers were derived from God. I had seen them in action. Hell, I'd felt the power flow through me, even if I wasn't aware of it at the time. But even now, I didn't truly believe. My mind looked for some other explanation of where the power could come from. I had easily accepted the powers themselves. My issue resided with the source.

Mr. Hager lifted his head and opened his eyes.

"The Covenant of Bishops is ancient. Older than most religions, possibly older than religion itself. Although our individual belief systems differ, one thing remains constant: we all believe that our deities are connected. There is some debate whether they are separate entities destined to guide different types of people, or if they are just distinct manifestations of one being. We do not argue about who is right, or whose religion is better. The key for each person is that you believe in your own faith. Whatever that is.

"There is a connection between many religions. I will put the parable into a Judeo-Christian context. Do you remember the story of Satan?"

"Yes," I answered. "Satan was the most beloved of God's children but was jealous of His power and wanted to rule for himself. So, God cast him out of Heaven."

"Close enough. It is believed that Satan wanted to get back at his Father for casting him from grace. But how does one go about hurting God?"

"The same way you hurt any creature that is more concerned for someone else's well-being: you hurt those they love."

"Correct. However, Satan had limited abilities to affect the course of humanity in his state. He, therefore, converted some of them into demigods."

"The Tainted."

"Correct again. He gave them abilities, both physical and metaphysical, which they use to cause chaos, pain, and suffering."

I started thinking about the wars, the genocide, the persecution, and the heinous acts that we have inflicted on each other over the centuries. I was sickened and yet somehow soothed. It was not humanity that felt the need to beat on each other. We had an outside influence.

"How many are there?"

"We cannot be sure. There isn't any documentation that specifies the numbers, but we have identified eighteen."

"Eighteen? That's it?"

"Believe me, that's more than enough."

"It just doesn't seem enough to cause all the problems in the world." Mr. Hager looked at me strangely. Then, to my surprise, he laughed.

It was a belly laugh that would have made me laugh right along with him, had I not been so surprised by the sight. Although the fit was short, he laughed so hard that tears streamed down his face.

"My dear boy, they do not cause all the problems." My relief disintegrated.

"Humankind is flawed, self-centered, and egotistical all by themselves. The Tainted are simply the grease for some grander scale acts. Oh sure, they dabble with the occasional individual, but I believe they do that just for fun. Well, that and to increase their ranks."

"They can recruit people?"

"Convert would be a more accurate term. It is also why we call them, the Converted. Not nearly as powerful, though dangerous in their own right. But that is a tale for another day." Mr. Hager took a final deep breath then continued. "To counteract the Tainted, God asked Michael to take action, and he created the Bishops."

"Why didn't God just smite the Tainted right there?" I asked.

"There are many theories, although we can never know. Nor can we know the exact circumstances which put us here. These are the stories that have been passed down and eventually, several generations later, documented. My belief is he looked at them like mischievous children. One does not simply smite them when they misbehave."

"Why wouldn't they write the stories down right away?"

"Remember, I said we were very old. Our existence predates formal writing."

"Okay. So, where does the fountain come in?"

"Now, that is an intelligent question."

He stood and walked over to the fountain. Laying a hand on it, he said, "this is the source of our abilities."

I followed, stopping next to him, and examined the carvings. "The fountain?"

"No," he said, scooping up a handful and throwing it into my face in one quick movement.

"The water."

That shock I felt back at the diner hit me again, only stronger. I fell to my knees. My whole body shook with the power. But it dissipated as quickly as it had come. I found myself breathing heavily as I recovered.

"What the hell!" I said when I could catch my breath.

"Not Hell, Mr. Bateleur, quite the opposite."

"Water doesn't normally do that to me."

"Nor should it; this is not your typical spring water."

"Holy water?"

"In a sense. This water is sourced from the same location where the tradition of holy water derived from. But this is not, strictly, holy water. While holy water may give you a tingle and a somewhat heightened sense of awareness, this water will do much more."

"Like what?"

"That comes later."

"Why later?"

"He who would learn to fly one day——"

"Must first learn to stand, and walk..."

"You have read Nietzsche?"

"No, Eddie Murphy."

Mr. Hager gave me a look, then said, "come, sit over here." We sat cross-legged on the grass that surrounded the fountain. "Wait, what?"

I brushed my hand across the thick lawn. "Real grass?"

"Yes, it is more cost effective than to have a poured concrete floor with artificial turf on top. Plus, the natural materials are more conducive to what we do."

"Huh." I grunted.

"Now, can we begin?"

I stopped examining the flora and returned my attention to my teacher, who nodded.

"Have you ever meditated before?"

The look on my face apparently provided the answer.

"I thought not. Close your eyes. Slow your breathing. Get into a rhythm. Count your breaths. One, inhale."

I did so, filling my lungs slowly all the way to capacity.

"Two, exhale."

Just as slowly, I let the breath out.

"Three, inhale."

Air flooded into my lungs again.

"Four, exhale."

I blew out the air as though trying to move a pinwheel. We continued that way up to ten, then started over. After a few rounds of this, Mr. Hager instructed me to continue counting in my head. My mind would occasionally wander, which he warned me would happen. I followed the prescribed method of simply starting back at one and continuing. My mind cleared. I was amazed that it was working, a thought which dropped me out of my meditative state again. I started over. It was like, when trying to fall asleep, you realize you are drifting off; that simple thought can pull you right back out. After several recounts, I could obtain the state and hold it.

Mr. Hager's voice skipped over the still lake of my mind, providing small ripples of information and direction.

When your mind is calm, feel the internal working of your body. Sense the air in your lungs. Focus on your heartbeat. Feel the blood flowing through your veins and arteries. Now go deeper, past the physical, into the core of your being. When you are there and at peace, you will sense it. A warmth. An energy.

Going deeper into myself, an image coalesced around me. I stood in a meadow, green grass all around, dotted here-and-there with wildflowers. I sensed water nearby, though I could not identify where this knowledge came from. Instinctively, I walked towards it and suddenly I was there. A vast lake splayed out before me, the surface like glass in its stillness. With childlike abandon, I stepped into the lake, laying back into it like a comfortable bed after a long journey.

The lake supported me without effort, and I floated out toward the center. I closed my eyes, giving my mind equal buoyancy. I was at peace here, unburdened by the discords of life. Free from the questions my physical form constantly fought with. I became one with it, my mind entangled with its depth. Drifting further, a current took hold that pulled me onward. I could feel something very faint. A sensation in my chest from an outside influence that was natural and awesome. Like a change in air pressure.

My mind tried to connect it to external experiences, to give it a name or a frame of reference. A thought skimmed across my lake, a dragonfly that bobbed and weaved, occasionally landing, causing undulations on the surface. Each concentric circle painted a piece of a picture for me. Together, they formed an idea. A waterfall. The flow of the water. The rumble deep in my chest. The sense of raw, natural power. Its awe of it took me in but didn't kick me out of this place of beauty and calm. I exalted in the sheer magnificence of it. It engulfed me. Then the rumble became a roar and I was no longer floating but falling.

Terror gripped me as I tumbled over the edge, dropping faster and faster. I could sense the mist and spray as the great falls reconnected with still water below. I knew I was lost.

Just as I sensed the impact was imminent, I felt myself being pulled back, dragged up through the layers of mist; the thundering sounds of crashing water calmed to a reverberation, then barely a feeling. I continued to rise. The lake waters receded, and the meadow returned, only to pass by, disappearing into the thickening mists. Thoughts came back to me. The most prevalent of these being; *who is shaking me?*

I opened my eyes and found myself lying face up, surrounded by the team. Mr. Hager was shaking me forcefully. Tira was lying next to me on the grass, panting. The rest of their expressions ranged from shock to concern. All except Mr. Hager, whose face registered a state that I had never seen before: astonishment.

I looked to each of them and finally asked, "Is it almost lunchtime? I'm starving."

Chapter Eleven

"I'M SORRY," I SAID between bites. "How long have I been sleeping?"

It was well past lunchtime, and the team sat around the kitchen table. Tira had a plate of homemade sushi. Soon-Li was nibbling at a pastrami on rye—I knew there was something I liked about her. Mr. Hager ate grilled chicken with some left-over pasta, and John had a small salad with a large piece of chocolate cake on the side. I attacked a sub sandwich, made from everything in the fridge, with the ferocity of a starving wolf. I described what I remembered about my dream: the meadow, the lake that led to a waterfall. My descriptions caused them to drop what little they had eaten back onto their plates.

"You weren't sleeping. You have been in a meditative state for several hours," Mr. Hager explained.

"Sounds like sleeping to me. How did you get me out?"

"My blessing provides me some telepathic abilities," Tira said. I stopped chewing and swallowed hard.

"So, you can read minds?" I asked.

She rolled her eyes. "It's not as easy as that. Don't worry, your thoughts are safe."

I tried not to show my relief. "Okay, so what *do* you see?"

She hesitated for so long I thought she wouldn't answer.

"I mostly get impressions, based on my own experiences." Tira paused for a second and I thought she was going to ask me a question, but then shook her head and continued. "Anyway, I felt you were at a precipice and guided you back."

"Even with all that, Amram still had to shake you to snap out of it altogether," John interjected. It took me a second to realize that he was referring to Mr. Hager.

"I do not understand," Soon-Li said, though the question was directed to Mr. Hager. "That sounds like the description of the Oneness."

"Indeed, it does." Mr. Hager agreed.

"Impossible. That level of connection to the power is rare and only attained by those who have studied meditation and self-discipline for decades," Tira added.

"Also true."

They all looked at me as I took another bite. I noticed the scrutiny and paused my chewing, looked at each, and gave an exaggerated shrug. John quietly shook his head, his dreadlocks swaying.

"But he has barely touched his power," Soon-Li stammered, practically unable to string the words together.

Mr. Hager acknowledged this with a mere nod of the head.

"But what does that mean about his overall potential? The accounts that I have read regarding this type of transcendence describe only..."

"Be that as it may," Mr. Hager interrupted, "we cannot deny the facts before us. To do so would make us as blind as the council of Elron."

I nearly choked on the last piece of my sandwich at the Tolkien reference.

"So, where does that leave us?" John asked.

"With a mystery, I would say. We need to proceed with his training, though cautiously. Perhaps you should accompany me this time, just in case? Can you spare the time?" Mr. Hager asked Tira.

"Not much choice in the matter. We need all hands on deck, and he needs to learn to defend himself. We can't waste resources on a security detail, and he is useless the way he is."

"Agreed." Mr. Hager said.

"Um, I am sitting right here." I said.

"And?" she responded, then got up and called the hidden elevator.

We had been trying for a few hours, but my meditation never went deeper than the meadow, and even that was rare. The distant sound of the waterfall, and even the lake shore, was too far out or gone altogether. Mr. Hager seemed mollified.

"So glad I could waste my time with you," Tira said, while walking away.

"I am not sure what I did to upset her, but, whatever it was, I didn't mean it," I said to Mr. Hager.

"I do not believe it was anything you did with your actions. I would recommend dropping it for now and letting her cool down."

"Okay."

"Are you ready to work?"

"Sure, anything but this meditating stuff. It feels like sleeping during the day, and I was never a fan of napping."

"Really? That is actually quite surprising." I frowned but did not reply.

"However, you will need to spend at least one hour per day in meditation."

My frown did not improve.

"I will ask Tira to work with you for a while until we are certain that there will be no further concerns."

"Great," I responded.

The thought of spending an hour a day in quiet reflection with her made my spine twitch. She made me feel guilty for no reason. Something was still bothering me though.

"First, I have a question."

Mr. Hager nodded.

"You compared what I experienced with a higher state of meditation. I don't get how falling off a waterfall is conducive to anything except dying."

"Think of it like surfing."

"I'm sorry, what? I've never surfed before."

"Do you understand the premise?"

"I've seen Point Break."

"Sufficient. What happened to the main character when he

attempted to surf for the first time?"

"He almost drowned."

He inclined his head. "The incredible force of the ocean, can be harnessed with the right training, experience and tools. You did the equivalent of paddling out into the perfect storm on a child's float."

I guess that made sense. I still remembered the power emanating from that place and doubted anyone could harness it.

"Now that you understand where our power comes from and have spent some time touching your connection to it, we need to discuss how that translates to abilities."

"Okay, I'll pretend I know what that means."

Mr. Hager nodded.

"The water is an enhancer. It doesn't give us abilities, per se. It enhances what we already have. It can make you stronger, faster, jump higher, and, in some cases, even enhance telekinetic or psychic abilities."

"What determines that?"

"You need to have some predisposition to that ability. If you don't have an ability, the water cannot enhance it."

"Makes sense. So, what's the catch?"

"Catch?"

"There's always a catch. You don't get something for nothing. There is always a trade-off or restriction."

He nodded again with a slight smile.

"Correct, Mr. Bateleur. The catch, as you put it, is that you cannot enhance more than one ability at a time. You can be fast, or strong, but not fast and strong."

"Why not?"

"We call it the supportive requirements factor."

"Excuse me?"

"Consider this, what happens when we blur?"

"We run faster."

"Is that it?"

I thought about the one time I experienced this phenomenon.

"Everything seemed to slow down. I was running fast, but it seemed like everything was normal to me."

"Good. That was because your senses were boosted to keep up with your speed. Now, can you extrapolate further?"

I nodded, already lost in thought, trying to take it to the next level. "To keep up with the added stress to my muscles, my heart and lungs would have to speed up. To support them, my whole metabolism would have to increase."

"Precisely. I also believe that the restriction is also a way to keep us in check—to ensure we do not become all-powerful and take advantage of our abilities."

"What about when you get stronger?" I asked, already going down that mental route.

"I suggest you pursue the effects of SRF on your own time. Feel free to come to me with questions."

It took effort to pull my head off the path. I nodded for him to continue.

"Very good, Mr. Bateleur. Shall we begin?"

We did, but with very little success. We started with every day running—me at the ready and Mr. Hager coaching me with instructions.

"Seek the calm. Find the power within and unleash it. Go."

I ran. At first, I thought I was doing it. My legs and arms pumped. I felt the rush as I cut through the air. My adrenaline started to build. Then I realized I was just running normally, not even that fast. I tried several more times until I lay on the grass, panting, but nothing kicked in.

We went on to other abilities. I tried throwing a shot. It went a measly few feet and I found new respect for those that could throw it over fifty in competition. Skill after skill, I failed. Dead lifting, jumping, trying to find a hidden object by sound or smell. We kept at it for hours with no indication that I was anything but an ordinary man.

After supper, I was given instructions to shower thoroughly. He gave me a brush and special fragrance-free soap, along with other instruments that were to be used in harder to reach places. I did so under scalding hot water, also as instructed, scrubbing my skin almost raw. I even used the bar soap on my hair—with some level of trepidation, as I once tried a similar experiment when I ran out of shampoo. Fortunately, this soap did not leave my hair feeling like the fur on a bear's ass. At least I assume that's what a bear's ass feels like. I made a mental note to find out where they got this timesaving super soap. The brushes and other instruments, on the other hand, they could keep. Although I had to admit, besides being a little raw, I did feel very clean.

When I emerged from the shower, I found a set of red robes laid out for me, along with a red... loincloth, was the only term that seemed to fit. Left to my own devices, I found a video online that gave instructions on how to put it on. It was not an overly complicated concept, but the execution was another story. It took me several tries to get it right. The robes were accompanied with a braided black-and-white rope-belt. Now thoroughly cleaned and appropriately dressed, I went to the Christian chapel—no pun intended—for quiet reflection and communion with my faith.

The chapel was quaint and somewhat reminiscent of the Church upstate where all of this started. I thought back to that experience as I slipped into one of the small pews on the right. That wedding put me on two interconnecting paths: one toward the Bishops, and the other toward a reconnection with the church. No, that wasn't right, not the church. But what then? The answer evaded me like a firefly on a dark night.

I sat for a second, then reached down, extended the kneeler, and lowered myself to my knees. At first, my butt was still on the bench, until my neck itched in anticipation of being scolded. I lifted myself into a more penitent position and folded my hands to pray. I felt self-conscious, like I was pretending. My brain must have agreed, since it started going over activity lists.

I called in my subcontractors last night and explained that I would be taking an extended leave due to a sick relative. It would lay the groundwork for my eventual departure without seeming odd. Plus, it would leave me an option to go back. I wasn't even sure if that was possible, but I didn't want to shut the door completely. Jackie was blowing up the new phone Soon-Li had given me. My vague answers were not satisfying her, and I needed to schedule time to bring her up to speed. How the hell was I going to explain this? She wasn't one who strayed towards the metaphysical. This was going to put her in a fit of laughter or push her to have me committed.

Then there was this whole messed up scenario. I was sitting in a church wearing a set of robes and a friggin' loincloth, which was about as comfortable as an atomic wedgie. I was about to pledge myself to a secret organization that fought evil and would grant me superpowers in exchange for my faith. Oh, and after this mysterious ceremony, they were going to inject me with a device that could basically track my every movement. I opened my eyes and looked around for a big bowl of Kool-Aid. The only point that was grounding me was Father Murphy.

He listened to and accepted my story without pause. He had prior knowledge of this group—that much was clear—and a supportive attitude. He poured the mojo water on my head. If I removed every other point, that strange action at a strange time shined a light on obvious facts. Not only was this Covenant thing legit, but Father Murphy was involved. While I could associate his appearance in my life over the years to his generosity, the scenario made more sense when the Bishops were added in. I wasn't just a lost child that needed supervision; I was also an extraordinary child that needed guidance to reach a specific destination in life. So, the only question left was, why hadn't he just told me years ago? Why all this cloak and dagger crap? When I was eighteen, hell, even fourteen, if someone told me I could have superpowers if I receive communion...

Okay, fine. I probably would have called bullshit. But that wasn't the point. Was it?

I shook my head and took a deep breath, tying again to clear my thoughts. I started the counting exercise in my head. I sought the calmness that I felt at the lake, but was hesitant to go there based on what happened last time. Instead, I pictured a hillside with the sun just beginning its descent but still high in the sky. A small stream babbled down one side. There were birds chirping, a light breeze rustling the trees that dotted the landscape, and the fresh, clean smell of the outdoors. The sun warmed the skin on one side of my face; light pushing through my closed lids. The other side was noticeably cooler without this direct source of light and heat. The brook gurgled past me as it ran over the rocks and into the lake. A dragonfly buzzed at a distance. It came closer to me, hovering, waiting. A loon called in the distance, and it seemed like the dragonfly wanted me to go toward it.

I felt a hand on my shoulder and the image shimmered. The dragonfly looked quizzically at me, then turned and flew away toward the sound of the loon.

The physical world began to assert itself back into my consciousness: the light smell of incense, the hardwood of the pew I leaned on, the sound of a truck as it rumbled down the nearest street. I opened my eyes and found myself back in the chapel. John stood next to me with his hand lightly on my shoulder. He was similarly dressed in red robes, with a stole draped over his shoulders that reached down to his waist. On one side was a symbol of the sun. The other had a symbol of a sword.

"You had me a little nervous there. Wasn't sure if you had gone catatonic again," John said in his deep, baritone voice.

"No, I'm good. They ready for me?"

"Yeah."

I stood up and followed John. We made our way down into the kitchen, through the secured vault door via the secret elevator, and into the long hallway. This time, instead of going right, we went left past several rooms until we came to the last door. Without preamble, John opened it and went through. All the lights went out. The shock of it nearly made me curse, but, at the last second, I caught myself. The darkness was absolute. I wasn't sure what I should do and so just stood in the doorway. Or at least I assumed I was still there. For all I knew, I could be standing on a precipice, the slightest step sending me to my death. My mind raced as I tried to remember if Mr. Hager had said anything, but nothing came to mind.

This was a test. But of what? How to trip in the dark? Without knowing what was in front of me, I could be walking into anything. I took a slow, deep breath, trying not to make any sound. I wasn't sure why I decided to remain quiet, but it felt right. Then I took a step. I felt dirt or gravel through the soft sandals I wore. After the stadium-like training area, walking on dirt inside wasn't much of a shock. Another step, then the earth gave way to grass. The feeling made a connection in my brain, and I realized I could smell the lawn as well. I paused for a moment, trying to determine what else I sensed. There was a musty smell that I recognized but could not place.

I took another step, and another, slightly wobbly. I was not sure if I was going in the right direction, but continued forward. About ten paces in, I felt the grass give way back to dirt and slope downward. My next step made a splash, and I nearly lost my footing. I waited for laughter, or a warning shout, but the silence remained. I continued forward, now struggling to keep upright as I walked into the rapidly deepening pool. The water was neither cold nor warm. I got the feeling that whether this water sat in the middle of the desert or in the middle of the Arctic, it would not change a degree. Once the pool reached my waist, my balance returned, now supported by the water on either side. I continued onward until the water was up to my chest. Then I felt a hand on my shoulder from someone in front of me.

"Why have you come?" It was Mr. Hager's voice.

The question, along with the break of complete silence, shocked and confused me. The answer that immediately sprung to mind was sarcastic and biting.

Think.

Several responses came to mind, and I chose the one that sounded the best.

"To become a Bishop," I said, my voice unsure.

"You're either a Bishop or not. No one can make you one. So why have you come?"

Okay, choice two. "To join the Covenant."

"That is tangential, not the purpose. Why have you come?"

My frustration was growing. I tried to think, then stopped. This was not a puzzle that could be solved through logic. I sought the calm of the hillside; I quit trying to think and began to feel. The pitch darkness aided my focus. The image of that place sprang into my mind and filled my senses. I walked up to the lake and stepped into the water, bringing the two areas together: a bridge between the physical and the spiritual. At first, nothing happened. But then an understanding started to grow in me. I felt a buzz to my right and found the dragonfly again.

"Why have you come?" Mr. Hager's voice was more urgent now, more demanding.

The dragonfly danced in front of my face, watching me, waiting. I knew the response. It formed in my mind, quick and solid like it had always been there.

"To defend those who cannot defend themselves. To guide the lost. To bring light to the darkness."

I heard a collective gasp run through the other unseen members of the room, followed by a more pronounced silence than before. Hager's voice, when he next spoke, was less demanding and sounded unsure. "Then be cleansed of who you were and be born again into the light."

I felt a hand on my head and was pushed beneath the water. As soon as it engulfed me, the shock wave hit, coursing through me as though someone had thrown a hairdryer into the pool. I opened my eyes and saw a light show, like I was in the center of a plasma ball. The surrounding water started to boil. Then everything went black.

Chapter Twelve

I AWOKE WITH A start, grabbing at my chest and gasping for air. The room was pitch dark, but at least this time I knew where I was. I turned the light on and squinted as my eyes adjusted. I was naked and wet; whether it was from the dip in the pool or from sweat, I didn't know. According to the clock, it was almost three in the morning. I knew I had been dreaming, but the images were disappearing fast. The only thing I could say for sure was that my mother was there.

My heart was still pounding and my throat felt tight. I wiped tears off my face while trying to control my breathing. Before the wedding, my mother hadn't entered my dreams in a very long time. Since then, she'd been making more cameos than Stan Lee. The result was often like this. I felt drained. Scrubbing at my damp hair and felt a twinge on my forearm. Looking down, I found an injection mark. Apparently, I was a full member of the Covenant now, with all rights and privileges. Not to mention tracking, or so I assumed.

I turned my pillow over to find a dry spot and grabbed the book off the nightstand. The title read: *The Accumulated Knowledge of Demons* by Garlon Burgos. The book was full of documented incidents of demonic possession, notes outlining the process of preparing a host, and a short chapter on how to dispose of them—which basically described methods that hadn't worked very well. Fire was the biggest mistake of all the bungled attempts which apparently makes them stronger. I was most interested in the chapter that explained how to identify demons, since they seemed like ordinary people. It wasn't something the author could put into words. It was just as Tira said, a bad feeling. All in all, the book was good, with excellent content and good writing that made a very complicated subject easy to understand. I noted when I grabbed it from the library that the same author had also penned several cookbooks. I guess Garlon was a chef that moonlighted as a demon hunter. That's what I call range.

After reading for a couple of hours, I gave up the idea of getting more sleep. I got out of bed, showered, ate, and used my new access to start my workout early. I had a ton of pent-up energy that made my skin almost tingle, and I needed to try to work it off. Hager arrived soon after. He seemed somewhat shocked to find me already up and about.

"That's quite the initiation you guys have," I said after the obligatory greetings.

"Yes, well, everyone reacts differently to their initial baptism."

"I don't get it. I've already been doused a few times."

"There is a vast difference between being splashed and being fully submerged in the Lord's Blessing."

"Apparently."

Hager worked me until I thought I was going to throw up, then pushed me harder. My drill sergeant could have learned a few things from this old man.

That evening was my first my guided meditation session with Tira. I hadn't seen her all day, so I wasn't sure what I was in for. Well, that wasn't exactly true. I had caught sight of her while being tortured by Hager as she ran through her own morning regimen. She was distracting, as well as impressive, and I felt myself pushing even harder when I thought she might be watching, then berating myself for even caring.

Her attitude that night was different. It was not the outwardly angry person of the day before. She was hesitant, almost unsure of how to relate to me. I connected it to a time when I was still in the army.

I was at the bar and this woman started up a conversation with me. Not flirtatiously, just two people talking. She seemed nice, down to earth. A short time later her bodyguard came over informing her she needed to leave, or she would be late for her next appointment. I had been talking to the senator of New York, the current front runner for president. For the remaining few minutes before she paid both our tabs and left, I struggled to hold up my end of the conversation. She was the same person I had spoken easily with minutes before, but knowing who she was practically struck me mute. It shouldn't have mattered, but it did. That was what I felt coming from Tira, and it didn't make sense.

Our session was very awkward. That is until I nodded off. She slapped me awake, yelling at me that I had been snoring. I guess she got over whatever her issue was.

Afterwards, back in my room, I decided to call Jackie before collapsing.

"Where the fuck are you?" That was how she answered the phone.

"And hello to you, too."

"Don't give me that shit! Where are you? I'm coming to pick you up."

"Easy, everything is fine."

"What do you mean, everything is fine? You have been gone for days. The only texts you're giving me are bullshit, and you won't tell me where you are."

"Jackie, I appreciate your concern, but everything is fine."

"Is someone there? If you are in trouble, say backgammon."

"If I was in trouble, how the hell would I work backgammon into a sentence?"

"How about 'don't worry Jackie, we will finish our backgammon game tomorrow?' Did you ever think of that?"

"Yeah, I guess that would work."

"Asshole."

"Bitch."

"Are you sure you're okay?" Jackie's tone held a note of genuine concern.

"Yeah. This is just not something I can talk about on the phone. But I promise, we'll meet up and I'll explain everything."

"When?"

"I don't know."

"You really suck at commitments of any kind."

"Will you get off my case?"

"Not until you set a date and time for us to meet. You did say backgammon, so I am within my rights to send the cavalry in right now."

"You don't even know where I am."

"Do you really want to test me?"

Although I didn't think there was a chance in hell she would be able to find me, I wasn't about to take that chance.

"Fine. Thursday at seven. Let's meet for dinner at Eataly. Happy?"

"No, but we are starting to move in the right direction. You can't meet any earlier?"

"Jackie!"

"Okay, okay. Fine. Thursday. Christian, whatever you're caught up in, be careful."

"Like always."

"Not like always! The last time you pulled this shit you ended up in basic training."

"I'm not far from that now."

"What?"

"Nothing, forget it."

"Did you reenlist?"

"Not really."

"What do you mean, not really?"

"I did not reenlist in the Army."

"That was very specific."

"Or the Navy, or the Marines, or the Coast Guard."

"Or any other military organization?"

I hesitated a hair too long.

"Christian, what the fuck did you do?"

"You curse a lot."

"You want to hear cursing..."

The string of expletives that followed were as inventive as they were scathing.

"Okay, so I'll see you Thursday..."

The next day was the same, this time with John guiding me. I thought he would be a little easier on me, but the opposite was true.

If Hager could teach a drill sergeant, then John would have been his star pupil. He didn't give me a moment's rest, pushing me to my limit. The following day was Soon-Li, who was gentle and supportive, then beat the crap out of me during our multiple sparring matches. I had a feeling she could take Bruce Lee on one-handed, without ever touching her blessing.

I held up a hand as I bent over, rested my other hand on my knee, and caught my breath.

"So, what's...the Oneness?" I asked in between panting.

"Eh? Why do you ask?" Soon-Li was not even breathing hard.

"I've just been thinking about it and wanted to know more."

"It is not for you to worry about."

"Why not?"

Soon-Li stared at me for what felt like an eternity. I felt stripped naked under her scrutiny, but at least she wasn't pummeling me.

"The oneness is a meditative state attained by only a rare few. It requires decades of training and thousands of hours of meditation. The last known Bishop to accomplish the Oneness was a woman from Persia, back in 1734. She had done so mere months before her death.

"What was her name?"

"She was unknown outside of the Bishop Chronicles."

"How old was she when she died?"

"A hundred and twelve. It was said once she attained the Oneness, she had no further reason to continue."

"Huh." I said, lost in thought. Then something occurred to me. "Tira is big into the meditation thing. Is she trying to attain the Oneness?"

"That is a question only she can answer. But ask yourself this: would you study martial arts with the intention of stopping short of the highest level?"

In-fact, I knew many people who joined a Karate class and stopped before reaching black belt. And almost no one reaches the tenth dan. I was still leaning over, hands on my knees, knowing that, if I straightened, Soon-Li would take it as a sign I was ready to continue. I had my breathing under control but was hedging for a longer break.

Flick, flick, smack. Soon-Li's foot shot out inside my arms, kicking one hand off my knee and taking the second out as she pulled back. The same foot drove into my chest, throwing me backwards. The whole motion lasted only a second, and I found myself on my ass again. Soon-Li's foot hadn't touched the ground once.

"Hey, no fair using your powers." I complained. She looked at me and raised an eyebrow.

"I didn't."

Dawn came on the fourth day. I groaned. My muscles didn't have time to recover. I'd been using different ones each day so the pain I felt each morning was cumulative. The bruises I received from Soon-Li earlier were now bright purple and formed patch work all over my body; they made me look like I had a skin condition. The worst were on my butt. She really liked to hit me there. I groaned again when I thought about what was to come, and not just because of the continued punishment my body was taking. Tira was guiding my workout today.

I rubbed my face with my hand and pulled myself out of bed, staggering to the bathroom. The scalding hot water felt good on my aching muscles, loosening them up. I even turned the shower head to the massage setting, hoping that would help. It didn't. But it was better than nothing. As I stood there whimpering like a child, I thought about what Soon-Li said yesterday.

Was that what's been bugging Tira these past few days? I had accidentally attained a level of mediation that she had been striving for and could not hope to attain for decades more. I mean, granted, she had never really taken a shine to me. But, since that day, she seemed angry with me. It was the only thing that made sense. I turned off the water and toweled off. I dressed, had breakfast alone, and made my way to the next day of torture.

She was already down there, running through some katas. I had advanced hand-to-hand combat from my military training, but nothing compared to the level that these people were on. Even without their enhanced abilities, I doubted I would be much of a challenge to any of them. Their technique was handed down, parent-to-child, from the days of the old masters, whose only focus every day was to improve their art. That art had grown and expanded with each new generation until what remained only vaguely resembled modern day martial arts.

I watched Tira's fluid movements, both beautiful and scary. Once finished, she immediately turned towards me, fully aware of my presence.

"Are you ready to work?"

"Absolutely."

I was wrong. Tira's version of training included quickly shifting from one ability to another. Running followed by lifting followed by running, then to jumping. I did parkour—in the loosest sense of the word—through buildings which I had, until now, only run past. She followed me through every move, always right behind, pushing me.

We stood in an alley between buildings. I was attempting a short wall run up to a window. In my high school, there was a ten-foot wall in the quad which seniors regularly tried to scale, then perched up there until the teachers made them get down. I couldn't do it then, and my skills did not improve with age. This was my fifth attempt.

I gauged the distance and leaped as if I was going to hip check the wall. My inside foot caught traction and boosted me higher. Then my outside foot finally caught too, just in time for me to grab the window's ledge. I hung there for a brief second, reveling in my success.

"Move it!"

Tira streaked behind me, practically floating up to the ledge next to me. She perched there one-handed, staring daggers at me. I turned away and lifted myself up to the next window, which was slightly higher. I missed.

I fell through the air and was caught. I looked up at Tira. She still held onto the window ledge with one hand and, with the other, held the back handle of my safety strap. I at first questioned the logic of wearing a device that was not attached to anything. I quickly learned that she just needed a place to grab onto. There were similar handles on each shoulder and one on the front. I hung there, looking stupid and feeling like a sack of potatoes. She lifted me up to the next window one-handed, making me feel like a child being held up to a basketball hoop so I could dunk. I rubbed my hands together to get feeling in them before grabbing onto the ledge. Then I twisted and launched myself to the ledge of the opposite roof. This time, I held on and struggled to pull myself up. Getting one leg up, I rolled unceremoniously over the lip and dropped the six inches to the flat roof. Tira's boot stopped me from rolling further. I sat there panting.

"Sorry." I managed to get out finally.

"For what?"

"I can't seem to turn my gift on."

"Everyone looks at our blessing like a light switch. It is either on or off. I would compare it more to a faucet. You can control how much flows through you, but it requires a higher level of meditation, an ability to reach a meditative state while still interacting with the physical world."

"How do you meditate...while being active?" I said between gulps of breath.

"Simple, I am doing it now," she said, not even breathing hard.

I scowled. Though whether it was at her or just from the exertion, I really couldn't say.

"Get up, keep going," she prodded.

I climbed to my feet, reset myself, and leaped back across the alley onto the opposite roof. The alley was narrow enough that even I could make the jump. I ran—well, maybe staggered was more accurate—across, then down the fire escape onto the far side. All the while, Tira continued her lecture, as though she were standing at a podium instead of a dead run atop a building.

"When a Bishop goes into a blur it takes a tremendous amount of energy. As such, it can only last a few seconds without severely draining reserves. With my technique, I can sustain a hyper-run for nearly twenty seconds."

She followed me down the metal stairway. As I slid down the suspended ladder, Tira leaped over the railing, landing cat-like next to me.

"Move," she said.

I took off at a sprint again, lungs screaming. Inside I was saying, *okay I get it, you're better than me. Can I just get a friggin' beer now?*

None of it helped. I still couldn't touch my gift. By the time we finished for the day, I hurt worse than I thought possible. My hands were ripped open and my knees and elbows were not much better, despite my clothing. My ego, in comparison, was in tatters. I was an Army Ranger, the bad-asses of the military. We used to make fun of the regular's training. Now I was a child among giants. An acolyte among masters. I was a baby bird being fed regurgitated food while everyone else soared among the clouds. I showered and chose to eat in my room instead of joining the team for dinner.

That evening, during my moderated meditation, I decided to confront her.

"What did I do?"

Tira opened her eyes and regarded me. "Excuse me?"

Her intense gaze nearly made me chicken out, but I pushed forward. "I must have done something to piss you off. I have wracked my brain trying to figure out what I did, but I can't come up with anything."

She looked at me, and her expression was... conflicted. So, I pushed on.

"Are you jealous?" Her eyes narrowed.

"What would I have to be jealous of?"

Oh crap. Warning bells sounded in my head. I was going down a dangerous path toward a cliff. Big signs flashed *go back* in neon colors. So, of course, I continued.

"The fact that I was able to attain the Oneness."

"So, you've not only decided that I am upset and felt it necessary to inform me of my—apparently unjust—emotions. You were also kind enough to determine the cause. Obviously, the only explanation is that I am jealous of you for bumbling into a situation, one which I had to drag you from before you were lost inside your own head forever. Does that sum everything up correctly?"

"Uh..."

I could hear the incoherent sound that was escaping my lips but could not make it stop.

"Thank you for that enlightenment. I think our meditation time is at an end. I will inform Mr. Hager that you no longer need my guidance."

I just sat there, unsure of what to do. At my lack of motion, Tira's eyes narrowed even further.

"You are excused, *Mr. Bateleur.*"

I ran out of the door.

Chapter Thirteen

THE NEXT MORNING, I visited the body of water where the ceremony took place in an attempt to connect with... something. I had no success. As I entered, I experienced a massive jolt of déjà vu. The pool was sizable, though it was not a pool in the modern sense of the word. A pond was probably more accurate. It was a naturally built structure made with sand as a base; stones created the semi-circular retaining wall. It could hold the entire team, plus several others, without anyone getting too chummy. The water flowed from a large statue that spanned the width of the pool.

It depicted many gods from different religions. I recognized the Judeo-Christian God as He was typically represented during the Renaissance. I also saw Buddha, but that was where my knowledge ended. The others varied between human-like figures and animals. One representation had a lion's head and a man's body. Water flowed from their hands, or whichever container they held, as though offering the liquid that supported the fight against evil. Well, that's how I saw it, at least. Mr. Hager told me later that the room's official name was the Fount. He explained this to me, with some exasperation, after I'd referred to it as 'the room with the pond.' My bad.

My frustration at my lack of metaphysical progress was growing. The upside, despite the pain, was that I was getting in the best shape of my life, thanks to the constant, ever-shifting exercise. It was like basic training without the yelling, crapping in public, and bad food. So not really like basic training at all. I was becoming good friends with John; although, since the ceremony, even he looked at me differently. I wasn't sure what happened, but I still felt I had done something very wrong. So bad that no one would tell me what it was.

It was about midday on Friday. Hager was putting me through my paces when my torturous routine changed. I was performing increasingly higher box jumps, hoping to trigger the enhancement, when Tira came in. I saw them talk briefly, then he turned to look at me.

"Mr. Bateleur, please come here."

Hager did not employ any pet names for me, but he did say my name with a little less contempt. That was something.

"What can I do for you, Boss Man?" I said, jogging over. Hager frowned.

"Tira is going to follow up on a possible sighting. I think you should go along with her."

"Sighting of what?"

"The Tainted," he replied.

"Ah, so you want me to go along for protection?"

Tira barked a laugh.

Hager simply said, "hardly. You are there to learn. Investigative techniques, who our contacts are, how to distinguish an actual sighting from a normal everyday occurrence..."

"Uh, okay." I looked at my new partner, who crossed her arms. "Do I have time to take a quick shower?"

"I would not accept you otherwise. I will meet you by the back entrance."

"Alrighty, then."

As I cleaned up and changed into my civvies, I took a lingering look at my mother's changing area. I still hadn't found time to investigate. Hell, I barely had time to do anything. I hadn't watched a ball game in a week and the itch was starting to grate at me.

The 'back door,' as the team liked to call it, was an elevator in the garage. It was something John had told me about, but I had not actually seen. Nor had I been in the garage itself. I walked to the end of the hall, went through the door, and stopped dead.

After witnessing, firsthand, the vastness of this house, I should probably have been prepared for what I saw. I was not. It was mostly due to my longtime residence in New York City. Sure, cars were everywhere, but most people didn't drive. I expected to see the truck that they picked me up in at the hospital and maybe one other car, based on the number of people. Instead, I stood in front of a row of vehicles of various makes and models: sedans, coupes, sports cars, light trucks, heavy trucks, vans-—all in different colors and states of repair. Tira stood by the elevator at the far end of the room, arms still crossed. I was surprised she was not tapping her foot.

"Why so many cars?"

"Some are for necessity. We have several corporate logos that can be adhered magnetically. Since the government doesn't acknowledge the existence of the Tainted, or of us for that matter, we sometimes work outside what is considered constitutional. The others are mostly for travel needs outside the city or for when traveling via public transportation would prove inconvenient. Can we go?"

We entered the elevator, which was large enough to fit any of the trucks. It was like being in the mouth of a whale. Tira pulled on the strap hanging down in front of us, and the doors shut. I may have preferred being swallowed by Moby Dick to this silence, broken only by the whir of the motor and the occasional squeak of friction.

"Still seems like a lot of cars for only four people?" I said finally, unable to endure the tension any longer.

"There used to be more of us." Her statement seemed to hang in the air, intensified by the moment of silence that followed. "And although the Tainted don't generally work together, we don't want to make it easy for them to track our movements. Any other questions?"

"Yeah, two. Who is paying for all of this?"

"This organization has been around for an extremely, long time. Our ancestors have been making wise investments for hundreds of years in the US alone. Despite Amram's complaining, we have very deep pockets. What was your other question?"

The elevator came to a halt and she yanked the doors open. "What would make traveling in public transportation inconvenient?" I asked.

"The MTA has a tendency to frown on bringing automatic weapons on the subway."

Tira started walking away, calling back, "please pull the doors shut behind you."

I did so and noticed a metal panel next to the elevator. I raised my arm with the implant and the panel slid open, a scanner like the one at the other entrance extended. I turned away and it retracted.

We took a set of stairs nearby, accessed by a solid steel door which opened noiselessly. The distinctive click just before Tira reached for the handle indicated another chip-responsive door. I got the feeling that much of the dirt, grime and age I saw down here was for show. If any personnel came down, they would likely just assume it was an old section that was no longer in service. The stairs continued up a few more levels, presumably to keep the elevator from being too close to foot traffic.

"Where does the road from the elevator lead?"

"To the VIP section of an underground parking lot."

"Let me guess, we are the only VIPs?"

"You're brighter than you look. All the cameras around the building and in the parking garage are connected to our implants. They are programmed to switch to snow as we get within range. No record of our passing."

"Neat trick."

We came to a door that opened onto street level next to a parking garage.

"Can I ask you a question?"

"Another one?"

"Well, I am supposed to be here to learn."

"I suppose."

"First, let me apologize for my blatant misinterpretation of the situation last night. I should not have assumed either your mood or the reason behind it."

Tira hesitated a beat, then replied, "Accepted. That was not a question, though."

I nodded and continued. "Did I do something to upset you?"

Without replying, she started walking off toward the nearest main road to catch a cab. I picked up the pace to catch up with her.

"Well?"

"Well, what?"

"You said I could ask a question and I did."

"I didn't say I would answer it."

She stepped off the curb and signaled for a passing cab with the typical arm raise. I sighed but let it drop. The cab stopped in front of a police station. That seemed odd, but I didn't push my luck with another question. At the front desk, Tira asked to see Lieutenant McDaniel. The officer made a quick call, then buzzed us through with directions to get to his office. Tira didn't seem to need them. She walked with purpose and confidence.

McDaniel was an interesting man, not what I was expecting from a police lieutenant. Then again, my only frame of reference was Columbo. He was dressed more like a businessman and sat behind a neat desk with a computer, medieval sword letter opener, and an open paper file. When we entered, he was jotting something down in a notebook with a modern version of a fountain pen. The small office he occupied was made mostly of plexiglass. As we walked closer, I noticed a family photo was also sitting on the desk, at just enough of an angle for me to see the subjects: McDaniel, a small child, and Tira.

What the hell?

He stepped around the desk and gave her a warm hug. "How have you been, Tira? It's been too long."

"I'm okay, Rich. How about you? And how is my niece?"

"Good. Kamala is growing like a weed."

"And Matrika?"

I noted a hesitance to the question.

"She's doing great over at the twelfth. She will make captain well before me. If she keeps this up, I am just going to retire and play Mr. Mom."

"That's great."

"How is it that sisters who shared a womb for nine months can be so distant? You two make me nuts," Rich said.

"We only lasted seven months in the womb. We couldn't stand being together then either." Tira answered.

Rich shook his head. "Who is your friend?"

Tira apparently just remembered that she wasn't here alone. She blushed slightly.

"This is Christian, the new guy. This is my brother-in-law, Rich McDaniel."

I stepped up and extended my hand. "Seems a little old for a new guy," Rich noted.

"Yeah, he is not what you would call our normal recruit."

"I am used to being thought of as abnormal," I said.

"Then you should fit right in over there," Rich said, smiling.

Tira rolled her eyes. "What do you have for us?"

"A woman came in yesterday with the telltale signs. The information just got to me when I called."

"Can we see her?"

"I'm having her brought up so you can talk to her without all the cameras and microphones."

"Isn't that against protocol?" I asked.

"A little, but she is not really under arrest, just in protective custody to determine if she was missing from a hospital psych ward. She will be cuffed, though, just in case. She was causing problems at a convenience store when we picked her up."

"What do you mean, telltale signs?" I asked.

"The Tainted are not allowed to act directly against humanity. They can't just make a bomb and drop it in the middle of Times Square," Tira explained.

"Why not?"

"We actually have no idea. If we could figure that out, it may be a tool to use against them."

"Then how do we know they can't?"

"Past precedent. They have never taken direct action. Everything the Tainted do starts by corrupting someone and getting them to take the action. The more innocent the person, the better the high."

"I'm sorry, what?" I asked.

Tira didn't have time to respond. A knock came at the door and an officer brought in a haggard-looking woman who appeared not to have showered in a while. She wore mismatched sweatpants and a sweatshirt, and her hair was a mass of tangles. The officer that escorted her had eyes that seemed to see everything at once. She had a hard cast on her left arm. I got the impression that she could make Tira's cool attitude look like a lover's embrace in comparison. This was a beat cop that has seen the worst side of this city.

"Sorry for the smell, Lieutenant. She isn't with it enough to acknowledge bodily functions. We cleaned her up as much as possible and she is wearing a diaper. The clothes are from the lost and found."

"Thanks, Sanchez. Any problems from her other than that?"

"No, sir. She didn't even struggle when we stripped her down to clean her up. Shame, I feel bad for her."

"You can leave her with us. Thanks," Rich said. "How's the arm?"

Sanchez smiled like a boxer going back in the ring to finish off his opponent.

"Cast comes off on Friday. Can't wait to get back on the street." Her expression shifted suddenly. "You gonna be able to help her, Doc?"

I wasn't sure who the officer was talking to until Tira responded. "I will do what I can."

"Doc?" I gasped.

"Surprised?" asked Rich.

"You'd think I wouldn't be by now...but yeah."

"She would never mention it herself, but Tira has several PhDs, as well as an MD," Rich said.

"No shit."

Rich smiled, clearly proud. Tira, however, was ignoring the exchange entirely and was wholly focused on the woman. She was looking her over tentatively, careful not to touch her. I wasn't sure, but it appeared as though she was inspecting her with her blessing.

Sanchez turned to leave, and my curiosity got the better of me. "How did you hurt your arm?"

It was Rich who answered. "Officer Sanchez single-handedly took down a three-hundred-pound suspect hopped up on PCP."

"Damn," I spouted, not able to contain my awe.

Sanchez smiled in a way that made me expect her to pick the remnants of the guy from her teeth.

"And if she ever pulls a stunt like that again without waiting for back-up, she will find herself suspended without pay. Right, Sanchez?"

"Of course, Lieutenant."

Sanchez turned and left the office, closing the door.

"Wow," I said.

"Yeah, tough as nails, that one."

"Seemed genuinely concerned for the woman, though," I noted. "Really went above and beyond."

"Well, that's partly Sanchez. Deep down she's a sweetheart, but she would never let you see it. But mostly it's her." Rich indicated the cuffed woman, now seated on one of the chairs.

She didn't look at anyone, just seemed to be in her own world.

"Sorry, I'm not following," I said.

"It is one of the indicators," Tira explained. "For some reason, a person who has been manipulated by one of the Tainted emits an aura that triggers sympathetic feelings for the victim. We think it may be something that was done to help counter the corruption. Or it could just be a kind of chemical response acting against a very alien attack. Since it has trouble fighting the corruption itself, it sends out a subliminal call for aid."

"I didn't know the body could send out signals," I said.

"Have you ever heard of pheromones?" she asked.

"Point taken."

"So, you said the sympathetic siren was one of the indicators. What are some others?" I asked.

"Sympathetic siren?"

"What, you don't like the name? I thought it fit."

Rich covered his mouth with his hand, but Tira was not amused. "Schizophrenia."

"Wait, are you saying that schizophrenia is caused by the Tainted?"

"God, no. Schizophrenia is a very real disease with a wide spectrum of symptoms. The contamination left by the Tainted mimics extreme cases. Now quiet for a second. I have to concentrate to perform this level of exam."

Tira closed her eyes, holding one hand up near the woman, but still not touching her. I stepped back as much as the small office would allow. Rich sat back down and grabbed the file off his desk. Turning towards the window, he started perusing the contents.

I looked out the opposite glass wall into the office common area. It looked to be a fairly typical police precinct, at least based on the TV shows I watched. I was looking at the back of an officer who was busy interviewing a man facing me. The 'perp' was tall, even sitting down. His biceps were clearly defined against the jacket of his well-tailored suit. His blonde hair was buzzed on the sides but long and slicked on top. The stubble of his beard gave him a rugged look that was at odds with his clothes. His most distinctive feature was the bright white silk scarf draped over his shoulders and chest. None of these things, however, first caught my attention. What did, was the fact that the guy was unabashedly smiling at me through the glass. Not in a *hey, want to grab a cup of coffee?* way. Nor was it a *you have a hair sticking up* look. This was a creepy, *I know something you don't know* smile.

I switched my focus on the faint reflection on the glass. The woman Tira was examining was clearly outlined, thanks to the desk lamp next to her. Her hand, which was supposed to be cuffed, was moving, snake-like, to the letter opener sitting on the desk. Her movements went unnoticed by anyone else in the room. In the seconds it took for me to connect the dots, her hand closed over the handle.

"Tira!" I shouted, turning.

Her eyes were just fluttering open from the concentrated trance she was in. The knife was moving towards her jugular.

Rich turned toward the noise. Tira's eyes opened and were now registering the danger without really being able to identify it. I moved with only one thought: protect Tira.

Everything around me slowed to a crawl as my gift kicked me into high speed. The hand holding the weapon slowed, but still seemed to fly to its mark. I was halfway to her, knowing full well there was no way I would make it in time, even with the added speed. I raged at my lack of ability, at my failure to protect her. Gritting my teeth, I willed myself to move faster.

Then I felt it. A barrier as soft as the seeds from a dandelion, brittle as the membrane of a soap bubble. I pushed at it from somewhere deep inside, felt resistance, then pushed harder and through. Everything stopped.

The weapon no longer moved. Rich was frozen in a half scream. Tira's eyes were wide and I could see a tear that had begun to form, lacking the time needed to take shape. I closed my hand over the woman's wrist; I might as well have been grabbing a mannequin for all the resistance it gave. I ripped the knife out of her hand and hit her square in the jaw, knocking her to the floor.

Everything started up again. Rich leaped out of his chair while Tira simultaneously launched herself backward, her own gift finally kicking in. It took them a few seconds to comprehend what had just happened. Even Tira had a difficult time understanding how I was now standing over her, holding the dagger that had been inches from her throat. She looked down and saw her attacker out cold on the floor. She seemed to be trying to form a sentence when I remembered the man with the scarf. I flipped the letter opener so that I held it from the blade and handed it to Tira. She took it, her mouth still moving wordlessly.

I rushed out the door, into the main area, and over to the desk. There was only an empty chair. The cop was sitting there, just staring into space.

"Where is the guy you were talking to?"

"Who?" he asked, sluggishly.

"The creepy German guy that was here at your desk." After a second, he came back to himself.

"Look, pal, there was no one here. Just me doing this shitty paperwork."

I was about to press him further, then realized he really had no clue what I was talking about.

"Sorry, my mistake."

Chapter Fourteen

"WHAT DO YOU MEAN, time stopped? You mean it slowed, correct?" asked Hager.

We all sat in the common room. Tira sipped a scotch with an unsteady hand. I couldn't imagine anything piercing through her aura of steel. But something had.

"It slowed at first," I said. "I watched the letter opener getting closer to Tira's throat while Rich was turning to see what was going on. I knew I would not get there in time at the speed I was going. So, I pushed to go faster, and I felt something blocking me."

"Please expand on that. You felt something?" Hager pushed.

"It's hard to explain." I paused for a second, rubbing the back of my neck, then continued. "Okay, how about this—you know how at the beginning of some football games, the team breaks through a paper wall with their logo on it?"

John nodded. "Yeah, I got ya."

"So, even if you have never actually done it, you can imagine what it would be like. You push against a thin layer. You feel a small resistance before you burst through. Now, imagine that barrier being invisible. It has no borders. It is just there. I pushed through it and everything stopped."

No one replied. They just watched me as I sat there on the couch, elbows on my knees, looking from my folded hands to Hager's face.

"It wasn't there before. I... I just knew that if I didn't move faster, Tira would die. I don't know why I had that feeling. I'm sure she could have just healed herself."

The team exchanged glances then Mr. Hager explained. "Arterial damage requires a lot of power to heal, especially one from a dull blade. Tira may have been able to heal, but there was also a chance she may not."

Tira took another sip. Back at the station, she seemed nonplussed by the incident. She had insisted that the woman be brought back to the house, saying that she would be able to pull her at least partially out of the trance. John had picked us up. After we got the mystery woman back to the house and settled, Tira became quiet and headed for the alcohol cabinet. She hadn't spoken since.

"Tira," Hager asked, "what did you see?" She took another sip and hesitated.

"I was delving into the woman, trying to find where the corruption was coming from so I could start to unravel it. Maybe not completely, but enough to bring her back into reality." She swirled her drink. "I heard Christian yell my name. It filtered through the layers much faster than any voice I've experienced when in that state." She looked up at me and met my eyes, then seemed to shy away. "I immediately started pulling my way out, and, as I did, I saw her with the blade in hand." She swallowed visibly. "I could see Christian from the corner of my eye. Saw him coming, saw him blur... knew he wouldn't make it." She took another sip and closed her eyes as it slid down her throat. "I kept my eyes on Christian... not wanting to see it coming. He hit a point and then he disappeared."

"Disappeared?" Soon-Li asked.

"There is no other way to say it." Another swirl of the drink. "He was there one second and gone the next." Tira stared deep into the amber liquid as if searching for something. "Then he was standing in front of me and the woman was on the floor."

Soon-Li, who was sitting next to Tira, put a hand on her shoulder. "I have never heard of this, never even read about it in the old texts."

"Neither have I," Hager concurred.

All eyes turned to me.

"Come on now, someone must have done something similar," I said. "You guys have been around for thousands of years. Are you telling me that no one in that amount of time has done something like this?"

"That is exactly what I am telling you." Hager paused, his focus never moving from me. "Even those of old, the pure of power, never wrote about anything like this. Even Jesus, who did things that none of us have even dreamed of, could not stop time."

"Wait, hold up, who?" I asked.

He just waved me off and said, "Nothing. Never mind."

"*The* Jesus. Jesus Christ. The Super Star. He was a Bishop?"

"Yes."

It was John who answered. Hager glared at him.

"What? Amram, you can't leave him hanging now. You took the shrimp out of the fridge. I'm just making the jambalaya before it goes bad."

John turned back to me. "Yes, he was a Bishop. He wasn't just *any* Bishop. Whether you look at Him as a savior or not still depends on your point of view and religious affiliation. The same goes for the rest."

"The rest?"

"Moses, Buddha, and pretty much every other positive religious figure throughout time."

"Next, you are going to tell me that the Ten Commandments were actually our idea."

John stared at me without comment. "Are you friggin' kidding me?".

"You have to understand..." Hager took up the debate. "...the world was plunging into sin and degradation. There was no mass media back then. The only way to get the word out was with stories told from person-to-person, from parent-to-child."

John tagged in. "I am sure you have played the phone game in school. How quickly does a message deteriorate from one person to the next? We needed a code for how people should live, and we couldn't just pass out fliers. It couldn't come from any mere human, either. It had to be divine. It needed weight. There needed to be consequences if the message was not adhered to."

I stared at them, dumbfounded. I couldn't believe what I was hearing. In just a few sentences, they pulled the rug out from under one of the most significant foundations of human history. Even me, whose connection with faith was tenuous at best, was shaken by this news. If it ever got out, the world would spiral down into chaos. My head dropped into my hands when a chilling thought hit me.

"What about the Bible?" I asked.

"What about it?" Hager asked.

"Who wrote the Bible?" My tone was accusatory.

"The Bible, as you may recall, has many authors..."

"That's not what I mean, and you know it. Were they Bishops? Was this another ploy to get people to act as they saw fit?"

Hager opened his mouth, but nothing came out.

"The Torah?"

Silence.

"The Quran?"

Only looks of guilt.

"You people are insane." I stared at each of them in turn. "Everything that everyone on this planet has ever believed is a lie. Every prophet that gave us hope that we are not alone, every parable that guided our decisions. All made up by a group of people..."

"Who were trying to save humanity," Hager interrupted. "Yes, feel free to judge people who are centuries dead, and were dealing with a situation you could not hope to comprehend. We have all done it at one point or another. Look back at how certain phrasing, instead of inspiring devotion, brought forth destruction. We weep for the holy wars that our ancestors helped to bring about, for the persecution of one religion over another. We rage against the shortsightedness of our forefathers, who denounced some forms of love as depraved and evil. And we shiver over those who still twist those words to justify extremist activities in favor of their God."

I stared at him. My arguments had been deflated; not against resistance, but against understanding. I grasped their plight, if barely. They didn't seem to disagree with me, nor did they shirk the responsibility laid upon them from their ancestors. But I was still pissed. I looked from face to face, searching for something to grab onto, something to ground me as I became utterly unhinged. Then I turned and walked out.

I'm not sure how long I sat there in the plush seats. My attention was drawn into one of the many worlds of Charles Dickens. An untouched glass of brandy sat on the side table next to me. I was continually pulled out of the story with every reference to faith and religion. My anger boiled under the surface, and continually bubbled up into my conscious mind. This betrayal was worldwide. The scope of it was staggering. I looked up to find Soon-Li sitting in the chair opposite me.

"How are you feeling?" she asked.

"Angry, confused, betrayed. Pick one."

She nodded.

"Confusion is normal. I was confused when I was told as well," she said in her staccato way of speaking. She spoke nearly perfect English, but it sounded like it should be Chinese.

"I just don't understand. How does a small group of people decide that they will play God? Not just once, but time and time again?"

"Christian, people have been doing it since the beginning."

I stayed quiet, waiting for her to explain.

"Every king and queen who made a decree. Every lord and lady that passed judgment. *Tā mā de*, every government that casts their votes based on who pays the check is doing the same. They do it for money. They do it for power. And mostly they do it because they think they are right. We did the same."

"We?"

"Yes, Christian. We. The Covenant that *we* belong to. Dedicated to protecting mankind. Without those fundamental rules, without people believing there were consequences to their actions, we would be fighting a losing battle. Governments make laws to keep people in line all the time."

"Yeah, but none of them were pretending to be God."

"Neither were we. None of the texts said that God came down and grabbed a pen."

"But they were based on divine intervention."

"Who says it wasn't?"

"But... John..."

"John stated that the authors also happen to be Bishops. How does that detract from their significance?"

My mouth opened as I searched for a response.

Soon-Li crossed her arms. "I would argue that it makes them more credible."

I sighed. "I have trouble seeing this as little more than manipulation."

Soon-Li cocked her head. "Why?"

"It was done deliberately to force people to follow certain precepts."

"So is the Constitution. And the laws that you live by. All were created by a group of people not divinely touched. How is that different?"

"None of them were saying that the message came from God."

"No, but they implied it."

"They do not!" I exclaimed.

"Really?" She held out a hand. "Give me a dollar."

"What?"

"Come on, lost time is never found again."

"Is that Confucius?"

"No, Benjamin Franklin. What, because I am Chinese, I have to be quoting Confucius?"

I shook my head but dug into my pocket for a bill, then handed it over. She took it, turned it over, and practically shoved it in my face.

"Read."

I looked at it and frowned. She had her finger next to four words appearing over the 'ONE.'

"Well?" She pushed.

"I see it."

"See what?"

I rolled my eyes, but complied. "In God we trust."

"They imply that God supports the American way."

"I wouldn't say that."

"No? How about the Pledge of Allegiance?"

I knew the line she was referring to. The same line that many people tried to have removed. The impetus for some parents having their children abstain from saying it. She watched me closely. I stayed quiet.

"Say it," she pushed.

I stared back at her, several other lines coming to mind. Instead, I acquiesced. "One nation under God." She nodded.

"I understand that you feel betrayed, but none of us had a hand in that. Not me, John, Tira or the boss man."

I smiled at her reference to Hager.

"You are misplacing your anger. No one on this team has tricked you or lied to you."

"No one told me, either," I countered.

"There, you are correct. Exactly when would have been the best time for that conversation? With children, it is somewhat easier. Even if they are shocked by the initial exposure, they are more open to change. Also, it is a fun game for them to know something that the rest of the world does not. Children have a fluid stance."

"Stance?"

"Yes, like in kung fu. If your stance is light, you are easily moved but are quick to recover. However, if you have a deep, solid stance, it is hard for people to move you. When something does, though, it is much harder to regain balance. Most adults have a very deep stance."

"Yeah, tell me about it."

"We, like you, have similar concerns and misgivings. Think about it this way: how did you think these things were written? Did you believe God pointed His will at a bunch of publishers who regurgitated disparate versions—some contradictory?"

"No," I admitted.

"So, tell me, who wrote them?"

"Humankind."

"Exactly. Men and women." She barked a short laugh. "Based on some passages, I would guess the women didn't have too much to say." She shook her head. "See, Bishops can be morons too."

I smiled again.

"They were possibly not the brightest group and were certainly flawed, but people all the same. Just as you have been taught, they were guided by the hand of God. Is that not the perfect description of what we are?"

I didn't reply.

"You are correct to feel the weight of it, to be concerned about the decisions of the time. But who is to say that the Covenant's decision to write those texts was not part of God's plan? Why are we less worthy of the same respect as those you did not even know, yet supported?"

I looked at her with a newfound respect. She had taken my concerns, turned them upside down, and made them seem foolish. I gave her emotions and she gave me logic, disarming my arguments.

"You got one thing wrong," I informed her with a smirk.

"What's that?"

"In God we trust didn't appear on our money until 1956, and the pledge didn't include it until 1954."

She stared at me for a minute.

"I know." She smiled. "I just didn't know you knew."

"You are a conniving old broad," I chided with a smile.

"Who are you calling old?" she countered with feigned outrage. We both laughed.

"Come, I want to show you something."

I followed her down to the lair, as I had melodramatically begun to refer to it. The additional door that I had noted between the garage and the stadium was, apparently, for interrogation and holding. Several of the cells were somewhat lavish, considering the reason for their existence. There was also an area for having "heart-to-heart talks" while being monitored. We entered one of the holding rooms. Tira was sitting in a chair, talking to the woman they had brought in. She seemed lucid, especially compared to the first time I saw her. She was also a lot cleaner and was wearing new clothes.

"How long was I in the library?" I said out loud.

The woman, hearing my voice, jumped up, ran over, and embraced me. I stood there, unsure of what to do or say. When she finally released me, she was able to find her voice.

"Thank you for helping me."

"Uh..." I wasn't usually thanked by a person I'd laid out cold.

"I could see clearly what was going on, but I couldn't do anything about it. I thought for sure I would end up killing Dr. Gupta."

"Uh, any time." I smiled awkwardly, extracted myself from the embrace, and extended my hand. "Christian."

She took it. "Denise."

"Sorry for the bruise, Denise."

"Understandable in light of the circumstances," she said, rubbing her face unconsciously.

"Please..." I indicated she should sit down again, and she did so. "How are you feeling?"

"Better, thanks to the Doc."

"How did you help her?" I asked Tira.

"Pretty much the same way I helped you when you went into your deep trance. I delved down into her psyche, found her, and pulled her out."

"Can I talk to you outside?"

"I suppose. Soon-Li, would you keep our guest company?"

"Of course. Denise, are you hungry?" Soon-Li inquired.

"Actually, I am. I don't know when I last ate something, but it feels like it's been a week."

We left the room and closed the door on the rest of the conversation. "What's the problem?"

"I'm concerned about this woman staying here."

"I have released her from that hold."

"And now she's cured?"

"Unfortunately, no. I have just put Denise back in control of herself. She will need to go through extensive psychotherapy. She will probably have nightmares, an inherent distrust of people, paranoia..."

"So basically, she has graduated from a mindless zombie to low grade schizophrenic."

"Mens Irrumabo."

"I'm sorry what?"

"It's the name of what she is dealing with. People misunderstand it, and many *so-called* doctors diagnose it as schizophrenia. That is just ignorance. I know some psychotherapists who understand how to treat it. I will send her to one."

"So, are you saying that she is no longer corrupted?" I asked.

"Correct."

"One hundred percent?"

She cocked her head to one side. "What is the problem?"

"Besides the fact that she had a letter opener an inch from your carotid artery today?"

"I understand your concern, but there are two things you need to know about this."

"Okay?"

Tira lowered her eyes for a second and swallowed before continuing. "The process of delving that deep into someone's mind is very revealing. You get to know them on an intimate level."

"So, you can read their thoughts?"

"No, it doesn't work like that. And before you ask, I cannot see images of their thoughts either. It is like walking through a dark room and getting impressions based on your other senses."

"Okay, fine, but I still have a bad feeling about this. You said two things I needed to know. What is the second one?"

"Where she works."

"You asked her about that already?"

"She has been lucid for over an hour now. She works at the Indian Point Energy Center."

The name tickled my memory.

"Wait, isn't that the nuclear plant upstate?"

"Yes, and guess what her job was?"

"Scientist?"

"No, worse. Waste management."

"So, she's a janitor. They wanted her for her keys?"

"*Nuclear* waste management," Tira paused after each word.

"Oh, shit."

Chapter Fifteen

WE TOOK THE CONVERSATION to a meeting room back up at the office level. It looked like your typical conference room that might be found in Silicon Valley, with every modern convenience. A large, round Arthurian table dominated the space; a credenza sat to one side, with a seventy-inch monstrosity of a monitor hanging over it. Everything was controlled by a digital display on the desk. A large camera was mounted under the TV and it locked on to whoever was talking at the time. It was pretty creepy. If it shot out and said *echuta*, I was out of there.

Soon-Li was typing away on the laptop that was connected to the wireless display system. Each of these people seemed to have multiple talents. Once again, I wasn't sure I measured up. I felt like the intern for a group of rocket scientists.

Soon-Li called up a real time satellite image of Indian Point and the surrounding area. I wasn't sure where she got it, but it definitely wasn't Google Maps.

"Indian Point Energy Center has been operating since the mid-seventies. It supplies two-thirds of the electricity that powers New York City and generates about twenty-one-hundred metric tons of nuclear waste per year. That is broken down into three types: LLW, MLW, and HLW. The HLW is the most radioactive. It is made up of mostly spent fuel rods. These are kept in large pools of water for about five years before being moved to dry casks for long-term storage."

"Okay, so what are the possible methods of terror attacks on this facility?" Hager asked.

"Well, you hardly need an attack with a facility as old as this one.

They've had regular issues since they opened. The first was the reactor housing structure, which buckled a few months after they opened. After that, the issues vary: Hudson River leaking into the nuclear cooling pool, radioactive steam purging, transformer fires...the last is the most common. Think about the computer systems that were around in 1974. Your phone has more computing power than the racks of servers that monitor the safety protocols. There have been upgrades to some side systems, but you can't just pause a nuclear reactor to rip out the technical infrastructure for an upgraded model. Still, the biggest concern that this, or any other, facility has is an earthquake."

"Although the Tainted are powerful, as far as I know they cannot cause an earthquake," Hager stated. "So that is out."

"Good to know," I said. "They seemed to have enough transformer fires to be fairly efficient in putting them out. So, I doubt that could be an issue. I think we can assume, at the very least, they will have backup systems to take over."

"I concur," Hager said.

"A direct assault would probably be out, since the military locks down these types of facilities," John added. "I think the key is our new friend, Denise."

"I agree," Hager said. "Out of all the people in that facility, he picked her. Why?"

"What does she have access to besides nuclear waste?" John asked. "Anything she can sabotage to cause a meltdown?"

"Not likely," Soon-Li replied. "With the number of redundant systems and the constant monitoring, there is little one person could do to cause a disaster of that magnitude.

"The critical part of her job is organizing the transition of the spent fuel rods from wet to dry storage. While in the pool, the water suppresses the radioactivity. If the pool runs dry, you have a stack of exposed, highly radioactive materials. Once they are in dry storage, they are flood proof, hurricane proof...you name it."

"So, could they do something to the pool?" I asked.

"I hate to say it, but that would not cause enough terror," John said.

"He's right," Tira jumped in. "With the limited number of people exposed to the contamination, and the fact that they probably have contingency plans in place, the worst-case scenario would still only be about one hundred dead. Maybe double that would get sick. That would only be a minor high for the Tainted. They get more than that in one day with some wars going on."

"That's the second time you said that. What does it mean?" I asked. Tira cocked her head.

"A small high." I clarified.

"Oh, simple, it's why they do it."

"Do what?"

"All of it," John said. "Cause pain, create chaos, kill. It is literally like a drug to them. They get a euphoric sensation every time they do it."

"But, also like a drug, they build up a tolerance," Hager added. "Maybe back in the early days, killing one person would give them their fix, as it were. Now, after millennia filled with horrible deeds, the only way to get back that feeling is to cause pain, suffering, and death on a mass scale."

"And we know this how?"

A sense of quiet commiseration descended on the small team until Hager finally spoke.

"That is a tale for another time. Suffice it to say that we are secure in our knowledge. So, what other possibilities do we have?"

My mind went into overdrive—bringing up options, following them to a conclusion and dismissing them, one after another. Each scenario laid out before me like the college basketball brackets during March Madness. A small explosive charge placed at a structural location, causing radioactive pool water to leak into the Hudson—-no, too easily patched. Siphoning off radioactive water to contaminate drinking water—no, the amount of water needed would be way too difficult to move. So not the water...what about the pellets?

"Christian, what do you think?" Soon-Li asked.

I didn't look up. I was in my process. Something I had done time and time again. I was not even completely sure how it worked. Things would click in my brain as either positive or negative, valuable or invaluable.

"Christian?" John probed.

I heard him somewhere outside my bubble of logic, but I couldn't stop now. The pellets were the key, but what could you do with the pellets? It had to be something that would cause enough destruction, pain, and panic to sustain a high for a set of immortal super powered drug addicts. Wait, that was it. Not panic. What had John said?

"Mr. Bateleur!"

Hager's voice broke through, but I was nearly there. I held a hand up, still not responding.

Shock, alarm, dread, dismay, fright, horror, terror...that was it. Terror. Something about that word sounded alarm bells. Terror, terror, terror...I kept repeating the word, over and over. My mind was stuck on it. Terror of what? Terror...ist.

"Oh, shit." I met everyone's gaze. "Based on this new information, I would say only one possibility makes sense."

Apparently, no one else had gotten there yet. "Okay, let's look at the facts."

I started counting off on my fingers.

"We have a facility providing the radioactive raw material. Based on what Tira said regarding the mass scale of destruction needed, we can eliminate the power plant as a target. Right?"

Heads nodded all around.

"Good. So, if you are not going to blow up a nuclear plant Chernobyl-style, then you need to do something else with the raw material. According to Mr. Potter, there are only two things you can do to create mass destruction with it.

"Who? Harry Potter?" John asked.

"Mr. Potter. My eighth-grade science teacher. He dedicated an entire month to nuclear power. It was both really interesting and really annoying. The number of gold bricks..."

"Mr. Bateleur, you were saying?"

"Right, sorry. Where was I?"

"Two things to do with the raw material." Soon-Li offered.

"Yeah. One is a nuclear bomb. Sure, they could cause some massive destruction, especially if they go fusion instead of fission. However, there is a problem with going nuclear. They would get one massive hit of mega ganja juice. Bang!"

I slammed my hand on the table and everyone jumped. All except Hager.

"But then New York would be a barren wasteland, unable to support further 'fixes.'"

I let that sink in for a quick second.

"The second option would still create large-scale destruction, with the added benefit of continued suffering for years to come."

Tira inhaled sharply. "He's talking about a dirty bomb."

They all looked at me, wanting me to deny it. My lack of response spoke volumes, and the silence hung there like a dense fog.

"Alright then," Hager said, his voice heavy. "I believe we have an idea of the type of atrocity they will be causing. If that's the endgame, they will not try to damage the plant itself, but extract radioactive material."

"Yes," replied Soon-Li slowly, as if just coming out of her own thoughts. "As I said, the spent fuel rods would make the most effective...device. The ones in the pool are technically easier to get to, but they are not easily transportable. They are not just in the pool for protection from radioactivity; they also need to be cooled."

"Cooled?" asked Hager.

"Yes. Based on my research on nuclear power plants, the fission process causes the uranium to heat up to extreme levels. It takes years to cool down sufficiently for it to be moved into dry storage. It consists basically of placing the rods into a big metal cask and covering it with cement. Those can be stored both on site and off site, at either government or privately owned storage facilities."

"So," John added, "if I were trying to get my hands on one of these casks, I wouldn't go after them while they are sitting in a high-security nuclear plant. I would hit one of these facilities."

"Agreed, but the security at those sites can't be that much less. This is radioactive material we're talking about. To get a government contract, you need to show a certain level of defense. They are audited regularly," Tira noted.

"Well, if we all agree that the most likely target is one of these storage facilities, let's make a list of the closest ones," John suggested.

They spent the next few minutes doing so. Soon-Li's fingers were a blur over the keyboard. Circles began appearing, one by one, on the higher-level map that covered New York, New Jersey, Connecticut, and a small part of Canada. There were seven in total. That completed, she began digging into the security protocols and downloading audit results that listed deficiency reports.

As Soon-Li finished scavenging the web for information about each facility, she sent them to our laptops with a swish of her hand. Each of us got a facility to investigate, in order to find one with enough lax in its security to be a target.

Four hours later, we were still at it. We had narrowed it down to three facilities, then spent the next two hours debating which one was the most likely target and not getting anywhere.

I thought for a second, feeling we were missing something, then a ridiculously obvious thought occurred to me.

"Can we print the map with the full list?" I asked Soon-Li. "Of course," she replied.

A few keystrokes later, a printer hidden in the cabinet whirred. I picked up the papers and left the room. After a few seconds (which I assume were filled with exchanged looks and more shrugging), I heard the team follow me. I led them all the way down to the sub-level. None of them asked any questions. They had argued themselves into silence. We reached the section where our guest/prisoner temporarily resided. I reached for the knob, hesitated, then decided to knock.

Despite Tira's help pulling Denise out of a deep-seated psychosis, the fact remained that she was being held here. It may not have been entirely against her will, but that didn't change the circumstances. If she wanted to go, she would not be able to. I thought knocking afforded her a little privacy and normalcy while costing us nothing.

"Come in," said Denise's tentative voice from inside.

I opened the door and entered. The rest of the team filed in behind me. Denise was sitting on the bed, reading a book from the library.

It was on Schizophrenia.

"Hey Denise, how are you feeling?" I asked.

"Okay, I guess, under the circumstances."

"We really appreciate all the help you're giving us. Everything we learn brings us closer to stopping whatever they're doing."

"I really can't remember anything else, but I'll do whatever I can to help."

"This should be easy for you. It has to do with what you know best."

She looked around, but the team stayed quiet. This was my show and they were giving me full reign, or enough rope to hang myself.

"Okay," Denise said tentatively.

"Good. We believe they are trying to obtain some of the spent fuel rods from dry storage. We looked at all the facilities and we have narrowed it down to three. But we would like you to take a look at the full list and pick the one you think would be the most likely target."

I handed her the satellite photo with the digital circles and facility names.

"Why didn't we just show her the three we picked to give her a smaller set to focus on?" complained Hager.

"You're missing one," Denise claimed.

I turned a pointed look at him. "That's why."

Soon-Li looked almost insulted. "I found all the active facilities within the surrounding states, I'm sure of it."

"You did. A new one is opening in Camden, New Jersey, next year. They are not officially operational yet, but we were running out of space. So, I worked out a contract to get in early for a discounted rate. They'll start earning revenue earlier and we will be paying less. Plus, it helps our bottom line, since we are closing."

"Is that legal?" asked Hager.

"It skirts the edges. The units we will be using have already been inspected, but the government contract doesn't start until their official opening date."

"Which is when?" John asked.

"Next summer."

"Not for another six-to-nine months," John said.

"Which means they are still under construction," added Tira. "And will only have a skeleton crew working while strangers are coming and going all the time," added Soon-Li.

"Yeah, but nobody knows about that contract. We kept it very hush-hush," said Denise.

"You were just compelled to kill someone you barely knew. I would say that if you know about it, it's a good bet she knows as well," Hager pointed out.

"He," Denise corrected.

"What?" John asked.

"The person manipulating me was a *he*. I still don't understand how he controlled me like that. I swear, it was like I was just a puppet."

I got a bad feeling.

"What did he look like?" I asked.

"He was European looking and attractive. That was what got me to start talking to him in the first place. I bumped into him at the coffee shop I go to every morning."

"Was he a cross between Dolph Lundgren and Hugh Jackman?" I asked.

The whole team turned to stare at me, as if I had just described a red man with horns, a pointed tail, and a pitchfork.

"Yup, that's him." Denise said.

"Oh, shit." I had never heard Tira utter any semblance of profanity. She looked at Hager and said, "Baldemar."

The whole team added their own curses simultaneously. Although they had come to the same conclusion, hearing it voiced hit a little too hard.

"How did you know what he looked like?" Tira asked me. "He was in the police station when it all went down."

"That's not possible." John exclaimed.

"Our intel has him in Iraq," Soon-Li added.

Hager crossed his arms. "Well, apparently, that is no longer the case."

Soon-Li suggested, "I think we should continue this conversation outside,"

They all turned to Denise, who glanced at each of them with wide eyes.

"You are quite right," Hager agreed. "Ms. Ellery needs her rest."

We all filed out, thanking her for the critical help she provided, and reassuring her that she was quite safe here. Then we moved one door down and stood around one of the black lab tables, which reminded me of high school science class.

"If Baldemar was there and directly controlling her actions, then he knows about my brother-in-law."

"Are you certain?" Hager asked.

"He has to. Think about it. He didn't need to push Denise as far as he did to get this information. This was not some deeply hidden secret or an idea that opposed her way of thinking."

She folded her arms and started biting on a thumbnail. She continued pulling her hand away, only enough to speak.

"This was a surface pull only. He could have gently pushed her in regular conversations for her to give this up without realizing. He went deep and stressed her sanity specifically to make her a target. Then he put her in the vicinity of Rich's precinct. He had to know that if she were brought in, it would get to me. Or why else do it? Why else be there when it happened?"

It made sense, I had to admit. Although I wasn't sure I really understood it all.

"Is this guy really *that* bad-ass?"

Hager looked at me, his expression more grim than usual. "In every encounter with him, a Bishop has died."

Chapter Sixteen

"WE NEED AN IMMERSION. Then we will prepare to depart," Hager said.

"Okay," said John, "It's a dip and dash."

"Dip and dash?" I asked.

"Soak and sprint?" John offered.

Hager made a face and I smiled. We all made our way to the lockers and changed into immersion robes. These were supposed to allow full exposure to the water while still preserving modesty.

"So, will this be like the last time?" I said to the collective changing room from my small enclosure.

"No, the first time is always the worst. Mine made me feel like a set of beads on Mardi Gras." John's voice drifted over the partition. I wasn't sure what that meant, but it didn't sound good. Or did it?

"And since then?"

"It depends."

"On what?"

"On how much of your blessing remains," Hager answered. "The more you need replaced, the more intense the reaction."

"How am I supposed to know how much reserve I have? Is there a dipstick I can check? Wait, that came out wrong." I could hear John laughing, and I even thought I heard Soon-Li chuckle.

"Dipsticks notwithstanding, everyone has a different reserve capacity." Hager's voice held a little more dryness than usual. "When you become more in tune with your gift, you will be able to feel how deep your well is and how much is left at any given point."

"How?"

"Do you remember when you first started driving that truck of yours?" John took over.

"Yeah?"

"So, in the beginning, you were tentative, right? Not sure where the bumpers were, unable to gauge which narrow alleys you could squeeze through."

"For the first few months, I was convinced I would take off everyone's side mirrors."

"Exactly. But now?"

"It's like I can feel the perimeter. I know when I'm getting too close to something."

"It's the same with your gift. You will just know how much you have left."

"I guess the intensity is a combination of how deep your reserves are, and how much of a top off you need?"

"Although I would not put it in those words, you are correct," Hager concluded.

I donned my robes and made my way to the Fount.

I was a little nervous despite the team's reassurances. I had used my power to perform a feat that no one thought possible, to break a barrier no one knew existed. I expected my reserves to be low and the resulting fuel-up to be extensive.

Tira stepped up next to me.

"We normally assist the newly baptized through the first few immersions just as a precaution. If you will permit me?"

Her voice was tense, as was her expression, as she held out her hand to me. I took it, and she relaxed slightly.

"Although the first time has the strongest reaction, the anticipation of the second is always the worst."

"Thanks," I said, and squeezed her hand slightly. Tira guided me into the pool.

"I will go first." She reached out, grabbing my other hand. We stood there facing each other. For a brief moment, she made eye contact, but then quickly refocused on my nose. "I should not need assistance, but keep hold of my hands as an anchor."

I nodded. Tira's face calmed, and her eyes closed. She lowered herself into the water, exhaling. As her head slipped below the surface, I could see the ripples caused by the infusion of power. After maybe five seconds, the vibration stopped, and she broke the surface again. She inhaled calmly enough, though she was breathing somewhat more rapidly than before. She released one hand and wiped the water out of her face.

"See, nothing to it."

"How much of a top off did you need?" I asked.

"I would say that was about one-third," she said.

So, to restore fully would take about fifteen seconds of being shocked while underwater, I thought.

I shook my head. "No sense putting this off any longer

"Listen, Christian, don't be nervous. Inhale for four seconds and exhale for eight, breathing from your diaphragm. Do that a couple of times. It's a technique free divers use to lower heart rate and blood pressure. It will also purge as much carbon dioxide from the lungs as possible. Then, squeeze your jaw shut and concentrate on that. It will be over before you know it."

"Okay," I said

She nodded. She held out her free hand, and I took it again. Out of the corner of my eye, I could see that the others had stopped to see what was going to happen.

Great, I thought, watching to see if the variety act is going to kill himself this time.

"Hey." Tira tugged slightly at my hands and drew my attention back. "You've got this."

I nodded again, trying to convince myself that I did. I closed my eyes, and breathed the way she had told me, then lowered myself beneath the water.

The buzzing started as soon as my head was fully submerged. This time, my muscles didn't spasm as if a toaster was dropped in the pool. This was more like the lowest setting of the muscle stimulator the chiropractor used. It gave me the mental image of static dancing across my skin. Then, as quickly as the tingling started, it was gone—lasting no more than two or three seconds. I stayed under for a few more moments, in case there was another wave coming. Nothing did. Tira gave a slight tug on my fingers and I emerged from the water, taking both my hands back to push the water and hair away from my face.

Everyone's expression seemed to mirror mine. I turned and waded out of the pool, grabbing one of the towels placed next to the water. I was getting tired of being an enigma.

John stood in front of a large Suburban. The back doors were open, and a large black box was visible—which he had stacked with several varieties of fully automatic rifles.

"That's quite a vehicle," I said as I walked up.

"Beulah? Yeah, she's great."

"You named the car after Ferris Bueller?"

"Not Bueller, *Beulah*. She's named after my Aunt Beulah, because she is big, black, and mean. But she always takes care of you."

"Sounds like quite a woman."

"You don't know the half of it."

John reached into the strong box, picked out a rifle, and threw it to me. It was an M16, the type I used during my time in the army rangers.

I examined the rifle. "Not bad."

"I did my research."

"Not to be picky, but do you have a holographic sight?"

"Yeah, sure. Follow me."

John led me to a large metal cabinet. He opened one of the drawers and pulled out the requested sight.

"Set the rifle in the vice."

Next to the cabinet was a worktable with a gun vise mounted on one end. I placed it into the rubber coated mounts and tightened the screws. John stepped up and started working with practiced efficiency.

"How did you get your hands on fully automatic weapons?"

"We have documentation that establishes us as a military subcontractor for many governments," John said as he loosened the screws.

"We must have friends in high places."

"We do. Unofficially of course."

He removed the optical sight and replaced it with the holographic one, quickly tightening it down.

"How does that happen?"

"Easily, actually. Like Amram said, the Tainted need to act on a large scale to get the type of hit they want." He placed a laser bore sight into the muzzle and removed the rifle from its perch. "To get the biggest bang for the least amount of effort, they target people at high levels who have the power to make things happen."

"Like those who control assault rifle permits."

John set the rifle on his shoulder and tucked the opposite elbow against his ribs. He rested the stock on his upturned open palm and aimed against the far wall.

"Yup. We help them, they help us."

"Convenient," I said.

He made a few quick screw-turns on the sight with his trigger hand until he was satisfied.

"You're all set." He, pulled the laser sight out of the muzzle, then handed the rifle over to me.

I examined his work and sighted down the rifle. "Impressive. You've got skills."

John nodded at me but said nothing. I got the message and dropped it.

A short time later, we were in New Jersey, headed for an unfinished nuclear waste storage facility that may be attacked by a band of immortal, drug addicts with superhuman abilities gifted to them by Satan. FUBAR would be an understatement.

Traffic was light at this hour of the night, even on the Turnpike. The plan was simple: find a suitable spot to set up camp and keep an eye on the facility. I watched the lights zip past us from the seat in the SUV's back row. The lack of space made sitting normally for an extended ride an uncomfortable prospect. Instead, I stretched my feet onto the floor of the opposite seat. I watched the elongated reflection of the passing streetlights in the window, which created a slow pinwheeling effect. I remembered a time from my youth when I would imagine there to be people in the lights acting as reverse gondoliers. They would use their oars of light to snatch our car and drag it onward to their fellows manning the next light. Pushed ever forward toward our destination. I was a weird kid.

Jackie came to mind. I wanted to talk to her about this whole screwed up situation. My powers, I could ever connect with them were transforming me into a giant among men—but one who is woefully inadequate when compared with the other giants. Her imagined response to that made me smile. '*Arrogant much?*'

If I didn't figure out how to connect with my faith, I'd be about as helpful as a knife at an Uzi convention. Somehow, I had the feeling that Jackie held the key. I couldn't explain why, just a feeling. Or maybe, being adrift in a sea of uncertainty and strangeness, I was just longing for the familiar. Maybe I was just hungry again. Being out of Manhattan was making me sappy.

Time to get my head in the game. Camden is a mid-sized town in western New Jersey; it's an equal mix of industrial and residential, with warehouses skirting the Delaware River and homes built mostly inland. I went through attack scenarios in my head, as was my habit while en route to any tactical encounter. The process gave me confidence that every scenario had been considered and would allow me to anticipate how the enemy would move.

I sat up so I could look between Soon-Li and Tira in the second row. "I have a question."

"Do tell," replied Hager from the passenger seat.

"What happens when we encounter...the non-Tainted?"

"What did you do when you encountered the enemy while in the army?"

"That's not the same," I said.

"Isn't it?"

"No, these people may be hypnotized."

"These are not common illusionists, Mr. Bateleur. They will not be thinking they are a turkey on Thanksgiving," Hager said.

"No, but they will not be in control of their faculties, either," I countered.

"Doubtful. The people they'll throw at us will not, in all likelihood, have been persuaded in any way. They don't do that anymore."

"Anymore?" I asked.

Hager ignored the question.

"They are more likely to hire an army than to do any overt persuasion," Hager said.

"Still, these people have no idea what they are fighting for."

Hager finally turned around to look at me. Even at night, two rows back, I could see the creases in his brow. "Mr. Bateleur, every war is fought by people who do no more than follow the orders of their superiors. They may be innocent. Or they may be as corrupt as the Tainted. What choice do most soldiers really have? Many countries have a mandatory service policy. And extremist groups recruit through fear and force as much as religious fervor. What other option does a father have but to serve when the alternative is letting them 'recruit' his son?"

The hand gripping the seat-back looked as though it was going to leave an indentation.

"Even those countries with voluntary service, soldiers must follow the decrees of others. Politicians decide which conflicts are worth sending loyal troops to the slaughterhouse. Wherever the hearts of the untainted lie, the cold truth of the matter is that they stand between us and keeping numerous people safe. While killing is the last thing we want, sometimes there is no choice."

I wanted to argue, but I had no basis. Hager was right. I didn't like it, but he was right. I didn't reply, and Hager held my gaze.

"We are about five miles out," called John from the driver's seat, finally breaking the silence.

I sat up fully and began to flex each of my muscle groups. I took deep breaths to get the blood flowing and to trigger my adrenal glands. I grabbed my rifle and started rechecking the settings.

Soon-Li looked sideways at me.

"We don't even know if the Tainted are there yet."

"We don't know that they aren't," I replied.

"I thought you were against using that."

I didn't stop my inspection. "I am. But that doesn't change reality."

The SUV pulled up alongside a long wire fence, in the blind spot between two cameras. Three hundred yards ahead stood the front gate security station. Hager aimed a pair of binoculars in that direction.

"The booth doesn't look occupied."

"This is a high-security nuclear facility," Soon Li muttered. "They don't just wander off for pee breaks."

"She's right," I added. "Let me out."

Tira jumped out and slid the seat forward. "What is your plan?" asked Hager.

"I am going to wander by, nonchalant like, and see if anyone's home. But I can't do that with this." I handed the assault rifle to Tira, who kept it low in case anyone was watching. "Keep it safe for me."

"Here." Soon-Li held out a small case. Inside was an earpiece tucked into a molded slot. I pulled it out and stuck it in my ear.

"Test."

"I got you," John answered.

"Try not to get yourself killed. Or worse, blow our surprise advantage," Tira scolded.

"Watch it now, you might sound like you care."

I reached for my sidearm, a well-oiled Glock. I pulled the slide back slightly, triple checked that a round was chambered, and put the pistol back in the shoulder holster under my black jacket.

"Don't miss me too much." I said.

"I won't"

I started walking toward the guardhouse, hands in my pockets. My training screamed at me to always keep my hands free, and it took all my will to do otherwise. If someone was keeping an eye out, I needed to look unimposing. At about the halfway point, I took them out and started to weave a little as I walked.

"Everything okay?" came a voice in my ear.

"Fine," I answered softly. "Just thought of a better way to get a closer look."

As I approached the outpost, my weave became a stagger, and I practically fell against the side of the small building, making over dramatic heaving motions.

"That's disgusting," said Tira through the com.

"Hopefully, anyone else looking will think the same and stop watching," I replied.

I lifted my head enough to look through the window of the security booth. A hand was visible, sprawled on the floor. I stumbled myself into a better view and saw the guard's body lying in a pool of blood. "Guard is down. Looks like a double tap to the chest. There's no blood splatter on the windows. This was either a low caliber weapon, or they made him kneel before they shot him."

"Somehow I doubt they are packing twenty-twos," John offered.

"I'd have to agree," I said.

"What now?" Tira asked.

"I have a feeling they are watching the gate in case someone shows up with a delivery, but they will not be watching all sides," I suggested.

"What made you draw that conclusion?" Hager asked.

"They are expecting this to be a quick job, since they didn't post a decoy at the gate. There's no one here to let people in, or at least come up with a crappy lie. They plan to be gone before anyone notices. I have basically used up my barfing time, so I am going to keep walking before whoever is watching gets suspicious. Pick me up about two hundred yards down the street."

"Copy that," John said.

I continued my faux drunken stagger, which took more energy than I had considered. Little by little, I trailed off my performance until I reached the rendezvous point. I pantomimed not needing a ride, then finally got in and we pulled away. Tira was now in the back and I had her seat. We followed the mid-construction semblance of a road. It forked one way that wrapped around the buildings and the other continued south. We exited onto Broadway and looped around the next building under construction before continuing along the river. John pulled into the west corner of a warehouse lot directly south of the main building.

"Sniper check?" I asked.

"Sniper check," John agreed.

We both got out. John reached into a duffle and handed me a set of military grade binoculars with night vision, then drew another pair out for himself.

There were ten buildings in the complex. Six of them formed a backward C shape and surrounded three others: the large main warehouse and two smaller buildings running parallel to its east side. The final structure was located on the west side, next to the dock that provided access via the Delaware River. We numbered them, starting in the center with the big warehouse and its sub-buildings, then working clockwise around the C.

John went to the left side of the southernmost building and I went to the right. From my vantage, I couldn't see much. The roof line obscured a complete view. "I have movement on the roof of building ten," John said.

"I have no view of building one. Need to get higher," I replied.

"Coming to you." This time it was Soon-Li's voice.

A minute later, she was by my side. She took the binoculars from me, looking up at the roofline. Then she followed a trail with her eyes back down to where we stood. She hooked the strap over her head and across her body, then turned and began to walk away.

"Watch this," said John over the com.

He had barely finished speaking when Soon-Li bolted toward the building at a run. At about ten feet away, she launched herself and covered more than half the distance up the three-story high warehouse. Pushing off the wall she drove herself further up. Two more of these mini hops put her at the top. She held onto the flat rooftop with just her folded arms, as though she was an elementary school student taking a rest on her desk. I just stood there, staring up at her.

"Soon-Li is the best at roofs," John said.

"Can you gentlemen focus, please?" Hager chastised.

"Sorry, boss man," I said. "Soon-Li, what do you see?"

"There is someone on building one, as expected. Her focus is on the front entrance. I guess the other guy is there to cover her six."

"How do you know it's a she?" John asked.

"I figured they would want their best person covering the gate."

"Okay," I interrupted before the banter could continue. "Any other guards?"

"Not sure. Wait, yes. Another on building one. I can just make out his heat signature. The first is just south of the gatehouse. The second is at the far north end."

"John, tactical options?" Hager asked.

"Building ten's guard needs to go first. He has a view of the south, as well as of the other two guards. Then, somehow, we need to take the other two guards down simultaneously, or we risk them sending up an alert."

"Soon-Li, can you get over to the other roof from where you are?"

"Spotter says it's fifty feet, which is just at the edge of my range for a single jump. I should be able to make it. But there is no way I can get to the north sniper before he raises the alarm."

"And I'm sure they are trained to recognize an enhanced attack," John added.

"Sniper rifle at this range would be like sending up a flare, even with a silencer," I added.

"Did you bring the new toy we were working on?" Hager's asked. "Oh yeah. I intended to run some tests while we were waiting them out, but it is theoretically field-ready. Christian, give me a hand back at the truck."

"Wilco."

"I will take out the guard at building ten," Tira said.

"How are you going to do that without him seeing?" I asked. "Leave that to me."

"Okay, that leaves Soon-Li and me to take out the other two. I will take the one on the north side with Snidely."

I double timed my way back to the SUV. Tira climbed out and took off like a shot, blurring in the opposite direction until she was in the protective cover of the next set of buildings. Then she eased back into her hyper-run.

I met up with John at the back. He was already climbing onto the roof box and sliding out what was inside. I reached up and helped him maneuver the jumble of metal and plastic. After about a minute of assembly, I could see what it was: a drone. It had a pitch-black frame with six rotors and a substantial remote control with a small screen affixed to the top. "Sweet," I said.

"These coms are waterproof, right?" Tira's voice broke in.

"Uh yeah, why?" John answered.

A strange noise came through the coms. I looked over at John before switching mine off.

"Did she just dive in the water?" I asked in a hushed voice.

"I think so," John replied, switching his off as well. "Damn. In this weather, that's badass."

"Shall I let her know you think so?" Hager's voice came from behind, making us both jump.

"Damn, you can be creepy sometimes," I said, catching my breath. "Will she be able to get into position in time?" I asked John.

"You haven't seen her swim. I am hustling to be in position by the time she is."

"Damn," I repeated.

John flicked on the drone and the screen came alive. He made a few selections and the view shifted to the camera display, then it switched to night vision. I whistled through my teeth. John nodded, accepting the praise. He got the drone up, hovering about four feet off the ground. It was whisper quiet. John turned to Hager.

"Ready?" John asked.

"Quite."

I looked from one to the other. "What do you mean?"

Hager removed his hat and placed it in the back of the car. John adjusted the height of the drone to hover just over Hager's head. He walked under it and grabbed the two reinforced landing struts.

"I'll have to take the scenic route over the water. Can you condense your frame?"

Hager casually pulled himself into a pike position, lying completely parallel to the body of the drone.

"Will that do, Mr. McCaw?" he said, as casually as if he was lounging on the sofa.

"Yup," John replied.

He guided the drone, with Hager attached, off toward the direction Tira had gone. I looked at John, who unsuccessfully tried to hide a smirk. These people were all badasses. My feeling of inadequacy grew deeper.

"Not up?" I asked.

"Don't want to take the chance that any of the snipers might see."

"Good call."

John snaked the makeshift Hager drone around the building and over the river. The viewer showed part of Hager's face at the bottom. Happy with the level of camouflage, John sent them shooting up. I tried to catch sight of the drone but couldn't—there were no blinking lights to draw attention to it. According to the viewer, Hager was about two hundred yards above the north side of building one and descending slowly. John made another selection and the viewer turned to thermal. It didn't show much.

"Amram, hang again so I can use the bottom camera."

Hager lowered himself to a hanging position. This improved the view, though not by much.

"Better but not great."

"I will guide you," Hager said.

With Hager's help, John got the drone in place, hovering about fifty feet above the third sniper. In the chill air against the metal roof, the sniper's outline showed up clearly.

"Christian, coordinate the strike," Hager said.

I hesitated for a second. Then the soldier in me took over.

"Roger that." For this part, at least I knew what I was doing. "Tira, sit-rep."

"In position."

"Roger. Soon-Li?"

"In position."

"Roger. Mr. Hager?"

"In position."

"All positions ready." I took a breath, knowing what I was unleashing. "Deploy, deploy, deploy."

Chapter Seventeen

JOHN AND I WATCHED the night vision enhanced screen as Hager released the drone and dropped to the roof. I heard a bone-crunching sound as he landed on top of the sniper—or maybe I just imagined it.

"Sniper three down," Hager said.

I picked up the field glasses and looked over the roofline in time to see a flutter of robes as Soon-Li launched herself into the air. Through the green-tinged world, she looked like a bird of prey descending on her game. Mid-leap, I heard a small grunt from the coms, followed by Tira's voice.

"Sniper one down."

Soon-Li disappeared past the roofline. Two seconds later, she reported in.

"Sniper two down."

"Good," replied Hager. "Let's move in. Soon-Li, meet up with Tira and enter from the west. John and Christian, enter from the east."

John joined me at the far end of building nine. He had strapped a combat knife to his left thigh. He wasn't carrying a rifle.

"You forget something?" I asked.

John did a quick check that ended on the knife. "Nope."

I lifted my M16 and gave it a little shake. John flashed a smile. "Nah, man. I don't carry those anymore," he said, patting his blade. "This is all I need."

That didn't align with the expertise I watched back in the garage. "Why not?"

"Long story."

I didn't press, though that was a story I wanted to hear.

John and I moved out, heading around the southernmost ware-house, which was still under construction. The area between the build-ings was littered with various machines, storage trailers, and other tools. We used them as cover, moving across the open area that made up the inner curve of the C.

"Amram, we have movement on the west side," said Soon-Li.

"I see him," Hager replied. "The warehouse doors are opening on the west side. John, Christian, move up and cover the flank. I don't want anyone circling back around."

"Roger that, boss man," I said.

John and I were halfway to the two small buildings next to building one. He turned to me.

"I'm going to blur up. Cover my six."

"Wilco," I said.

John blurred out of sight, appearing a few seconds later at the southeast corner of building three. I cradled my rifle and took off at slightly under my top speed to conserve energy. I was unconcerned with being picked off, since the snipers were already out of the picture, but I still had the feeling that I was being watched. John started skirting around at normal speed to the east, away from the central warehouse. I got to the south corner of building three while John was at the north corner of building two.

A weird feeling came over me—a sense of dread that, for some reason, was focused on John. It was like that feeling you get when you're a kid walking through a dark room. You know it's empty, but that imagined presence causes you to run in fear. I had that same feeling now and, like the old days, it spurred me to move faster.

Time began to slow down, an alien feeling that was becoming more familiar. My footfalls increased. The stress on my lungs receded. My vision became clearer. I didn't go left as I was supposed to; instead, I followed behind John, catching up quickly. John was five steps from the corner when a figure stepped off a small path that separated buildings one and two. The guard raised his rifle just as John began to turn around, clearly sensing that something was wrong.

I blurred in next to the guard, my hands slapping either side of his trigger arm. My inside hand slammed against the P6 pressure point on his forearm while I hit the back of his hand with the butt of my knife. The combination caused him to drop the rifle. Before it hit the ground, my knife slipped in between his ribs. It slid up through his lung, silencing any cries of warning, and into his heart.

He died quickly. One second, he was a human being, with dreams and goals. The next, he was a bag of flesh and bones. A wave of pain hit me. My breath was gone. My legs went rubbery. Screams ripped through my head, voices both young and old. I dropped to my knees, still trying to support the body of the man I had just forcibly ripped from this world. John was back at my side, releasing me of at least the physical weight. He dragged the body between the two buildings, out of sight. A fog pushed in around my brain, getting thicker until it obscured my vision, threatening to blind me. I felt as if someone was pushing a needle through my temple. I struggled to repress my own scream.

"Yo, brother, you okay?"

Slowly, the pain and the screams receded until I was able to focus again. I started breathing, unaware that I had been holding it in until that point.

"Yeah, sorry." My breath was now coming in gulps and I searched for something to say that didn't sound insane. "I just got lightheaded for a second."

"Uh, right. You sure you're good?"

"Hundred percent." I shook my head to clear the voices, then forced myself to stand.

"Okay," John said, though he didn't sound convinced. He nodded to the corpse without looking. "Thanks. How did you know he was there? How did you get it to kick in? Your blessing?"

"No idea on both counts. Until I figure it out, how about you wait for me from now on?"

"Good plan."

"Take your corner. I will circle around to the west side."

"Copy that."

I went back through the alley that the sentry had come from. I stalked around the next corner, making sure no other surprises were waiting, and took up position at the open hangar door. The interior was vast and dark. It took my eyes several seconds to adjust to the point where shapes began to coalesce. I started to see the outline of several large trucks, along with some figures moving around.

"How many?" John said over the com. "Hard to tell. Looks like about ten."

"Why is it hard to tell? You just blurred to my rescue. You can't peer into the shadows?"

I rolled my eyes. "Well, apparently, I only rolled a four on my twenty-sided die."

"What?"

"Why don't you take a look?"

"Gentlemen, if you please," Hager prodded.

I saw John poke his head out. "Ten enemy combatants confirmed inside. With the guard on the west and the one Christian took out on the east, that makes a total of twelve. Eleven active. I say again, eleven active combatants. Possible target identified."

The nearby truck suddenly roared to life, headlights flooding the interior. Several vehicles of various types, as well as machinery, were illuminated. The running truck slowly moved toward the opposite door facing the river. It looked monstrous and heavy, and resembled something built out of LEGO—a flatbed with a huge beer can mounted on top.

"Make that definite. Target acquired."

"Okay, what's the plan?" I asked. "We were supposed to stop them before they got to this point. I don't think we want to start a firefight around a tin can holding nuclear waste."

"That would be inadvisable," Hager added unhelpfully.

"I have a slightly dangerous idea," Tira said.

"Would you care to share?" I asked.

"Since they opened the west door, my guess is they will try to get it out by boat. If it can't reach the boat, problem solved, right?"

"How do you plan to stop it?" Soon-Li asked.

"Take out the tires," I added, seeing where Tira was going.

"I thought we already covered the no shooting at the radioactive truck part," John said.

The truck was nearing the garage door, moving slowly because of its dangerous payload.

"Once we start shooting, they will start shooting back. We are good, but I don't think any of us can dodge bullets while aiming accurately," Soon-Li added.

"I have a better idea," I said. "Boss man, can you drop in on the driver from above and get the key?"

"I can't blur through a closed door. I will need a distraction."

"One distraction coming up. Give me a go signal."

"Acknowledged," Mr. Hager said. Then after a brief pause. "Confirm readiness."

The small tractor-trailer rolled towards the hangar door at a snail's pace. The guards surrounded it, keeping pace while looking in all directions. John blurred up to the opposite side of the door, peeked around for a second, and then pulled back. He gave me a thumbs up. I pulled up my rifle and sighted down, picking a target. I placed the sight's red dot at the back of his head. The screams still echoed in my mind. My training, telling me to shoot center mass, fought with these new voices of questionable origin. I took a breath and moved my focus to his right shoulder.

"Distraction ready," I said. "Steady..."

The truck crept forward.

"Now!"

I saw John blur from the corner of my eye. He appeared behind two of the mercenaries who were walking too close together. John grabbed one and, in one quick movement, snapped his neck. As the other guard turned, John grabbed his rifle, flipped him onto his back and drove the butt end of the gun into his face.

I let out my breath and squeezed the trigger. The rifle coughed. A pink mist plumed from my target's shoulder. He yelled in pain, which got the attention of all the others who had missed John's show.

"We're under attack!" someone yelled.

I took another few shots, aiming at random metal pieces—trying to make noise more than anything else.

"Contact east!" another yelled.

"Two down," John said, already back in his spot. "Make that three," I added.

"Four," said Soon-Li.

"That leaves seven active. I repeat, seven active."

I dropped low and peeked around the corner. The rest of the mercs had found cover and were starting to pepper the area with suppressive fire. I caught sight of Hager dropping quietly down onto the roof. I sent a few blind rounds into the warehouse, making sure I aimed well away from the truck. When I heard breaking glass, I risked another look. Hager, kneeling on top of the roof, reached in and pulled the driver out one-handed before tossing him to the side. In one swift movement, he swung into the window.

The mercs missed the gymnastics. They were unaware that their defensive ring was already breached from above. They did notice, however, when the truck engine went silent. They turned to look, only to find Hager running down the length of the payload, bounding back onto the roof from the top of the truck. I took advantage of the confusion to send a few more rounds their way.

"Truck is down," Hager said. "It is out in the open, but it's not going anywhere."

"Great," I replied. "What now?"

"Start pulling back. That nuclear waste is not getting on any boat." Bullets ripped into the wall next to me.

"Roger that."

I looked over at John. A smile broke across his face. Then, it turned to confusion and he looked up. That bad feeling came back and my senses went nuts like back in the diner. It took another second before I heard it. The distinctive *whomp whomp whomp* sound coming from the north.

"Oh shit," both John and I said in unison. "Hager, get off the roof now!" I yelled.

He landed next to me, nearly making me jump out of my skin.

"Everyone, find cover," Hager's voice was irritatingly calm.

The helicopter swooped in overhead, a searchlight scanning the area.

"Let's get inside," John said.

"Copy that," I replied.

We made our way quickly but cautiously inside the hangar, watching for any more sentries. We found none; they were all surrounding the immobile target.

"We made it to building ten," Tira said.

"Acknowledged. Stay put for now. We need to figure out our next move."

We were just coming around a maintenance truck when my hearing went into overdrive. The din created by the helicopter blades faded out and small details became sharper. I could hear the ticking of Hager's pocket watch. His heartbeat was elevated but steady. In the distance, I could pick out John's footfalls, faint but still distinctive.

Then I heard a strange voice. "I have movement in the hangar."

Followed by another. "Fire at will."

"Drop!" I yelled, turning and tackling Hager.

Rifle fire tore a line in the truck, where our chests had been. I half expected a snarky comment from Hager about my overreaction, but none came. We crawled further back into the hangar to make sure we were out of sight.

My enhanced hearing was still working and caught more chatter. "Movement in the small building."

"Overwatch, open up with the Minigun."

My head jerked up. "Soon-Li, Tira, get out now!"

I heard the whir of the M134 high-powered, rotary machine gun mounted on the helicopter. It was followed by what sounded like a poorly muffled minibike. The massive fire rate of the minigun was laying waste to the building in a hail of bullets. I could hear windows shattering, and walls being torn apart like the paper target from the old B.B. gun carnival game. After what seemed like an impossibly long time, the gun quieted.

"Are you guys okay?" John said in a whispered voice.

"Yes, we blurred out just in time, thanks to Christian's warning," Tira said.

"Thank God," Hager exclaimed.

"What's the plan?" asked Soon-Li.

"Good question," I replied.

"What are our friends doing?" Hager asked.

"I have a line of sight," John said. "I see a winch being lowered. Looks like they are hooking it up."

"Is that even possible? That thing must weigh five tons," Tira said.

I couldn't let that happen. "We have to stop them. I'm pushing up."

"No, wait!" John yelled.

I moved forward, sighting down my rifle as I went. As I came into view of the truck, I saw three guns aimed at my position. There was no time to move. Just as the bullets started flying, I was yanked backward, as if pulled by a parachute. I heard the buzzing of the rounds passing by my head. I landed flat on my back, staring up at Hager, who was frowning at me.

"That was stupid," he said plainly.

"We are pinned down, Soon-Li," reported John. "Anything you can do from your position?"

"Not with that machine gun aimed this way."

"It's too late. They are hooked up and starting to climb," Tira said.

"Can you get a shot at the pilot?" I asked desperately.

"And risk the helicopter coming down on the rods? No, thank you," Hager said.

I couldn't watch as these guys made off with the raw components of a dirty bomb. I made my way back to the east door, picking up speed as I moved. Hager launched into a tirade questioning my sanity, which I ignored. I just needed to stop them. I wasn't sure what was driving me. I skirted to the right, out the door and between the buildings. I hopped up on an electrical unit and launched myself fifteen feet up onto the roof of building two. I knew I would make it. There was no thought to it—just action. It was like something I had done a thousand times before. I turned to see the container lifting above the roof.

I took off at a run, leaping the twenty feet to the roof of the warehouse and slipping into a blur. The helicopter continued to climb, pulling its payload higher by the second. My speed increased until I was close enough, then I launched myself up. As fast as I ascended, another figure slid down the thick cable. We met at the base.

The figure solidified into Kali. She lashed out with her foot, driving it into my chest, hurling me away from both the chopper and its payload. I landed like a rag doll almost half a football field away.

I sat up—somehow still unmarred—and looked up at the lifting helo. My enhanced vision was working. I focused on the open side door. A lone figure leaned out, staring right at me. The interior light came on, clearly outlining his facial features: Baldemar. Before they lifted further out of view, he waved. The asshole actually waved at me. Then he dropped something and closed the door.

I knew what it was without knowing how. "BOMB!"

I saw John skid around the other side of the hangar door and take cover. I did the same, scrambling for the protection of building two. The concussion wave knocked us both over, despite our huddled forms. Debris rained down all over, falling as muted collisions thanks to the ringing in my ears. I opened my eyes to a body leaned up against the far building, or rather half a body.

Panicked, I turned toward where John had taken cover. He was still there, hands over his ears, staring up at a large piece of metal that had penetrated the wall about four inches away from his head. John met my gaze and said something that didn't filter through, but the intent was clear enough.

I looked back remorsefully at the man's torso; moments ago, he had been my enemy.

"He killed them," I said in disbelief. "He killed his own men."

Chapter Eighteen

"CHRISTIAN! JOHN! AMRAM! ARE you guys okay?" Tira's voice was muffled, but clearly panicked through the earpiece. I was still trying to focus on my surroundings, trying to assess the current danger level.

"Christian, please answer."

I could hear Tira, could connect that it was her and that she was calling for Christian; but I felt like it was a different Christian. Possibly even a different world entirely. Thoughts came to me and just as quickly disappeared. Hager appeared at my side.

"Bateleur, sit-rep!" he barked.

That order bypassed all the haze and activated my training. The fog in my head lifted enough to acknowledge and respond.

I looked up at him. "Copy. IED Blowed up. Status green. No visible injuries."

He reached under my arm with one hand and helped me to my feet. "Let's get to the extraction point," Hager ordered.

"Wilco."

I looked around the corner and saw that John was on his feet again. "John, come to me. I'll give you cover," I said.

I looked over at where the advance team had been. I doubted there was anyone left alive, but I wasn't taking any chances. John blurred, ending up behind me. Nothing moved in the hangar.

"Let's move." John said. "This place is going to be crawling with badges soon, and we have no reason to be here."

The three of us started making our way back quickly, though none of us were pushing with any advanced abilities. I tried to re-engage mine and was met with failure again.

"I need help with a package on what's left of the south side of building one," said Soon-Li.

"This is no time to pick up your laundry," John replied.

"Was that a crack about my being Chinese?"

John smirked. "Touché."

"The package is large. Maybe we should bring the car around, so we don't have to carry it."

"Keep your eyes open. There could still be resistance left over," I said.

"Will do."

"I'll get the car," Tira said.

Hager, John, and I continued along the building; I faced forward and kept an eye out through the sights of my rifle. John was walking backward, covering our retreat, knife in hand. We got to the end of the building just as the SUV was approaching.

"John, catch—fragile."

"Copy."

He sheathed his knife and looked up. Soon-Li was standing on the edge of the roof, holding a bundle in her arms.

"Ready," he said.

She dropped the package, which let out a muffled scream as it fell into John's strength-enhanced arms. It was a woman dressed in the black fatigues favored by many mercenaries. She was hogtied and gagged, staring wild-eyed at John. Tira screeched to a stop in the SUV.

"You want to take it from here?" John lifted the woman slightly in explanation.

Tira tripped the switch for the liftgate and jumped from the driver's seat. She grabbed a bag from the back, and hopped into the third row, leaving room for John to place the woman. After "the package" was secured, he closed the rear gate and jumped into the driver's seat. Hager was already climbing into the front passenger side when I opened the backdoor. Soon-li, who had apparently gotten down from the roof and jumped in without my even noticing, patted the seat next to her. I shook my head, climbing in as the first cop car pulled in through the main entrance.

"Okay, back way it is." John threw the SUV in reverse and gunned the engine.

I struggled to get the door shut while maintaining my seat. I finally won with Soon-Li's helpful hand on my belt. We watched two more cruisers follow the first before John yanked hard on the steering wheel, putting us into a controlled slide. He rammed the shifter into drive and gunned the engine, launching us forward.

"Could you throw me around a little less?" Tira called from the back. "I don't want to stick myself with this."

I turned and saw her holding a syringe. She had the woman's sleeve pushed up past the elbow.

"No problem," John retorted. "I'll just call the three cop cars and ask them to chase us a little slower, since we are having a hard time sedating our kidnap victim."

"That's all I ask." Tira filled the vial. She asked the woman, "Are you allergic to any sedatives?"

She received only an icy stare in response.

"Okay, I asked. No sudden moves, John."

I couldn't believe what I was seeing. "Tira! You can't inject someone in a moving car."

She gave me a pointed look and held the filled needle for my inspection. One heartbeat it was full, the next it was empty.

"You can when you move faster than the car."

The woman's eyes rolled back and closed. Tira checked her pulse and nodded to herself. Then yelled, "Clear!"

She adjusted the restraints so she could get the guard into a sitting position before buckling herself in.

"Potent stuff," I said.

Tira smiled. "Would knock out a horse with a slightly larger dose."

I frowned. "Remind me not to piss you off."

"Words to live by."

I turned back and found Soon-Li watching me. The woman had taken out a trained sniper by disarming and hog tying her.

"You neither."

The maniacal grin would have made the Joker proud.

The car jerked to the side and brought me back to the issue at hand. "So, what's the plan?"

"I was thinking we ought to escape the cops. Then perhaps question the sniper, find the secret lair, and save the day," John replied.

"Good plan."

We were screaming down Broadway when a train whistle rang out.

John whipped his head around, smiled, and said, "I just thought of a better one."

I looked back and saw a long freight train coming up fast. "You're kidding, right?"

"Nope."

John's gaze kept moving from the road to the side mirror, apparently doing the math in his head and adjusting his speed to fit.

"Isn't escaping a high-speed pursuit with a freight train a little cliché?"

"God works in mysterious ways," Hager said.

"Not funny," I replied.

I could see the crossing that he was aiming for now, flashing lights and all. My brain filled with the sounds that generally accompany an active railroad intersection. The clanging bells added to the tension. He looked back to check the train's position relative to our own.

"Don't you think you're letting it gain a little too much?"

"Relax, Mr. Bateleur. Mr. McCaw is an expert driver," Hager assured me.

"Easy for you to say. Remember, I can't become hard as a rock at will."

"Sounds like a personal problem," John retorted.

I would have kicked the driver's seat, but I didn't want to take the chance of distracting him. Plus, I had to admit, it was a good jibe.

I looked back and watched as both the train and the police slowly gained. John secured a decent lead at the beginning, but was forced to slow his pace to allow both to catch up. To make this work, he needed them right behind us.

John serpentined down the road to prevent the cops from passing him. If they did, this little joy ride would be over in a very anticlimactic way. Luckily, since the lead car was doing everything possible to overtake them, it forced the following vehicles to stay back. This was where glory hounds played to our advantage. The train was now past us by about two cars. I could tell when John fully extended his senses. I couldn't say why; it was something in the way he settled into his seat and gripped the steering wheel. He reached over and flipped up a cover, revealing a thin metal toggle switch.

"Use the force, John," I said in my best Obi-won voice.

He smirked in the rearview mirror. "Come on Beulah, time to make the biscuits. Hang on."

John stomped on the gas and flicked the switch. The Suburban, weighed down with six adults and an arsenal of weapons, took off like a shot. The souped-up interceptors might as well have been in park, considering how quickly our larger vehicle left them in the dust—literally, since we sped over a patch of sand.

We were all pushed back in our seats. I watched us start passing the train cars again. The turn was coming up at an incredible rate. I didn't think there was any way for us to make it without flipping. We were past the train now by ten-car lengths, and still rocketing forward at full speed. It took all of my self-control not to yell, *you can break any time now!*

At a point that seemed way too late, John finally yelled, "BRACE!"

He pulled up hard on the emergency brake. Everything not secured flew toward the front window. He held the brake there for a count of three before pulling on the steering wheel. Then he released the brake and gunned the engine again. The tires went into a drift, back wheels screeching and spinning on the asphalt as we crossed the tracks. My position gave me a perfect view of the train's conductor as he stared, open-mouthed. Beulah skirted gracefully across the tracks with about three feet of clearance between the rear bumper and the edge of the train. He didn't even have time to pull the air horn.

We all sat in stunned silence as John let up on the gas, allowing the rear tires to catch. He set us back on a straight course at highway speed.

"I told you that John was an accomplished driver," Hager said.

"Vin Diesel, eat your heart out!" I yelled. "Now we just need to worry about the police net dropping around us."

"That's going to be difficult with no communications." Soon-Li's computer was back on her lap. When it got there, and how she managed to do anything during that roller coaster ride, I had no idea.

"What do you mean?"

"I hacked their cars and shut them down. Our normal jammer was doing its work while they were close enough, but they would have called for a BOLO once we were out of range. So, I had to use other methods. However, I think we should turn it off."

"The jammer, why?" Hager asked.

"Figure it this way: when we slip through their non-existent net, they will check the traffic cams. Those will be suspiciously blank in a linear sequence from our origin point."

"They will play follow the blank space right to our door," added John.

"But if we turn off the jammer, they'll follow us anyway," Tira said.

"I think the most prudent action would be to switch cars," Hager offered.

John shot a look at Hager. "Ditch Beulah?"

We pulled into a used car lot wedged in between a Liquor Barn and a small strip mall. We parked. Under cover of night and the video jammer, we picked two nondescript cars. We put two sets of license plates on them—one from Iowa, the other from Utah—and slipped an envelope through the mail slot containing enough cash to cover both.

"You just happen to carry huge sums of cash and extra license plates around with you?" I asked.

"Like the Boy Scouts say, 'always prepared,'" replied John.

The team moved quickly, parking the big truck—with yet another set of out-of-state plates—in the lot of the mini strip mall while I stood and watched. They pulled out all the visible indications that this was used for anything but a family car: including the automatic weapons and hi-tech devices like the jamming device. The tech was replaced with typical family truckster paraphernalia—toys, magazines, coloring books, fast food containers, and even a booster seat—all of it pulled from a hidden compartment in the back. They completed the picture right down to a distressed Disney World bumper sticker, and a set of silhouette people for the back window. A *Star Wars* character represented each member of the family. I watched in silent awe as everyone worked together, finishing the transformation in minutes. The only thing that didn't fit was the drone, which John quickly programmed to go home.

The two cars backtracked slightly, going the wrong way down route one-thirty and pulling a quick U-turn onto the on-ramp of route seventy-six. About twenty miles later, we turned off the jammer. If anyone connected the gap in the video to our escape, they still wouldn't be able to identify our current cars. At least not for a while. The chances that these two data points would lead anyone to our door were slim. I settled back into the uncomfortable seat of the compact car and allowed my adrenaline to ebb.

Chapter Nineteen

I STARED THROUGH THE two-way glass into the interrogation room. Tira sat across from the woman Soon-Li had captured, now handcuffed to the table by the large metal ring mounted in the center. Her name was Jelena Torres. I paced in the small room, listening to the back and forth. There was very little coming from our guest. I glanced at the clock. We had been at this for fifteen hours with minimal traction. Oh, sure, we knew all about Jelena since Soon-Li had hacked into her life. From college to boot camp to sniper school, plus her tours in Afghanistan and the incident with the IED. Jelena just wasn't telling us anything herself.

"Did you know what the target was, or was it compartmentalized?" Tira asked.

No response.

"The package they took was filled with the spent rods from a nuclear power plant."

No response.

"We believe they are trying to make a dirty bomb with the material."

No response.

"Do you know the bomb's target?"

The same questions over and over. Jelena had barely moved.

Soon-Li sat pouring over the screen, flipping from one piece of our prisoner's life to another. At one point she had even been looking at Jelena's Netflix account. We tried everything from threatening, to begging, to pushing on her military background. Nothing affected her, nothing moved her.

"Ah, ha!" Soon-Li exclaimed.

"What?"

"She has a child."

"What? No way."

"I just confirmed it. She must have a connection that buried it because this was not easy to find."

"How did you figure that out?"

"My first clue was the large number and frequency of Disney Movies watched on her Netflix. I mean, I like *Moana* as much as the next person, but come on!"

"That it?" I asked.

"Do you want to hear the whole process?" she asked.

"No, not really," I admitted.

"Okay, then." Soon-Li turned the laptop so I could see. The screen displayed a scanned copy of a birth certificate for an Enric Torres. I stared at the screen, then looked back at the printouts of her files. The woman on the other side of the glass had such a faraway look in her eyes. Everything clicked.

"We need to pick him up now. Can you get John on it? Have him brought here. The kid may be in danger."

"On it," Soon-Li said. "Her mother is probably watching him at home. I show her living at the same address."

I nodded and went into the interrogation room. Tira's face registered annoyance at my appearance. Jelena looked up out of habit, before quickly staring out into space again.

"Hi again, Jelena."

I pulled a set of keys out of my pocket and proceeded to unlock the cuffs. Tira shot me a glance but didn't interrupt whatever play I was making. They weren't necessary, anyway. If she actually managed to overpower three Bishops—well maybe two and a half—and get out, there was no escape from the underground fortress without a key card.

"Remember me?"

She looked up at me, then down at the cuffs being removed, but said nothing. When they were off, she rubbed her wrists but made no move to escape. Nor did she make a quick visual assessment to turn the situation to her advantage. There was only placid acceptance.

"I am here to offer you a job."

"What?" It was a stereo response from both Tira and Jelena.

The two women stared at me, but Jelena looked like she had a gleam of hope in her eyes. I could almost see the conflict. I stayed quiet and let her think a little, let her mind develop options and hopes that I could not possibly make up on the fly. She would be able to create the best, or worst, case scenarios all by herself.

"I figure it this way," I said, gambling that it was time to push. "Your boss thinks you're dead. He would assume there was no way we were getting past you without taking you out. Plus there was the whole dropping a bomb on everyone thing. And even if he doesn't think you're dead, we can assume he plans to remedy that later, based on his past method of cleanup." I paused to let that sink in and mentally made a slow count to five before continuing.

"You, however, have a bigger problem. Your only decent source of income has just dried up. You can't just pop back up in the same circles for fear of word getting back to your old employer. You could just bail. If you can get out of here, that is." I waved my fingers vaguely in the air. "But since you haven't been working at this job too long, you don't have enough saved up to just start over. Especially with your mother and son in tow."

Jelena's expression fell.

"I must say I'm impressed; you hid Enric well. But if we found him, then so can they."

I let the silence hang and chanced a glance at Tira to ensure she would do the same. She had adopted a look of concern for Jelena. She was good. The silence dragged on.

Jelena must have been running through all of her options and the likely outcomes for each. Could she hide him? She probably had a plan for that inevitable day when she didn't return from a mission. It probably included her mother getting out with the boy, a strategy which would have been easier with a few more years and a larger escape fund. Then they could still get to safety and have a relatively normal life. But for them to do that, she would have to...

"How much?" she asked.

Tira picked up the narrative. "Enough to give your son a good, safe life."

"That's not a number."

"How much was your old employer giving you?"

"One-fifty."

"Yeah, I don't think so. With your knee, a short career in the military, and few options, you could not be pulling in more than ninety."

"Ninety? Are you serious? I can shoot a popsicle stick out of your mouth at 1000 yards without a spotter."

"Yeah, but could you climb a tree to get into position?"

"Depends, do I have to argue with morons while doing it?"

We went on like that for about fifteen minutes. We were just hitting a decision point when the phone rang. I pulled it out of my pocket and put it to my ear, my eyes never leaving Jelena's.

"What's the verdict?" I said.

"I'm at the place, but they won't go with me," said John. "Amram's watching the street and a van just pulled up. We believe it's a pickup team."

"Hang on," I said. Then I put the phone on speaker and placed it on the table. "Repeat that so Jelena can hear."

There was a slight pause at the other end, then John repeated it, but in a much gruffer voice. I tried not to smile at John's tough guy act. Jelena's eyes went wide.

"Decision time. Employees we can help; otherwise, Johnny can just leave them where they are."

"Bastard." It was a statement of fact, not an accusation. "Give the phone to my mother."

A rustling sound emitted from the speaker as John handed over the conversation on his end.

"Who is this?" The voice was demanding.

"Mom, it's me."

"Jelena? What the hell's going on? Who is this man? Where..."

"Charlie, Charlie, Charlie."

The phone went silent for a second. "This guy?"

Jelena met my eyes before she responded.

"Friend. But others are on our doorstep that are not."

"Can he handle himself? I don't need anyone slowing me down," the woman said.

"I think he should be alright."

"Okay, we are bugging out. See you soon."

There were some muffled sounds and John came back on the line. "This should be interesting," he said.

"You all good?" I asked.

"Piece of cake." John's voice became distant. "Woah, lady, easy with that cannon. Is that a Desert Eagle? Okay, maybe not cake."

The last part, he said back into the phone before the line cut off.

Jelena was grinning, her fingers happily drumming on the table. "Is your mother looking for work?" I asked, half kidding.

The grin got wider.

"How about I show you to the locker room where you can get cleaned up and maybe get a fresh set of clothes?"

"Wait, seriously?" Jelena asked.

"Sure, it's in the employee handbook. Full use of the facilities for bodily functions and general hygiene. When you're done, we'll see about food. You're not a vegetarian, are you? This one is." I gestured to Tira. "And it can be a real pain remembering not to put bacon on her stuff."

"Hell no. Bacon on everything is good with me."

"Can I have a word with you?" Tira said.

I looked over at her, sighed, and tilted my head towards the two-way mirror. "Soon-Li, are you still there?"

The speaker clicked on. "Right here."

"Great, would you be able to take care of our new member while Tira yells at me?"

"My pleasure."

"Thanks."

"Just let me know what happens after."

Jelena looked at me, not believing that she had gone from captive to employee so quickly.

"The door's unlocked. Soon-Li will meet you in the hallway."

She stood up tentatively and made her way towards the door, never taking her eyes off either of us. Her expression barely contained her genuine shock when she turned the knob and the door actually opened. She took one last glance at us, then hesitantly stepped out through the door and closed it behind her. I turned back to Tira and raised an eyebrow at her.

"So, you have decided that you're our HR department now?" she asked.

"Do we have an HR department? If so, I would like to discuss hazard pay."

"For last night?"

"No, for now."

"What makes you think you can just start hiring people? We have never recruited the unblessed."

"Unblessed?"

"Those who are not Bishops."

"I think the terms are a little backward. And I think not hiring regular people is shortsighted and utilitarian."

"We are a secret society that needs to keep its anonymity."

"Really? Secret, except for all the officials who are covering for us.

"Plus, extended families of all the Bishops, including your brother-in-law. And what about the other side of the equation? You have been trying to battle hundreds with only a few; meanwhile, there are thousands out there who would line up for a chance to fight on the side of righteousness."

"Like Jelena?"

"Yes, as a matter of fact. She joined the military to fight for what she believes in. Like her mother did before her. Got injured but not sufficiently enough to draw a large pension. She went to school for criminal justice but no law enforcement agency would take her. My guess, based on everything I've seen, is that she's an adrenaline junky. The only thing that would check all the boxes and pay enough to give her son the life she was denied is doing this crap.

"In these organizations, everyone except the most senior operative is kept in the dark. They get their individual mission parameters. She would never have known what the actual target was."

Tira folded her arms.

"Are you done mansplaining?"

"You already figured all this out?"

"Psychology is one of my PhDs."

"Then why are you making me work so hard?"

"It's fun." Tira smiled then stared at me quietly for a minute. "Do you trust her?"

"I think so. Something in my gut is telling me to." I wondered internally if my trust was coming from the fact that she had a child. Was I that simplistic? "Do you?"

"I trust her situation. She will depend on us to keep her family safe. She believes we are just as bad as her previous employer. We already know about her family, so she will behave for two reasons: fear of reprisal and the need for money. As she gets to understand who we are and what we fight for, she will give us her loyalty. But we haven't earned it yet."

"Makes sense," I said. "Right?"

Tira walked to the door and opened it.

"It's not like she can really go anywhere. Let's see how cooperative she is. Then we will be able to determine if your play is smart or stupid. At the very least, it will be fun to watch the show."

"What show?"

"The one where you explain to Amram that you hired a highly paid sniper."

Chapter Twenty

"YOU DID WHAT?"
We were in Hager's office, so Tira couldn't listen in. "It's logical when you think about it."

"Who gave you the authority to hire someone? We don't even have anyone come in to clean, but you thought it prudent to hire a sniper?"

"Well..."

"Not just a sniper, but one who, until last night, was hired to kill you!"

"Funny you mention it. She told me that I was in her crosshairs until I started fake vomiting. Apparently, she has no problem with splattered brains but can't stomach bodily functions." Hager stared at me with a combination of anger and pure shock. "So, my drunk idea worked even better than I thought," I explained, assuming he was not getting my point.

Hager shook his head as if trying to dispel nonsensical thoughts from it. "Where did you think the money to support her salary was going to come from?"

"Sorry, I understood we have deep pockets."

"Where did you get that idea?"

I looked dramatically up at the ceiling. "Eve, what is the status of our current financial portfolio?"

"We have seventy-three separate portfolios for the New York Covenant. Which one do you want details on?"

I looked back at Hager.

"Any requests? I especially liked number 34. The gains realized last quarter were especially..."

"You have made your point," Hager said. "But what made you think you had the right to spend it?"

"Each Bishop shall have discretionary spend allowances no greater than one percent of the total monthly income of the Covenant house to which they are assigned," I quoted.

Hager stared at me, blank-faced.

"I had trouble sleeping one night and found the by-laws. I presume that total equated to a lot less back in 1853 when they were last updated."

"Mr. Bateleur." Hager really had the scolding voice down pat. "This Covenant reports to a higher power. How would you like me to explain that our newest member just broke a six-hundred-year-old rule?"

"I can explain it if you'd like?"

Hager took a deep breath and let it out slowly.

"In the future, I must insist you run any new hires past me prior to offering employment."

"I think I can manage that."

"You may go."

I nodded and left. Tira was casually leaning against the wall in the hallway. She watched me for a moment, then gave me a slow clap and walked away. It looked like she might be smiling, but I wasn't sure.

The family we adopted was welcomed warmly by all the Bishops—even Hager, who rejoined everyone in the common room shortly after our little talk. Having only had time to bring the bare essentials, they were settling in as best they could. Soon-Li hurried off after seeing the little boy and returned with an old box of toys circa 1980. There were He-Man action figures, coloring books, and board games like Candy Land and Chutes and Ladders—all in perfect condition. I wondered at their value to the right collector.

Soon-Li, thinking nothing of it, ripped open some packages and started playing. Jelena's son, Enric, cautiously approached at first, but was playing right alongside her within minutes. Jelena was talking quietly to her mother in one corner of the room. They kept glancing in my direction. Finally, after some animated conversation, the mother approached. Her daughter trailed, shaking her head. "You

Christian?" she asked.

It sounded more like an accusation. "I am. Misses?"

"Torres. That useless moron of a father was little more than a DNA dump and run."

"Mom!"

"Names mean something. Heritage, tradition, family. His held none of those. So, Jelena kept a name for Enric that did."

"Understood." I said, my hand still hovering in the air. "Nice to meet you, Mrs. Torres."

She looked pointedly down at my hand, then back up at me. After a few seconds, she took it in a grip that could have come from a truck driver.

"Call me Janice."

"Oh, I'm gonna like this one," John said, smiling.

Janice eyed him sideways and John's smile disappeared.

"The last place Jelena got involved with nearly got her killed, from what I hear."

"I assure you, Janice, we do not consider any of our team expendable."

"Talk is cheap, Chris."

"Mom," Jelena tried again, but her mother waved her away.

"I want to take steps to make sure of that," she continued.

"And how...?" I tried to ask.

"I want in."

I looked at her for a moment, not willing to start another sentence that I couldn't finish.

"I want a job," she continued. "A way to keep an eye on your activities. Also, it would be a way to earn my keep. I won't be living here on someone else's dime."

I continued to stare at her, waiting. Finally, I asked, "finished?" To her credit, she didn't back down at all.

"Yes."

I turned to Hager.

"This is your call. I have an opinion if you would like to hear it."

He regarded me for a heartbeat or two. "Please, continue."

"An unused asset can quickly become a liability. From what I have seen so far, Janice can be an asset. I suggest we put her to work."

"I would agree. Do you have a suggestion as to what she should work on?"

I turned to Janice. "Skills?"

"I was a communications officer in the Navy."

"Perfect," Soon-Li piped up. "I have been wanting to set up a central dispatch. I will put you to work. But I will need to buy some new equipment."

"Of course you will," Hager said, rolling his eyes.

I smiled and turned back to Janice. "Good enough?"

"Yes. Thanks, Chris."

"It's Christian," I said. "Names have meaning."

Not waiting for a reply I took the opportunity to extricate myself, heading back to the meeting room. I needed a whiteboard. Somewhere I could get the information out of my head and visualize it. I settled down at the large table and opened my laptop, which I had picked up from my room on the way. I pulled up a web browser.

First question: how to build a dirty bomb?

I wrote that on the whiteboard in red. I really didn't want to type that into the search engine, figuring it would raise red flags all over the country. But I didn't need to. A dirty bomb wasn't really anything more than a regular I.E.D. with some radioactive material thrown in to extend the resulting damage. Putting things like nails or ball bearings in served the same purpose. The explosion would create a concussive wave that would propel shrapnel in all directions. That shrapnel just happened to be nuclear waste.

So, what could the bomb be made from? According to MacGyver, it could be just about anything. Mixing a stack of household cleaners together to cause an explosion seemed cool. It would, however, be less stable and produce questionable results. Somehow, I didn't think that these guys would be cheaping out by mixing bleach and borax. I had to consider more stable explosives.

I started listing them out on the board as they occurred to me: C4, dynamite, nitroglycerine. What were those chemicals used in the third Die Hard again? A quick internet search informed me that they actually existed but were not nearly as volatile as the film made them out to be. I also discovered, overall, there are about one hundred different explosive chemicals. I concluded that figuring out the type of bomb would not narrow down the search. I needed a new perspective.

I knocked on the door of the holding unit in the bunker. That was John's name for the lower level. Since it not only fit but also seemed to perturb Hager, I took up the charge as well. I checked the time before coming down. It was still early evening, so I was hoping our prisoner/guest, Denise was still awake. It only took a few seconds for the door to open. The room was not spacious. She was wearing sweatpants and a tee-shirt, her brown hair pulled back into a ponytail with a scrunchie. The fact that I knew the name for it kind of bothered me.

"Sorry to disturb you."

"It wasn't like I was in the middle of anything critical."

The sarcasm in her voice was evident. I couldn't blame her. During the first day or so of her detainment, she was recovering from the demonic manifestation of a mental disability. Going with the flow, at that point, was pretty easy. But now, thanks to regular sessions with Dr. Gupta, she was starting to feel more like herself. As a consequence, she was less inclined to be okay with being locked in a bunker for her own safety.

"Sorry."

"Stop saying that, please."

"Okay."

There was an awkward few seconds of silence.

"I was just thinking I could use some coffee. Want some?" Denise asked.

"Always."

She gave me a half smile, then walked past me into the kitchen area. This section functioned as a holding area, guest accommodation (for those in the know), and a break area for when we worked down here. We didn't want to have to go all the way up to the main kitchen every time we needed a snack. It was kind of like a break room in an office, including a round white table with six matching wooden chairs. It had the basics. Nice but no-nonsense.

Denise set to work putting on a pot of coffee. It was a practiced routine. She had been here too long already. I sat down at the table and waited, letting her play host. It probably provided her a sense of control, which she sorely lacked at this point.

"So, how are you feeling?"

"Besides being stir crazy and dealing with the onset of claustrophobia?"

"Yeah, besides that."

Denise inserted the filter basket filled with coffee and switched on the brew cycle. She turned to look at me, and I could see the tension in her jawline. She took a breath and seemed to relax a little.

"Sorry. I appreciate what you guys did for me, really. I literally owe you my life." Denise paused as though searching for the next sentence. "My emotions are all mixed up. They come and go in spurts. One minute I'm content, the next I'm paranoid, then depressed, then angry. I go from binge-watching random shows, to reading for hours at a time, to just lying in bed curled up in a ball. Crying one minute, laughing the next."

She flushed and turned back to the coffee, willing it to finish so she could have something to do.

"I need your help with something."

Denise's head cocked slightly. She pulled stray hairs behind her ear, still facing away from me, and rested her hand lightly back down on the counter. Her thumb gently traced the edge.

"I am trying to piece together the requirements to build this bomb. Hopefully, you can give me a direction to pursue."

Denise took a deep breath. She grabbed cups from the cupboard and filled them with hot water from the tap.

"I'm not a bomb maker."

"No, but you are a nuclear engineer. You've been around these materials for years. You know how they need to be stored, what equipment they will need. I am counting on the fact that a Venn diagram of the required tools and available places will reduce our search area."

She turned and looked at me.

"You don't sound like a soldier."

"Why do you think I'm a soldier?"

"Tira mentioned it."

"Why did she mention it?"

She tried to cover a smile. "I may have asked."

"And what are soldiers supposed to sound like?"

"The ones that are assigned to the plant don't say very much. When they do, it is usually about sports or weapons. They are very cocky, very full of themselves, and have never referenced a Venn diagram."

"Believe it or not, there are all types of soldiers with all kinds of interests. Some of us even like math and science. What about you? Where are your thick-rimmed glasses?"

"Touché."

The coffee maker beeped, and the smell permeated the small room. Denise filled two cups. "Milk and sugar?"

"No thanks, black is fine."

"Tough guy, huh?"

"Milk doesn't travel well. So, when you're deployed, it is either the powdered crap or black."

"It's light and sweet for me."

I had to resist commenting on that one. Denise brought the two cups over and sat down.

"Thanks."

"My pleasure. So how can I help?" Denise asked.

"I'm not sure yet. I figure the place they're holding up will have special needs for storing and working with that uranium."

Denise held the cup in both hands, the handle curving around her middle fingers, and leaned back to stare out at something I couldn't see. "Well, there are only a few substances that you can use to shield yourself from the gamma radiation that comes off the enriched uranium."

"Lead, right?" I said.

"Yes, but the weight and cost of lead are both prohibitive."

"I didn't think lead was that expensive."

"It's not, generally, but try building a small house out of it."

"Got it. So, lead is out. What else?"

"The two most common are concrete and water."

"Water?"

"Yeah, water is actually an excellent radiation barrier and has the added capability of keeping the uranium cool."

"You have to keep it cool even when it's not in use?"

"Yup. In fact, when the fuel rods come out of the reactor, they need to stay in a radioactive fuel pool for a few years."

"Years?"

"Yeah, usually you are fine after three or four, but government regulations state five years minimum."

"Okay. Water. So how much water are we talking here? Like a swimming pool? Could I set up one of those liner-only jobs that is held up by a metal skeleton?"

"No, absolutely not. You would need at least twenty feet of water to block that type of radiation. The radiation pools we use are forty feet to provide a larger barrier. It allows divers to perform mainte-nance functions."

"Wait, people dive in pools full of uranium?"

"Sure, all the time. It's safe."

"And people think I'm crazy."

Denise smiled.

"Okay, so twenty feet minimum. Let's check Google to see how deep an Olympic pool is," I said, turning to my laptop.

"Ten feet for racing, and up to sixteen feet for platform diving."

I stopped typing and looked up at Denise, who quietly sipped her coffee. Her eyes twinkled behind the mug.

"So, not just a nuclear nerd, I guess."

"I was on the swim team in college."

That was intriguing, but I forced myself to focus.

"Okay, so more questions: could I just dig a big hole in the ground and fill it with water?"

"Interesting thought, but no."

"Why not?"

"Well, for one thing, the uranium would heat the water to a boiling point without a filtration system continually extracting the heat and keep contamination levels to a minimum."

"Okay. So, I would need a location that has a pretty sophisticated filtration system already embedded in a pool that is greater than twenty feet in depth. Well, that seems pretty rare."

She nodded. "Yeah, generally the pools are also cement lined with steel. But that is mostly to guard against seismic activity and less to do with radiation blocking."

"Okay, so in all likelihood, this is not the method they would use."

"It depends. Performing all the operations underwater is more complicated but safer."

"So, I am either looking for a large water container that doesn't appear to exist, or some kind of concrete bunker. Luckily there are not too many concrete buildings around here. Oh, wait."

Chapter Twenty-One

EATALY IS, AS THE name would indicate, an Italian restaurant and market. Almost everything on the main floor is sourced straight from the boot country, so you can make authentic Italian anything at home. Little mini eateries sit within the shopping area, offering wine and cheese, seafood, pizza, and—of course—pasta. On the roof, a faux Italian countryside garden and restaurant serves up a large variety of beers. It's open air in the milder months, but has a retractable roof for when the weather isn't cooperating.

I sat at one of the inner tables. While the ability to gaze at the building was nice, I wasn't about to make a sniper's job that much easier. I took another swig of my Peroni as I waited for Jackie. What, I'm supposed to drink Budweiser at an Italian restaurant?

Jackie arrived and looked around before spotting me. She was dressed in a no-nonsense business suit with a form-fitting overcoat. I caught several men and a few women eyeing her as she approached. If anyone was there on a blind date, they were praying she was it. I stopped noticing this reaction a long time ago. Jackie was always pretty, even as a child. I don't remember her ever going through an awkward phase. Annoying, yes. Then, when she hit seventeen, she became drop dead gorgeous. At the beginning, I used to tease her about how much attention she would draw. The joke got old after a while. Now, it was like witnessing her for the first time again. Why she ended up hanging around with me, I'll never know, but I thank... well, you get the picture.

Jackie walked over. A waiter appeared next to her, offering to take her coat.

"No, thanks, I've got it," she said.

I got up and gave her a hug and kiss on the cheek. The waiter gave me the evil eye as if I was cutting in on his dance.

She sat down and told the waiter, "I'll have what he's drinking."

He hesitated, seeming confused as to why such a refined woman would order a beer—clearly a drink not worthy of her status. Or maybe he was just calculating a way to extricate me from the equation. I felt like telling him he was wasting his testosterone on a pheromone addict, but I knew it was a useless endeavor. Besides being bad form, men generally fell into two categories with her: those that couldn't believe she was gay and those that felt sure they could turn her. He finally nodded and walked away after saying the archetypical, "Very good."

"Peroni, right?" She asked.

"Of course."

"You are so cliché."

I shrugged.

"So, how's Father Murphy?" Jackie asked.

"No change. It's a miracle he's alive at all."

"I've never heard you use that word before."

"Yeah, well. It's been a hell of a week."

"Are you going to tell me about it?" she finally asked.

"Best wait for the drink."

We didn't have to wait long. Garcon, or whatever the Italian equivalent was, may have been a Bishop based on his speedy return. More likely, he was one of the Tainted in disguise. Maybe he just went behind the bar and poured the beer himself for added brownie points. We took only a minute to order, and the waiter disappeared again. I had already perused the menu, and Jackie, the consummate lawyer, was excellent under pressure.

Once our hovering friend finally departed, Jackie said, "So, what's the deal?"

"I think I'm a superhero."

After she stopped laughing, I laid it all out for her. The Bishops, the Covenant, the war against evil raging since the dawn of time. Her expression took on the look she got when we visited the comedy club and the comic was in the middle of a very long joke. When I got to Denise and Indian Point, her expression changed. I rounded out my set with the attack on the Camden facility.

"That was you?" she asked. "That whole facility exploded."

"Shhhh. Keep your voice down. And it wasn't the entire facility."

"Christian, you have to go to the police."

"That's just it. The police come to us. No one else can handle these...things."

"Are you hearing yourself? They have a manhunt going for the people who did that. They are calling them terrorists."

"We didn't do that; we were trying to stop them."

"And maybe if your hall of religious fanatics had gone to the police they would have been stopped."

I wanted to be mad that she didn't believe me, but I couldn't blame her. Her dig at the Covenant was a play on the Hall of Justice. How could I be mad at that?

"I know it sounds stupid. I walked away from it at first, but I got sucked back in at the diner."

"Wait." She held up a hand and looked down to the left. It was her thinking pose. She looked back up at me. "They said a random patron took out the gunman. The reports were fantastical. Everyone chalked it up to the stress of the situation. Amazingly enough, everyone was too scared to whip out a phone. That was you?"

"I am a Ranger, remember? What, you didn't think I had it in me?"

"No. Spill it, I want details."

I proceeded to give her the short version of what happened. I left out the holy water, as Hager was reluctant to talk about that in public. I wasn't quite sure why, and I made a mental note to ask him about it.

"Show me."

I felt myself blush.

"That's one of the problems, I can't do it at will. With me, it kind of just happens when I need it."

I could see her dissecting my story as she would a witness's testimony. She was deciding which direction the cross-examination would go in, now that their weak point was revealed.

Whatever she was about to say was interrupted when our coffee was delivered. When we were alone, I preempted her.

"What is the verdict, councilor?"

She made a face, then said, "Okay."

I expected more. Instead, she added some milk to her coffee and took a sip.

"Okay?" I said.

She only nodded.

"What do you mean, okay?"

"Christian, I love you. You have come to me with a ridiculous story about a secret magical society that has existed since the dawn of man. You say that you're one of them. You're New York's only hope against demonic terrorists."

"That about sums it up."

"If it were anyone else, I would have called the police, a mental hospital, or both."

I waited.

"Here is what I know." She counted off on her fingers. "One: you are not a liar. You are many things, but not that. Two: while I would not call you exactly sane, you are also not that bat shit crazy."

"Gee, thanks."

Jackie smiled and nodded like she had done me a service. "Three: you are highly intelligent, despite your juvenile sense of humor. It would take an extraordinary amount of cost and planning to pull something over on you."

I rolled my eyes.

"Thank you for proving my point. And four: you're not that creative. You could not have come up with this on your own."

I watched her with trepidation.

"That adds up to a high probability that this is all true. But you have no proof. So, you are asking me to accept it on faith."

She reached into the collar of her blouse and pulled out a chain.

At the end was the Star of David.

"Lucky for you, I am a woman of faith."

I released a breath that I didn't realize I was holding. I reached out and took her hand, feeling an unfamiliar lump in my throat. Looking in Jackie's eyes, I saw only trust and love. I couldn't find the words—something else that I wasn't accustomed to.

"So, is she cute?"

I cleared my throat and wiped a hand over my face. "Who?"

"Tira."

"You're kidding, right?"

"While I have always wanted to have sex with an Avenger, I didn't mean for me."

"Then why...oh, you are nuts."

"What? I can hear how you talk about her. You have a thing."

"I don't have a thing. Besides, she hates me."

"Two things that will never change about you: your unhealthy love for the cinema and your inability to tell when someone is interested."

"If you witnessed the workout she put me through, you would be singing a different tune."

"Oh, a woman who wanted to see a man sweat and pushed to his limits. You're right, not interested at all."

"It wasn't like that!"

"When do I get to meet them?"

"Let me run it by Hager. I've pushed the envelope a little as of late. I think it might be the last straw if I bring you around for a guided tour of our secret lair."

"I'm not waiting long. Although I said I bought your story, your description still sounds like a cult. If you disappear on me again, I am going to show up at the front door."

"See, it does sound like a cult. That's what I told John." She cocked her head at me and frowned.

"Yeah, yeah, I got it. Keep you in the loop or you will go all Eddie from *Christmas Vacation*, and kidnap me with your RV."

She nodded, satisfied.

Chapter Twenty-Two

"THE ACTUAL EXPLOSION IS nothing compared to the devastation that would follow."

Denise was giving us a lesson on the results of a dirty bomb being detonated within the confines of Manhattan. We brought a portable white board down to the kitchenette outside of her room. On it, she had drawn a quick but very passable representation of New York City. If the nuclear waste management thing didn't pan out, art school could be an option for her. She drew a circle around a random spot, which represented the initial detonation.

"Concentric rings would extend out from the blast site for blocks." She drew them emanating from the blast radius.

"Some particles will vaporize, become airborne and spread the contamination. Each ring would have a number assigned to it; that number would equate to how long the exposed populous in those areas would live. The number of dead and dying would overwhelm the hospitals. Large sections of Manhattan would need to be evacuated. The cleanup would take months and cost billions."

We sat around the table in the kitchenette, watching in shocked silence as Denise outlined the repercussions if we failed. We didn't even exchange glances.

"How long will it take to build the bomb?" Tira asked.

"It depends."

"On what?"

"A couple of things: the type of facility, how many people were working on it, their skill level with uranium pellets..."

Tira nodded.

"Oh, and how many bombs they're making." Denise added.

"What?" Soon-Li interjected.

"How many can they make?" Hager asked, a little too calmly for my liking.

"That will also depend on what size of bomb they're making. I figure they have enough uranium to make two big bombs or about seven smaller ones."

"Can you give us an educated guess?" I asked.

Denise looked at me for a somewhat uncomfortable few seconds. "I would have to say two to four days for extraction, but I wouldn't know about the bomb assembly."

John shook his head.

"We are running out of time."

The clock read 12:23 AM. It was the hot time of night. I threw the blanket off, propped up the pillow, and laid back down. How could my body temperature go from comfortable, to hot, to cold in a room that stayed at a constant sixty-five degrees? As my upper back hit the pillow, I felt its cold dampness. Gritting my teeth, I turned it over to get at the dry side. My pajama bottoms clung to me, and my lower back told me that the sheets were in the same condition as the pillow. I edged over into the corner to find a dry spot. When I was deployed in Afghanistan, I learned to deal with sweating at night. What couldn't be corrected was ignored. Too many years out of the desert had made me soft.

I ran through the latest raid in my head. The lack of actionable intel was starting to get to me. We were taking straws of information and trying to build a bridge to a solution. Soon-Li was cross-referencing electricity usage with likely locations. So far, nothing helpful. Some were pot houses, which we provided as anonymous tips to the police. One building had been settled by a homeless guy that had set up three old air conditioners and a T.V. in a corner room. He was not very happy at our intrusion, especially since he had been entertaining, so to speak. Apparently, we ruined the mood for him and his two lady friends. I shivered at the mental image all over again.

I closed my eyes and tried to let sleep take me. One phrase kept repeating in my head. *The actual explosion would be nothing compared to the devastation that would follow.* After about twenty minutes, I gave up. I put on sweatpants and a tee-shirt before heading downstairs, pouring a glass of ice water and moving into the common room. Switching on the large TV, I settled on a feel-good movie that I hadn't seen in a while, hoping it would lull me into slumber.

A few minutes later, Jelena wandered in and sat on the opposite side of the couch. "Couldn't sleep either, huh?" I asked.

"No, I was sleeping fine. I always set my alarm for one AM so I can catch up on some late-night television."

"Funny," I replied.

Jelena gave me a duh look and turned to stare at the TV. We sat in silence for about ten minutes before Tira entered. She sat on one of the chairs, pulling a blanket over her legs, which were exposed below her nightshirt. From the corner of my eye, I could see that Jelena was taking a longer look than what might be considered appropriate. John, Soon-Li, and Hager joined us shortly after. John was wearing a full nylon sweat suit.

"You going out on a hit?" I asked him.

"It's what I pulled out of the dresser and is more appropriate than what I wore to bed."

I didn't ask for more detail. Soon-Li wore a flowered, silk nighty with a matching robe. Hager was amusingly wearing a complete pajama set. I could see the collar of the shirt sticking out of his robe, and it matched the light blue pants that were visible below the robe's hem. When I mentally added a small shirt pocket, I had to hide my wide grin behind my hand.

It was quiet for a while. All of us seemed as tentative to start up a conversation as I was. Talking could lead to the discussion of our current failures, the last thing I wanted.

Eventually, the silence was broken. I couldn't say who threw out the first tentative words, but it quickly became clear that an unspoken agreement was in place to avoid certain subjects. The discussion became almost boisterous. John suggested we ordered from an all-night pizza delivery chain. It was basically cardboard with sauce and cheese on it. Everyone's combined dietary requirements or preferences made toppings impossible. It did, however, ease the stress in the room, which made it palatable.

"Jelena, Enric is so precious." Soon-Li said.

"Thanks. Yeah, he's great. Not sure how much credit I can take, though. Between the Army and the merc unit, my mother has been doing most of the raising."

"That can all change now."

"What made you join the Army instead of following your mother's career in the Navy?" I asked.

"Water."

"You're afraid of the water?" John asked.

"Let's just say I'm not a fan."

The team was smiling and swapping stories. Jelena talked about Enric and her issues in the military. Tira spoke about India; the things she liked and missed—family mostly. Soon-Li had a host of stories about her many travels, several of which I was sure would make a sailor blush if the details were revealed. She had lived in pretty much every country at one point. Not for very long, of course; a few months here, a few weeks there. My God, could she spin a yarn. When Soon-Li described a place, she did so with all five senses. What she saw and smelled, the things she ate, the bustle of the crowd or the call of the surrounding wildlife. I swear I could feel the dry heat of the Egyptian desert one minute, and the mantle of cold that covered the northern parts of Russia the next.

It was the end of one such story when John turned towards the TV and asked, "what the hell are we watching?"

"*Free Willy.*"

Jelena's head shot up. "What?"

"*Free Willy.* You know the one about the killer whale who was in a show and befriended—"

"No wait, shut up!" Jelena exclaimed.

"What? What's the matter?" Tira asked.

"Just be quiet. Let me think for a second before I lose it."

She was sitting forward in her seat, staring at the empty pizza box—or rather through it. What she was seeing was anyone's guess. "*Free Willy.*" Pause. "*Free Willy.*"

She started shaking her hand as though pointing at some unseen image that floated in front of her.

"That's it!"

She looked up at us as though we should have all gotten it too. "*Free Willy!*"

"We will need a little more context if you please," Hager prompted.

"Sorry, right. When I first joined the mercs, we went out to a local bar. Apparently, it was something they did with all the new recruits to help build camaraderie. One of the officers got a little drunk and started talking more than he should have. He made a joke about one of the current projects being an abandoned aquarium—called it 'Operation Free Willy.' I had forgotten all about it until now. I think I had a little too much that night as well."

Jelena looked at me expectantly. I smiled at her and nodded. I turned to the rest of the team.

"Anyone know how deep a whale tank is?"

Chapter Twenty-Three

DAWN WAS STILL A few hours away as I looked eastward past Hager, who was sitting in the passenger seat. One of the benefits of being an early bird is the regular ability to watch the sunrise. It always surprises me how few people take advantage of this earthling privilege. No amalgamation of camera settings can capture such beauty.

We were on Interstate Eighty-Seven, heading upstate to a town north of Lake George called Whitehall.

"How many ways did you phrase your question to the Google?" Hager asked.

"It's just Google. Or Google the all-knowing." I replied.

"And yet, it took a human to make the leap from a whale to a location for nuclear extraction."

"Yes, all hail the human race. Skynet has no chance against our movie trivia."

"Well, at least *some* humans are superior."

Thanks to Jelena's revelation, we were on the road once again. "What's the name of this place again?" I asked.

"Poseidon's Hideaway," Hager replied.

"It's hidden away, alright. I didn't think anyone lived this far north, apart from bears and moose."

"Have you ever heard of Canada?" asked Jelena from the back seat.

"I believe you just made my point. And who would think it's a good idea to create a cheap version of Sea World up here?"

"Its business model assumed a cheap local labor force on cheap land," Hager informed me. "The location is still close enough to larger communities who, based on the poll, would be willing to take the drive for a killer whale show."

"Sounds solid," I said. "What went wrong?"

"According to this article, shallow rivers."

I gave him a questioning look from the driver's seat.

"They miscalculated the depth of the river coming in from the Atlantic, where all the deliveries were being routed. It was adequate for the smaller fish, but the whale required a larger and deeper hold then could be navigated through two or three narrower points. At the time, there were no other methods of transport."

"Well, sucks for them." I said.

"Indeed." Hager agreed.

"Who cares?" Jelena piped up. "Can we talk strategy, please?"

"Fine," I said. "Let's go over it again. How far out did we estimate their sentries to be, based on recent satellite photos?"

"Since the place was designed with a theme park in mind, there is a perimeter fence which funneled traffic to a single entrance. It doesn't have a gate to prevent entry so it was most likely built for the security of visitors and their cars. Inside is a large, wide open parking lot with guard posts six-hundred-yards out at the northwest and northeast positions—about the midpoint of the lot."

"Patrols?" I asked.

"Impossible to calculate based on random pictures that Soon-Li was able to upload from the past few weeks. We can't even say for sure how many guards there are. You know, we really should invest in our own satellite."

"Great idea, Jelena. How 'bout it, boss man?"

Hager didn't answer.

"Looks like it's a no go on the launch," I said.

"Damn, that would have been cool."

"Wonderful, now there are two of them," Hager mumbled.

"Any thoughts about how to secure the guards without giving us away?"

"Sure, I can make both shots from a central location. But the bullets breaking the sound barrier are going to be a little telling," Jelena almost sounded cheery about the possibility.

I sighed. "I don't want them killed if at all possible."

"That will be a little more difficult."

"Mr. Bateleur, we are fighting for the greater good. These men are on the side of evil," Hager pointed out.

"So was I until a few days ago," Jelena added. "But I still agree with Hager."

I noticed him nodding silently in the passenger seat.

She continued. "It's true that most of us are not read in on the actual mission. But we know we're not involved in anything whole-some—it's just not really a concern."

I glimpsed in the rearview mirror and caught her staring at her feet. "Honestly, there are good people on the team and not so good people. But far more of the latter."

She sighed deeply. When she continued, she was all business. "There are two kinds of people who become mercenaries: those that have run out of options, and those who don't care who or what they are fighting as long as they get paid. None of us are deluded. If any of the team feels that their post is threatened, they will kill to protect it and let the cleanup crews take it from there. You are thinking of them as human."

She paused, and I saw her look out the window.

"They are thinking of you as a walking corpse waiting to join their confirmed kills. The only variation among them is how much sleep they get after the job is done. Either way, it will get done."

I chewed on that for a few miles while we drove in silence. It was an argument I had heard before, but it was not a mindset that was easy for me to adopt. I can and have killed. It was always accompanied by some physical or mental reaction, though nothing compared to what I had felt in Camden. I wasn't sure what it meant, and didn't feel like dwelling on it.

"Amram."

Soon-Li called out through the audio system in the car. She had connected the two cars so we could communicate through the central console with the click of a button. Hager reached out and toggled the mic on.

"Yes, Soon-Li?"

"We need to stop at a diner near Whitehall."

"I told you to go before we left," I piped in before Hager could reply.

He frowned at me. I was starting to enjoy it. Then he turned toward the radio as though facing Soon-Li.

"I assume there is some reason beyond bodily functions and stale coffee."

"I found a man in the area that has been publicly complaining about the current residents of Poseidon's Hideaway. His description of their activity seemed a little too strategic for a civilian, so I did some digging into his background. He is ex-military. Tira called and convinced him to meet with us. He suggested the diner. He may have valuable intel."

"She called him in the middle of the night and convinced him to meet at a diner before dawn?" I asked.

"I am very persuasive," Tira replied over the audio. She sounded pleased with herself.

The name of the diner in Whitehall was, astonishingly enough, The Whitehall Diner. It was reasonably clean and had '50s decor. A few patrons sat at booths eating their early breakfast or very late dinner. I expected to be greeted by a heavyset waitress in a tidy uniform with a name tag identifying her as "Gladys" or "Marge." Jackie has told me I am a sexist. She is probably right.

The guy behind the counter, however, looked to be in his twenties. He was wearing a polo shirt and reading a particle physics textbook. He did have a name tag. It read "Jed." I looked around to see if Rod Serling was in one of the booths. Jed noticed. He looked at me as if he was trying to figure out what was so interesting, then apparently remembered that he didn't care.

"Help you?" Jed asked in a tone that didn't entirely suggest it was a question.

"I need four coffees. Two black, one with just milk, and one light and sweet," I informed Jed.

"And a bear claw," John interjected.

"And a bear claw," I repeated. "Hager, you want a sarsaparilla or something?"

Hager frowned and said, "Water, if you would be so kind. Bottled if possible."

Jed nodded at the order and moved off to get it together. Jelena and Tira left to find the restroom.

Jed returned with the coffees, marked on top with the green high-lighter he was using on his textbook. The two women returned from their bio break at about the same time, and I started handing the coffee out.

"How do you drink it like that?" I asked, shaking my head. "I like my sugar."

"Your bear claw," Jed said, handing over the pastry.

I transferred ownership and John had the courtesy to look sheepish. "What do you weigh? A buck eighty with zero percent body fat? You have a sweet tooth with a torso out of a superhero movie. Are you sure you are not an alien?"

"Don't hate the player," John tossed his dreads to the side with a twitch of his head as he maneuvered the bear claw into his mouth.

An older gentleman approached us from one of the booths. He was thin, but only a fool would label him frail.

"Can I assume you are the NRPA?"

"Yes. You must be Morty. I'm Tira." She practically leaped forward before any of us could screw up the cover story.

"What does that stand for again?" Morty asked.

"The National Resource Protection Agency," Tira replied.

"And why y'all need my help again? You got me out of bed, and Mary was wearing my favorite nightie."

"Favorite?" I asked.

He nodded. "Pink with purple flowers."

Morty returned his attention to Tira.

"We are trying to force Hammond Enterprises to break down the site completely and replant the area."

This was clearly a test to make sure she didn't stray from the original conversation. Whoever this guy was, he was quick.

"National, huh? And who'd do the work of breaking 'em down and replanting, a Fed construction crew?"

"Of course," Tira continued. "With a contract stipulation that twenty percent of the workforce had to be hired from Whitehall and its surrounding townships."

"White-hall." Morty pronounced it with a bit of a pause between the two syllables.

"I'm sorry?"

"It's pronounced White-hall."

"But it's spelled..." The rest of my sentence was cut off by an elbow to my stomach. While I was hunched over, Soon-Li smacked me on the back several times.

"Coffee must have gone down the wrong pipe," she explained.

"This some kinda joke?" Morty asked.

"No, sir. It is the NRPA's opinion that what's been done to the area is criminal. Hammond Enterprises' negligent lack of due-diligence is directly responsible. We're looking to make an example of them, and to give back a little of what was promised to the surrounding neighborhoods."

John looked utterly shocked. Hager looked visibly sick. Soon-Li and Jelena's faces seemed to dare anyone to question Tira's words. I continued to cough up imaginary coffee.

The old man nodded. He stuck out his hand and said, "I reckon that'll do. Tell me what I can do to help."

Chapter Twenty-Four

MORTY'S INFORMATION PROVED TO be extensive. He had a private war going with Hammond Enterprises which included tracking movements around Poseidon's Hideaway. His records included shift change times and how many guards there were—at least the ones that he knew about. He even had patrol frequencies, thanks to a set of very powerful binoculars he used to keep tabs on their movements. He smiled ear-to-ear the entire time Tira was bleeding him dry. We left the diner well caffeinated and well informed.

It was approaching sunrise when we reached the furthest point of the outside perimeter. Hammond Enterprises had cleared fifty feet of trees around the fence. No one could hop it and commit grand theft auto without exposing themselves to either the cameras or the guards. The guard booths were stationed exactly where the satellites had indicated: one was at the entrance, and two were strategically placed at central points in the middle of the immense parking lot.

"Man, all this place needs is a mouse wearing red shorts and suspenders," John said.

The team sat just within the tree line. Soon-Li had her laptop out and was trying to hack into the security system. I climbed the nearest tree to get a more unobstructed view and scouted the two raised security posts in the lot. They were shaped to look like an old-fashioned diving helmet. There was a four-foot-wide strip of plexiglass that wrapped around the circumference of the booth. It provided the guard an unblocked view in all directions but detracted somewhat from the overall image. The posts themselves were made superfluous by the security cameras. Although not as small or high-resolution as units of today, they were still prevalent at the time this facility was built. I assumed the booths were designed as a combination of customer service and deterrence.

"What did you see?" asked Hager as I lightly hit the ground. "Both guards are awake, if not completely alert."

"Shit," Jelena cursed. "I was hoping Johnson would be on duty. He was famous for napping, especially in the predawn hours."

"Okay, so we do it the hard way." I said.

"And that is?" Hager inquired.

I glanced at the group. Each of them looked back expectantly. "Hey, I'm the new guy!"

"Not anymore," Jelena said. "Now I am."

"Okay, new guy," I retorted. "Where I was perched in that tree looks like a good spot for overwatch. Get on it."

"Sir, yes sir," she said with a mocking air, but she started climbing.

"Maybe we should try Operation Thunderbolt?" said a voice.

"Wasn't that a strategy from World War II?" John asked.

"Nah, Korean War," the strange voice corrected.

I glanced behind me.

"Morty! What the hell are you doing here?" I yell-whispered at the figure crouching in the shadows.

"There ain't no NRPA. I looked it up after you called and there was nothing. After you left, there was suddenly a website. I got to wondering what y'all were really doin', and figured I'd take a gander."

"Morty." Tira drew his name out and made it sound like a scolding.

"Don't you try them wicked wiles on me again. I'm a watchin' out for 'em now."

"How the hell did you get the drop on us, old man?" Jelena asked from halfway up the tree. "I didn't hear a thing."

"Bah," Morty scoffed. "I've been hunting in these woods since before you were an itch in your daddy's pants. Besides which, the war made me learn to keep quiet. Less'n I wanted a North Korean dirt nap. So, who are you people and what are you doing here?"

"We cannot say who we are," offered Hager. "But we believe

terrorist activities are occurring in there."

"Amram!" Tira exclaimed.

"Appologies. Did you think you would get him to vacate by employing another four-letter acronym? If he believes our actions suspect, he will alert the authorities. One more distraction we cannot afford."

"He's got you there," John said.

"What are we supposed to do with him?" I turned to Soon-Li. "I don't suppose you've invented a neuralyzer?"

"Listen, fobbits. I have been doin' just fine without you. I'm the one who's been bugging these guys the past eight months. I've been the thorn in their sides. They cringe when I wander in. It's because of me that you have the information you do."

"You're right," Tira placated. "We do appreciate your help, but these people are dangerous. We have an edge that—"

"Wait, that's it," I interrupted.

"You've got an idea?" John asked.

"Yeah, a really stupid one."

"Is there any other kind?" Hager offered.

I ignored the slight and directed my attention to Morty. "Where did you park your car?"

"Truck. Back up the road a piece."

"Truck, outstanding. You and I will get it. Soon-Li, how's it going with their security system?"

"Piece of cake. They didn't bother to upgrade it from its original design, so the PHP coding didn't have the newest defenses against SLQI. I slipped in, inserted myself into the admin list and voila!"

"Sorry, again in English?" I asked.

"That was English, Mr. Bateleur. She has hacked the system and has access to the cameras."

Soon-Li hooked a thumb at Hager. "What he said. Before you ask, I already created a video loop and deployed it. Dawn was approaching quickly, and I didn't want a bird flying by over and over again. The darker, the better."

"Genius," I replied.

"I know. What would you do without me?"

"I hope I don't find out. Tira, you are the fastest we have. I need you on the other side."

"Sure, what did you have in mind?"

"Okay, here's the plan."

Chapter Twenty-Five

I was uncomfortable. The tarp covering me did little to keep out the cold predawn air. Something was pushing through my back. I think it was a tire iron. These were minor distractions as I lay in the back of Morty's pickup, watching the live cameras on my phone.

"About to pass the gate," said Jelena through the com.

I watched as the headlights brightened the view as the old truck came into view, then quickly passed.

"Slow down, Morty. Give Tira time," I yelled. We were still far enough out that I wasn't worried about alerting the guards.

Morty had the window open so he could hear me, since we didn't have an extra com for him.

"Okay, boss, we have their attention," Jelena said. "Go, Tira."

I switched cameras and watched as her outline approached the northern fence. In the dark, at her speed, I barely caught it. She slowed slightly before jumping, giving me a pretty good view of her front flip over the ten-foot fence.

"Damn," I whispered as she landed, once again taking off like a shot.

I changed cameras to check our location. We were about halfway to the booth, moving slowly without being obvious. I switched views to the top of the security outpost so I could watch Tira's approach.

"Uh-oh," said Jelena.

"What?" I asked.

"Something has guard two's attention."

"The one that Tira's heading towards at high-speed," I added unhelpfully.

"Shit."

"What now?"

"I did a quick check of the fence and found a motion detector," she said.

As if to punctuate her sentence, the flood light on the guard tower flared to life.

"They must be brand new or Morty would have known about them." Another thought occurred to me that nearly caused a panic attack. "Turn the guard house camera live!" I said, trying to keep my voice down. We had to be close to the guard house by now.

"What?" Soon-Li responded. "That'll give Tira away."

"The guard will definitely notice the lack of a spotlight on the camera. Just do it!"

"God might be shining light down on us," Hager said. "The flood-light is facing the entrance and is moving slowly towards Ms. Gupta's position."

"Well if He's not, something else sure will," I said.

"Amen," John added.

I watched the darkness on my phone slowly start to give way to the flood light. I couldn't see Tira, but it was just a matter of time.

"Tira," I said. "You can do this. Keep moving. You can make it. Soon-Li, is there a camera that will give me a better view?"

"Camera six," she replied.

I scrolled through the images until I found the one I wanted, then tapped it into full screen. The camera was west, halfway between the guardhouse and the fence. It had the perfect vantage point. At this angle, I could clearly see her predicament. Tira was moving fast. She was visible but running at the speed of a cheetah. Unfortunately, she had a long way to go. The large floodlight turned slowly.

The truck rolled to a stop. I pulled my attention away from the drama on the screen.

"What can I do for you tonight, Mr. Keane?"

The guard's voice was patient ambivalence. They knew his full name. Not good.

"I noticed you put up motion detectors around the fence," Morty said.

"Is that why you decided to take a ride out here at o-six hundred?" the guard asked.

I checked my phone to verify the time. 6:04—thirty minutes until sunrise. We were running out of time. The view on the phone showed that Tira was halfway there. She informed me before we started that this was going to be her longest run. She was *mostly* sure she could pull it off. I was beginning to think my plan was doomed.

"Don't play coy with me, I know what is going on around here," Morty continued.

"Oh yeah? And what would that be?"

"You are performing experiments in there. Illegal experiments."

"I can assure you, Mr. Keane, nothing like that is going on here. Did you just come from the lodge? Out late having a few pints with the good ol' boys?"

"Where I've been is none of your business. Have you been watching me?"

"Why, of course not following you." Slight pause. "Or Mary." The mention of his wife's name sent a jolt of fear through me.

"I am sure you don't want to cause any problems. Mary will be worried if she wakes up to your six-thirty alarm and finds that you're not home. You wouldn't want her to worry, right? Up in that log cabin with the green door. All alone."

My mouth went dry. I had a feeling Morty's did, too, since he didn't reply.

"I see I have made my point," the guard continued. "Why don't you run along back to your wife and cuddle up with her? Maybe get a little action this morning and forget about the surveillance operation you have going. Believe me, nothing here would be as interesting for you as what is under Mary's pretty pink nightie with the purple flowers. Have a nice night, Mr. Keane."

I heard the guard's boot scrape as he turned around and walked back to the guard booth. I broke out in a cold sweat as I listened to the guard's footsteps retreating. I checked on Tira.

"She's not there yet," I hissed under my breath, knowing he could not hear me.

Conflicting thoughts tugged at me. I could intercede before Tira gave the clear signal. But they were watching his house. They knew too many details. They had been in his house—in his bedroom.

I made up my mind, tapping my boot against the back glass of the cab. I was hoping to spur Morty into action. It worked a little too well. He croaked out a word that made my heart skip. The footfalls stopped. I heard the gravel grinding under the guards' boots as he turned.

"What did you just say?" he asked.

"Oh shit," I let the words slip out.

"What?" Hager asked.

"Nuclear," Morty repeated. "I know you have nuclear material in there."

I could feel the threat radiating off the guard from under the tarp. His footsteps were quick and staccato. He opened the driver's-side door. I heard shuffling and grunting. I wasn't sure what was happening until I heard a thump right next to me.

Not wanting to chance giving myself away, I scrolled through the cameras until I found one that showed the truck. Morty was slammed backward in a painful position against the truck bed. It was probably popping several vertebrae out of alignment.

"Where did you get that idea from, old man?"

All previous niceties were gone. The now enraged security guard was holding a rifle off to the side, still strapped around his thick neck. He must have manhandled Morty out of the car and into chiropractic hell one-handed.

"From the helicopter...heard reports a few nights back... the explosion in Camden." Morty had found his voice and was picking up speed as he talked through the obvious pain. "Then there's the trucks that came screaming through town, early that morning. Y'all were at least intelligent enough not to land a helicopter on the lake. 'Septin anyone who can put two and two together could see this were'nt no coincidence."

"You've got some imagination, old man. One that just got you in a world of shit. Who else did you tell about this?"

I had to chance a look. I needed to see where they were in relation to me. Using the cameras was like trying to touch something on the back of your head while looking through two mirrors. I eased the tarp to the side. The guard was about even with where my calves were—any closer and he would be at point blank range. Morty was being pushed backward, nearly into the bed.

"She's almost there," Soon-Li said.

I eased my weapon free of the tarp. I kept it close to the side of the truck bed and out of sight. Morty was looking directly into the man's eyes.

Morty's eyes narrowed and he said, calm as you please, "Fuck you."

"CLEAR!" Tira said, gasping through the com.

I pulled the gun sharply up, aimed, and fired. At such close range, the leads for both ends of the taser didn't get the spread I would have liked. One hit him in the pecs, the other in the ribs. It was enough. The guard's whole body locked. He fell forward, smashing his face against the edge of the truck before hitting the ground.

Without the tension holding him up, Morty fell forward onto the cold blacktop. I threw back the tarp and leaped out of the truck bed. I pulled out a set of plastic zip ties for the guard's hands. It was an unnecessary precaution. The hit on the truck had knocked him out cold.

"Clear," I said. "You okay, Morty?"

"I'll live, I think," he said.

I helped him to his feet. He rubbed his chest where the guard's hand had been.

"I aint never seen 'em react like that. They're dismissive or evasive, but always courteous. Least'n the fake kind when they really want to tell you where to go."

"It means the pressure has either increased or become lax."

"What he said about my house, about Mary…"

Morty visibly shivered.

"That's quite a mouth you have on you," I said, trying to distract him. He smiled and rubbed the stubble of his beard. He hadn't had time to shave this morning, thanks to us.

"I haven't said that in over a decade. Reckon I have a reason to go to confession."

"Somehow, I think God will be okay with it," I said.

Two cars were approaching from the gate; one towards us while the other was aimed at the second booth. The floodlight was out again. Mr. Hager stepped out alongside Soon-Li. Together, we moved the guard back into his raised stand and secured him in the chair. If any patrols came around, they would at least see a figure in the booth. By the time we came back out, John and Tira had arrived in the other car. Tira went immediately to Morty to check on him. After that, she kept to herself.

"Okay, so are we ready to go?" I asked. There were nods all around.

"Where d'you need me?" Morty asked.

"I'm sure Mr. Bateleur would agree that, while your services have been invaluable, it would be advantageous for you to retire back to your home."

"You're shit canning me."

"Hager is right, Morty. I've put you in enough danger tonight. You've already spent years in service of your country. I'm not sure what's in there, and I can't guarantee your safety."

"I'm not looking for any guarantees."

"But I couldn't live with the idea that any harm came to you," I said.

"Nor could I," added Tira.

She approached him, grabbing one of his hands and looking him in the eyes.

"Go home to your wife, Morty. Don't let her wake up without you next to her."

Morty looked at her and smiled slightly. Hager looked up as though to say something but seemed to change his mind.

"Whatever agency you guys *do* work for, y'all are good people. Good luck in there."

He insisted on giving us his phone number in case we needed help. Then he got in his truck and drove away.

Chapter Twenty-Six

WE MADE OUR WAY back to the cars. Before John walked away, I grabbed him by the arm.

"Is she carrying a book in a handkerchief?" I nodded towards Tira.

"Yup, and don't ask about it."

I was about to say something else, but the look in John's eyes stopped me.

"Okay."

To avoid being seen, we took a somewhat circuitous route toward the large glass-front doors. The motif reminded me of a Disney World attraction with a demonic edge. The depictions of Poseidon were a little too elongated and painted in muted colors, giving the images a menacing tone. The coral reefs and marine flora looked poisonous or like something was lurking within them. While no set of red eyes peered out of the gloom, I wasn't left with an overall cheery feeling.

"Nice place," Soon-Li observed. "Very welcoming." I gave her an incredulous look.

"What? It's almost like Disney."

"Let's focus on the task at hand, shall we?" Hager said. "We need to hurry. The daylight will begin to draw attention to us—anyone with a security monitor and a window will be understandably skeptical." We moved toward the door, approaching from the left. John pulled out a small camera on an extendable rod, attached it to his phone, and eased it slowly in front of the door.

"One guard, sitting at the welcome desk," he said.

"Okay, how do we distract him long enough to get the door open?"

"I have an idea," Tira said.

"What's the plan?" I asked.

"Trust me."

She crept up next to the glass doors. She placed a palm on the wall and closed her eyes. First, she moved her hand onto the glass, then followed with the rest of her body. I inhaled sharply, waiting for a yell from the guard. None came. She continued to move into the center of the doorway. I shifted into a position where I could see the image on John's phone.

The guard was not paying attention; he seemed distracted by whatever was on the desk. He momentarily looked up, then back down. I glanced to where Tira was now standing—center stage and in plain view, palm still flat on the glass. The guard looked up again, slowly this time. He stood up and walked around the desk, heading for the door. His eyes locked on Tira. Stopping right in front of her, he stared directly into her eyes without moving. The guard pulled out a set of keys. He bent to the floor and unlocked the door, then stood up and pulled it open. The door barely made it halfway through its arc before the guard was face down on the concrete, Tira's knee in his back. She shoved her two thumbs against either side of the base of his skull, rendering him unconscious. The handkerchief wrapped book was still gripped in one hand.

"Nicely done," John said.

John and I dragged the body into the aquarium and out of sight. I pulled up the floor plan on the tactical display strapped to my left forearm. The structure was laid out to mimic the side view of an orca. The main entrance was where its mouth would be. Its shape and the interior color scheme gave visitors a distinct impression of being swallowed. To the right, a hallway funneled you through the exhibits; it led up the back of the whale until it reached its tail fin. The return route, through the belly of the beast, guiding tourists back to the mouth by way of the gift shop. You were then vomited into the parking lot, heavier in knowledge and lighter in the wallet.

In the tail fin, a stadium of seats were arranged around the main attraction: the orca pool. That was our target.

"Okay, Mr. McCaw, you and Mr. Bateleur take the north corridor. Ms. Gupta will lead Ms. Yuan and myself along the south."

"Roger that," John said.

We moved around the bend and came upon the first set of tanks. I moaned softly. John chuckled.

"Not what you expected?" he whispered.

The tanks were empty. Debris littered the sand floor. What remained of the faux coral had lost its luster in the open air and was covered with several years of dust. Cleaning equipment was discarded all around. It resembled a post-apocalyptic theme park.

"Now, that's just disap..."

A curse rang out from a room just up and to the left. It was followed by the scraping of wood on a tiled floor. John and I exchanged glances. A second later, three guys burst through the door, running straight toward us. They carried sub-machine guns, which they were readying for combat.

The group stopped short; one standing in front of the other two. The standoff lasted only a few rapid heartbeats. John blurred. One second he was next to me, the next he was holding one of the rear guards by the rifle and twirling him into the wall. I took advantage of the shock and launched myself at the one in front. I hit him in the air at chest height, driving him painfully to the floor, his rifle pinned between us.

As we landed, I shifted my weight and drove an elbow into the man's gut. The involuntary contraction of muscles brought the guard's head off the floor. I followed up with a backhand to the face.

I looked up to see the third guard being flipped onto his back. John ripped the rifle from his hands and drove the stock into his face. All three were down. We took a second to assess and catch our breath. "What the hell just happened?" I asked.

"Apparently, they know we're here."

"No kidding, but how?"

John shook his head in response. "We'd better find out."

"Boss man, we have been compromised. Three aggressors down. We're investigating."

"Very good, Mr. Bateleur. We are continuing."

The door from which the guards attacked us had a mechanical push button lock. It gave way to John's prodding.

"Cute trick," I said.

He gave me one of his dazzling smiles. "I am multi-talented."

"I'm sure."

Inside, we found the culprit. The guards had paused a local news channel broadcast during a traffic report. There was a jam up on the Thruway—a deer had picked an inopportune time to cross. The scene was gruesome, to say the least. The remains of the animal were splattered across the three-car pile-up, which could be seen clearly in the morning light. The word Live was displayed in red lettering across the top right corner of the screen. The picture was in direct conflict with the security monitors, which still showed only the beginning stages of early dawn.

We dragged the guards back into the security office. Well, I dragged one. John picked the other two up by their belts, one in each hand. Showoff.

"What'd you think?" He asked.

"These two seem freshly showered. Uniforms are still pretty crisp. I'm figuring shift change. No other reason to have three guys in a security booth at night."

"Agreed. We have two daisies and four corn chips. I figure we have an hour before the remaining relief arrives. Max.

I cocked my head at him. "Corn chips?"

"What do you think they smell like?"

"Let's not go there."

John updated the rest of the team while he and I secured the guards in the small office. Once done, we moved out into the corridor and continued scouting through the abandoned aquarium. When we reached the whale tank viewing area, we found the rest of the team already there. They were all staring into the tank. This time, there was water in it, and I could see a sizeable cylindrical shape at the bottom of the pool. I rushed forward to get a better view, then stopped short as my mind put the pieces together.

Instead of relieved, the team looked shocked and disgusted. The pool water had a faint tint to it. As I approached slowly, a face came into view. A woman was floating near the bottom. Her expression was fixed in a death scream, and her hand was still reaching out for unfound assistance. Worse, she was not alone.

"Sweet Jesus," John said quietly from behind.

The scene inside the theater was worse. The water cleaned those floating in the tank, freeing them from the gore of their deaths. But those outside were lying in pools of their own blood. Most were shot. A few were killed by a knife—stabbed and slashed multiple times, with large gashes across their throats.

"Kali," Hager said with disgust.

I looked up from examining one of the bodies.

"She loves to cut throats," he said by way of explanation.

"Rigor hasn't set in," Tira said. "And this man is still warm. We just missed this."

"Those guards were waiting for the cleanup crew," John added. "All right, we have limited time," Hager pointed out. "Please execute a thorough search for anything that will tell us what their next step is."

The orca pool had been jury-rigged with equipment to facilitate the underwater extraction of the fuel rods. There was an arc cutting tool bolted to the cement floor with mechanical arms that could reach to the bottom of the pool. The dry containment unit was no longer dry, sitting at the bottom of the tank. The top had been cut off and five fuel rods were strewn around next to it.

I turned to Soon-Li.

"Do you think you can work that robot arm?"

"I can, but don't ask me to do anything delicate without a few hours of practice."

"Can you grab one of those fuel rods?"

"And do what with it?"

"Get it close to the viewing area. I want to take a closer look."

"Not too close. Radiation is still beyond tolerable levels, even for individual rods," added John. We all looked over at him.

"Well, according to Denise, anyway."

"Understood," Soon-Li said.

She found the controls for the mechanical arm and got it operational. It looked like it could control a plane—or at least a DeLorean. She ran it through a few test movements to get the feel before she nodded at me. We went inside where we had a better view through the porthole. Trying to determine distance through the refraction of the water's surface would be nearly impossible.

We tried to ignore the floating bodies as Soon-Li maneuvered the arm towards the rods. It took her precious minutes getting aligned. She required several attempts to close the pincer grip onto the thin tubes, and several more to get it in place without dropping it. Once she got it up to eye level, we were able to determine if it was empty, then spent the next fifteen minutes examining the rest of the rods. By the end, I bet Soon-Li could have picked up a banana and peeled it. She moved with confidence as the final tip came into view.

"Okay, that one is sealed, too. Only five of the seven rods have been utilized. I hope that means that we interrupted them."

We packed up and moved toward the door, picking up the rest of the team as we went. John found the location where they were building the devices. There were spare parts, wires, and a form of plastic explosive. But nothing pointed to how many devices there were or how much nuclear material was in them.

"Let's stop by the security room and clone the guards' phones. They may hold a clue," Soon-Li suggested. "The ones belonging to the workers were missing." We reached the security office and a sense of dread came over me.

The door stood ajar.

"We closed that, didn't we?" John whispered.

"Yup," I said as I readied my rifle.

I stood in front, already aiming down sights. I indicated via hand signals that I would check left and that John should focus right. John gave a thumbs up and put a hand on the door. I silently counted down from three with my fingers, ending with a fist. John pushed hard. I breached at a fast walk, John right behind me, checking opposite corners. There was no one there except the guards that had been secured. Each throat had been cut. The room had been cleaned of anything that might have held a clue, including the cell phones.

"What the hell?" I said.

"Time to go, gentlemen," said Hager.

We started our way back to the front door, me in the lead. John brought up the rear, walking backward. We reached the entryway and found the guard there dead as well, his phone missing.

We exited and made our way to the cars, hyper-vigilant.

"The cars are fine," Soon-Li said as we reached them. "I expected the tires to be slashed or something." She popped the hood while John checked underneath. "No devices that I can see," she reported from the driver's seat.

"None here either," John agreed.

"That's strange," I said.

"No, it's a message," Hager said.

"What message?" I asked.

"That we are free to go, since there is nothing we can do to stop them."

We got in the cars without further comment. We didn't have to check the guard house in the parking lot—the blood spray was clearly visible across the windows of the massive diving helmet.

"Okay, it's possible that someone sneaked by Jelena from another direction. But she would not have missed someone coming in here and slitting the guard's throat."

"Jelena, sit-rep."

There was no response.

"I repeat, overwatch sit-rep... Shit."

I stomped on the accelerator and tore off towards the main gate. The sun was starting to peek over the trees, casting long shadows and pushing the depth of the tree line into darkness. As we shot through the gates, our headlights reflected against a large metal object that stood just inside the tree line. It resolved into a vehicle. An early model Ford pickup truck sat in the middle of the road. The driver's side door was open.

Tira was the first out, leaping from the car before it stopped. She ran to the open door and looked in. Finding nothing, she slammed the door and glanced around. I followed. The truck was empty, the glove compartment open.

"We have to find him." Tira's voice was an octave above normal.

"We will," I said.

"Don't patronize me." Tira's voice was venomous. Her eyes sparkled in the combination of headlights and sunlight filtering through the trees.

"Ladies and gentlemen, perhaps we could focus our attention on more pressing matters?" Hager interrupted. "It is my opinion that, since this spot is parallel to where we left Ms. Torres, we might start our search in that direction."

"Agreed, I see footprints leading toward the right," Soon-Li said from a squatting position near the tree line.

The team moved off quickly but cautiously, leaving some space for better coverage. It was unlikely that Morty would have left his truck unattended for no reason. I had a bad feeling that I couldn't shake. The search didn't take long. We found him covered in blood, sitting against the bottom of the tree where Jelena had been perched. He had a hunting knife in his hand; also bloodied. He was breathing but just barely. Tira rushed up next to him and started to examine his wounds. There were too many. He opened his eyes at her touch.

"Ah, I knew you'd be back," he wheezed. "What are you doing here?" Tira choked out.

"Heard a ruckus. Coming from her perch. Wanted to know. If she was okay." It took a few seconds for him to catch his breath. "Got here. Red was down. Hanging."

They looked up, and Jelena was indeed hanging from her safety line, mostly hidden behind the branches. Soon-Li was up the tree in seconds. She secured Jelena and dropped lightly to the ground again. Since Tira was ministering to Morty, I did a quick triage. Jelena had a throwing knife in her abdomen. It looked like she had packed around the blade with gauze and secured it in place.

"Crazy bitch... taunting her," Morty said between gasps. "Tried... scare her off. Moved like lightning." His talking must have been causing extreme pain. He panted through it for a few seconds. Then he smiled. "Pattern. Got a piece of her."

He lifted the knife in hand, barely a movement. His breaths were coming short and ragged. I looked around the site. There were splotches of blood all over, mixed with the undergrowth. I looked down at Tira, who met my gaze and shook her head. I kneeled down next to Morty and put my hand on his shoulder.

"Semper-Fi."

Morty looked up at me and barely whispered, "hu-rah." It was the last thing he said.

"Why didn't you just go home?" Tira sobbed.

I took his knife, wrapped it in a small cloth, and put it in one of my pouches.

"We need to extricate ourselves from this," Hager said.

I nodded, then reached into Morty's pocket and remove his cell phone. Tira cocked her head but didn't move to stop me. I activated it with a push of the button, then grabbed Morty's thumb and pressed it onto the emergency icon on the home screen. It left a bloody finger-print. The screen turned white. I touched his thumb to the green dial icon. The display started blaring out a warning signal along with a countdown. I dropped the phone next to Morty's hand.

"Let's go."

Soon-Li held Jelena in her arms as if she were a small, sleeping child and took off at a run. The rest followed her lead—all except Tira. I rested a hand on her shoulder, about to say something. She whipped her head around and silenced me with a look. I removed my hand.

Tira touched Morty's arm. "I'm sorry."

She stood up without looking at me and ran towards the car.

The blaring signal stopped. I looked down at the phone. A faint voice said, "Nine-One-One, what is your emergency? ... Hello?... Hello, can you hear me?"

I looked at Morty's body again. "I'm sorry too," I whispered.

I hurried to follow.

Chapter Twenty-Seven

"WHAT WERE YOU THINKING?"
The ride back to the city was silent. Jelena was laid in the back seat of one car while Tira tended to her. She repacked the wound with fresh bandages and started a saline drip to keep her hydrated. We didn't have blood, but with the knife plugging the hole and the I.V. replenishing fluids, we made it back without an issue. Once we got back to the house, and Jelena was stabilized, the silence was broken.

"Excuse me?" I asked.

Tira stood right in front of me. Her eyes blazed with rage. One hand was clenched; the other held a paperback book in a white-knuckled grip. She hadn't bothered to clean any of the blood off her.

"You wanted to know why we don't enlist help from outside the Covenant? This is it."

The rest of the team was silent as we stared each other down. She had been in the basement medical facility with Jelena while the rest of us gathered in the meeting room trying to come up with possible scenarios.

"The unblessed don't have our defenses. Sending them against one of the Tainted is like sending an ant up against a lion."

"Have you ever seen what an army of fire ants can do? Don't underestimate the value or the strength of those you incorrectly think of as weak."

Tira's face softened. She walked up to me and took my hand. She placed my palm gently, almost tenderly, on her side. It felt damp. She looked up at me.

"You killed Morty."

Although her tone was soft, her words held a hard edge. I tried to respond but found I couldn't.

"You almost killed Jelena."

She guided my hand off her and held it up for my inspection. It was coated red.

"Their blood is on your hands."

She turned her attention to Hager as I stood there staring at my bloody palm.

"Amram, if you are going to continue to let Christian call the shots, I am going to need a larger medical ward."

Tira turned and left the room.

I wanted to be angry, to yell at her, say she was wrong. It had been her who persuaded Morty to give us the information. She provided the lame backstory, and Soon-Li should have documented that back story sooner. All of that may have been true, but it didn't change how I felt. Guilty. Responsible. I was bumbling around where I didn't belong, and I had gotten a good man killed.

A towel appeared in front of my face, blocking the view of my blood-stained hand. Soon-Li was next to me. She cleaned it off and guided me to a chair.

"Just give her some time to cool down."

Hager stared at the door Tira had exited. "I have never seen her react like this to a civilian's death. Even it if was... Kali that did the killing."

"It wasn't just him. Tira also killed a guard, trying to stop him from raising the alarm," John's rumble of a voice was low. "It was an accident from what little she said about it. She hit him at full speed with enhanced solidity."

Soon-Li sucked air through her teeth.

Hager simply said, "Oh, my."

"I'm guessing that's bad," I prompted.

"You would have a better chance of surviving being hit by a car. This is akin to hitting someone in the chest with a sledgehammer. A tremendous force in a very concentrated area."

I tried to curse but couldn't find the strength. I just shook my head and stared at the floor while Soon-Li continued to clean my hand like I was a toddler. The gesture was soothing.

John leaned forward. "Those types of hits tend to result in a slower death, generally one the person is awake for. My impression is that she watched the lights go out."

"And it was my plan that put her in that position."

"You could not have known that would happen," Soon-Li comforted. She finished cleaning me and I let my head sink down into my hands. We were always two steps behind. At every turn, it was like they knew we were coming. Even in the diner when Father Murphy was shot. How did they know we would be there? We picked a different place every week. Someone must have followed us. Even now, the Tainted must be keeping tabs on what we are doing.

Something tickled my mind and I got a chill. "Soon-Li?"

She picked her head up, drawn out from her own introspection.

"You said you looked through the security footage from when Father Murphy was shot."

She nodded.

"Do you still have it?"

"Of course." She returned to her laptop. Her fingers flew across the keys, and the main screen came to life. It showed the Tainted's minion walking into the diner and shooting at us. It was the first time I had seen the footage. From the angle, it was blatantly clear that he was aiming at me. The camera was positioned near the door, perfectly inline with the gunman's aim.

"Are there any other angles?" I stood up, my self-loathing forgotten thanks to a spike of adrenaline.

"None that have a better view of the attacker."

"I'm not worried about the attacker."

"What are you looking for?" Hager asked.

"I'm not sure yet. Move forward, slowly."

The image advanced. Father Murphy turned and saw the gunman. He leaped protectively in front of me. The muzzle flash bloomed. I could just make out the blood spray as we fell together. People in the other booths were taking cover or running for the doors. "Stop."

The image froze.

"Now, look for other angles at the same timestamp."

Soon-Li started typing again. The image shrunk to the top left quarter of the screen. Other pictures filled the other quadrants. The top right was an angle from the opposite corner, catching only the gun. The next was from the back wall. It pointed at the door, showing the attacker from the opposite angle. The last camera showed Father Murphy and me from the kitchen opening.

"Stop. Can you enlarge that last one?"

Soon-Li complied. I stepped right up to the screen and peered at it. "What do you see?" asked John.

"I see everyone ducking for their lives." I pointed. "Except one."

They all examined the monitor. John jumped from where he was sitting to get a closer look. He spun back around to stare wide-eyed at me.

"Dear Lord," Hager said. "That's Denise!"

I said nothing, just stared at the screen.

"She's been playing us this whole time," mumbled John, almost too low to hear.

"Pull up the camera for the detainment area."

The screen shifted. Tira and Denise were sitting at the kitchenette.

I headed for the door, the rest following in my wake.

We burst into the area. Tira turned on us. She opened her mouth. Her expression changed as she took in our faces.

My focus was on Denise. She looked back at me, her eyes wide and eyebrows arched high. Then her expression changed, replaced with a look of pure malice and cunning.

"You finally figured it out," she said.

Tira glanced back at her, shock and confusion etched on her face.

"It took you long enough."

"How have you been communicating with him?" I asked.

Denise's laugh, filled with mirth, danced over my spine, making my skin crawl. When she spoke again, the voice was not her own. "Seriously, did you think this little girl of yours could reclaim what I have taken?" It laughed again, real humor behind it. I'm not sure what I expected—a voice somewhere between James Earl Jones and Freddy Kruger, maybe. What emanated from Denise, though, was more of a cross between Arnold Schwarzenegger and Colonel Sanders. It has a singsong tone to it, with elements of a southern gentleman and German aristocrat.

"I have been turning humans into my puppets for thousands of years. Whatever power you have is nothing compared to what I possess. I have been here the whole time, watching, listening." Baldemar was not threatening, nor condescending. He was simply passing along information, more aloof than anything else.

Tira sat there with her mouth open, trying to form a word but failing. I said nothing. I just stared at Baldemar behind Denise's face.

"But I healed you," Tira finally managed to say. "I know I did." Denise turned to face Tira.

"Ah, children. They think they know everything, desperate to be the keeper of all knowledge. When shown up, they become jealous and aggressive."

It turned back to me.

"So, you are the second. I'm not impressed. You denied your birthright for half your life, and stumble around in the dark looking for the light switch." Baldemar shook Denise's head, "Fool."

It nonchalantly regarded Hager. "Amram, have you told him yet? No, of course not, I can see it in your eyes. A fool being led by a coward. Well, it has been fun. Perhaps we can do it again sometime." This last comment held the tone of a guest saying their afternoon tea goodbyes.

Denise's body stood up and walked over to the coffee pot. She grabbed it as if she was going to pour herself a cup; instead, she smashed it on the counter. Baldemar turned to face us. Its expression changed, and for a split second, she was Denise again. Her face pleaded with us for help, but the mocking grin returned. It lifted a jagged piece of glass and dragged it across Denise's throat.

Chapter Twenty-Eight

WE LAUNCHED FORWARD, EACH crying out. Tira had finally pulled herself out of the fog and called for towels. We worked fast, all the while knowing it was too late. The jagged gash that the glass made had completely severed the carotid artery. Denise was bleeding out quickly. There was no sign of Baldemar. I kneeled next to her. She looked up at Tira, meeting her eyes and then mine. She held onto Tira's shoulder, fingers tearing at her shirt.

Her back arched in pain and her face drained to a deathly pale. She was splattered with her own blood.

"I'm sorry," she mouthed.

Her hand slowly lost its strength, falling back to the floor as her spirit fled the now empty vessel.

Tira let out a choking sob. I fell backward against the cabinet, smashing my elbow against the base before resting my head in my bloodied hands.

Hager closed Denise's eyes and mouth. He wiped his hands, then found a clean towel to place over her face. He pulled out a shawl and draped it over his shoulders, then took out a small copy of the Torah and began to read in Hebrew.

I found that I couldn't watch. I pushed myself off the floor and headed for the door, not sure where I was going.

"Stop!"

Hager's voice froze me in place.

"No one leaves yet. Out of respect, we will all remain until her soul has transitioned." His voice was soft but firm. "We were unable to provide Mr. Keane the same courtesy, but I will not allow that to happen again."

I nodded and turned back to attend in silence. Hager completed one prayer, then started on another. When he finally finished, he sighed heavily and nodded to me. I turned and left the room.

I went into the training area, thoughts bombarding me. I replayed each conversation with Denise, looking for hints I should have seen, moments when she may have been asking for help. I thought about Morty, the nice old man who only wanted to help. Now dead, his poor wife left alone. I replayed the diner incident over and over. My walk had turned into a run. I raced around the track as my mind reeled. The clues were there but I missed them all. I had been blind, and because of that, two people were dead, and one was in a coma—not to mention the dozens killed in both Camden and Whitehall. All preventable if I had just paid attention to the details.

The run turned into a sprint. I tried to engage my blessing, but it was still out of reach. The frustration spurred me even more. I tripped over myself, tears streaming down my face as I ran. More images flashed across my memory. Returning home from school to hear that my mother died, the picture I drew for her still clutched in my hand. Then my drill sergeant stopping me on the obstacle course to inform me that my father had committed suicide. My only response was to complete the course, just as I pushed through the circuit now.

Once finished, I headed for the shower, still running at full speed. Bursting through the door, I staggered around, trying to catch my breath. I walked in large circles but still couldn't control my breathing. I finally stopped, leaned forward and put my hands on my knees until my panting slowed. Sweat poured off me. Only one thought broke through: shower.

I picked up my head and froze. I thought I had stopped in front of my locker; instead, I was facing my mother's. I stared at her name, following the curves of the letters. Angela Bateleur. I stepped forward and opened the door.

I'm still not sure what I expected to find. This wasn't a secret room, safe, or even a safe deposit box. This was a locker. Any valuables or important documents would have been in her office. Still, I stepped reverently into the small area.

As expected, the spot where her uniform should have been, was empty. The clothes she wore before donning that uniform for the last time still hung there. I stared at them for a while, trying to picture her. The shoes were navy blue with a short heal. Flowers were subtly stitched along the sides and the toe was buffed to a high shine. The shelves were empty apart from the top shelf, which held a small decorative box. I stared at the reliquary for a full minute. I had nothing of my mother's. My father could not stand any reminders of her. I reached out, afraid that touching it would make it disappear. The wooden box had inlays depicting the five symbols of the Covenant.

It was lightweight and delicate. There was no lock or combination to guess; no mystery to solve. I marveled at its very existence, at its possible contents. I waited until I could no longer restrain my fingers, then lifted the lid.

Inside was a necklace with three pendants: Saint Christopher, a crucifix, and the crest of the Covenant. It sat atop a plain white envelope with a single name written in flowing script: *Christian*.

I nearly dropped the box. Emotions came in rapid waves; I felt like I was in the middle of the ocean during a storm. It wasn't just a relic from my mother. It was direct communication. I refused to even hope for this possibility. I'd heard too many stories of children yearning for letters like this one, only to be woefully disappointed. Searching the belongings of the dead only turned up unpaid bills, private collections, and sometimes money. But it rarely revealed what was really longed for—closure.

My hands shook as I sat down on the changing bench and set the box next to me. I removed the letter, letting the necklace slide off the envelope. The inside of the box was lined with red satin, and the chain fell onto it with a dull thunk. I turned the envelope over in my still trembling hands. The flap was only sealed at the very tip, leaving ample space in which to slip my finger. I did so, then hesitated. There were answers beneath that glue, but did I want to read them? What if this letter shattered the perfect image of my mother that I held in my mind? Reality rarely measures up, and I wasn't sure if I was ready for it. Not now, when all else was crashing around me. Finally, I ran my finger along the seal, popping it open cleanly. I moved quickly after that to eliminate second guessing.

Christian,

You probably have a thousand questions, and this letter will not answer them all, so this is only the first. Seek out Amram for the rest. He will give them to you when the time is right.

I want to start out by welcoming you into the Covenant. This place and these people are dear to me, more than you can know. It was my sincerest wish that you join their ranks as soon as possible, to give you the support you need while growing up. I am sorry I missed your communion. I wanted very much to see you in your fancy new suit, sitting at the Lord's table for the first time. I can see you in my mind's eye, and you look very handsome.

The work that we do here is of the utmost importance to the world. You are blessed with unique talents, as are all the people in the Covenant, and we use them to help others. Yours were unlocked when you had your first communion. You start young because learning to use your gifts is a long road, and the earlier you start, the better off you will be. Some religions don't introduce their children until later in life, and many of them have a hard time connecting with their powers. Some don't start until they are fifteen! Can you believe that?!

So, you are kind of a superhero! And as such, it is your duty to use your powers to help those that cannot protect themselves. Your responsibility, if you will. This is not an easy thing I lay before you. It will be trying and dangerous, but it will also be fulfilling. Our abilities are God given. You need to always remember that, because the connection to our gift is based on faith. The more faith you have, the better your link, and the easier it will be to call upon your abilities when needed.

Since you are always filled with questions and rarely take things on faith, I wanted to give you the symbols of mine. The necklace in the box has been handed down over many generations. The three symbols all have significant meaning. The Saint Christopher medal—the bearer of Christ. He carried the Jesus as a boy across a river experiencing the weight of the world. It reminds us that it is a heavy burden we carry, but to do otherwise would betray our heritage and our faith. The Crucifix reminds us that Jesus died so that we may live on. He suffered greatly, both physically and emotionally, but held steadfast in His beliefs and His dedication to God. And the seal of the Covenant is the reminder that we are not the beginning or the end of faith. While we celebrate our individual beliefs and customs, we must recognize that they are not the only way. It is not how we worship, but simply that we have faith in what we worship.

Faith is the strongest of all human traits. It allows us to make sense of life when it becomes confusing, gives us confidence in trying times, and fills our hearts with joy. Support all faith, not just those you were taught. Faith in God, faith in family, faith in friendship, faith in love. Never let it falter, for a faith that is nurtured is stronger than anything in this world.

Wear these symbols always and I will forever be with you. Love, Mom.

Tears streamed down my face, blurring the words as I struggled to read. When I finished, I went back to the beginning and reread it several times, making the words part of me. They were a salve to a wound I had forgotten, one that had scarred over but never fully healed. Each time I read her letter, I felt a little more whole.

When I was finally done, I placed it carefully down on the bench beside me, then withdrew the necklace. My hands shook once more as I lifted it to the light. I now recognized its age. These were not the feather-light charms of today; these were solid pieces. I could feel their presence. The style was reminiscent of the Renaissance period. The chain did not have a clasp. It was long enough that it slipped over my head—a closed, unbreakable loop. Each pendant was attached to a separate link and soldered in place. They rested against my heart. This was a symbol of faith, of my family's commitment. I felt the weight immediately.

I took a deep breath, feeling resolved and renewed. I picked up the box and placed it back on the shelf. Then I picked up the letter and envelope, still holding them carefully.

I headed for the door.

Chapter Twenty-Nine

I FOUND HAGER BEHIND his desk, reading a book. I burst in without knocking, which did not elicit any kind of reaction. His complete lack of response to my entry put me off so much that I stopped before I got a word out.

"I assume there is something important you wish to discuss, since you left your manners wherever you came from."

Hager never even lifted his head from his book. I blinked, then came back to myself.

"I understand you have some letters for me."

Hager stopped and looked up at me. His eyes focused first on the letter in my hand, then on the chain around my neck. He closed the book, laying a hand on it, and continued to watch me. He looked to be searching for something.

"Nothing to say?" I asked.

"What would you have me say?"

"Maybe an explanation."

"For?"

"What do you mean, for? Isn't it obvious?"

"Apparently not."

"Why didn't you tell me you had letters from my mother?"

Hager visibly relaxed. "Very simple, actually. I was asked not to speak of it until you found her first letter."

Hager stood and walked over to a bookshelf. He pulled out a book and reached behind it. I heard a faint click, and the small section of books swung outward, revealing a safe. It required another biometric palm print authentication. After doing so, Hager opened the safe and took out a stack of envelopes wrapped in ribbon, then closed both doors and replaced the book. He did it all in complete silence.

Hager handed the stack to me. "There you are. I was instructed to provide one each year on your birthday until the age of eighteen. I think at this point we can forgo that."

I reached out and took them.

"I expected more of a fight."

"Why? They are yours. You needed only to ask."

I looked up into his eyes and saw something incomprehensible there. "Why did she want you to wait until I found the first one?"

"I have no idea. If that is all, I would like to get back to my research." He supported the statement by moving back behind his desk.

"Hager."

He stopped and looked up at me once again.

"How did she know?"

"That her time was short?"

"Foresight was one of her gifts."

"She could see the future?"

"In snippets. Some were clear, others more of a puzzle."

"So she saw her own death."

Hager sighed deeply. "She saw a way to solve a particular problem we were having. That solution required her sacrifice. No one was able to talk her out of it."

I thought about that, then held up the envelopes. "Thank you."

Hager seemed about to say something, probably nit-picky, but stopped. His expression changed.

"You're quite welcome," was all he said.

I turned to leave, intending to head for the library.

"Amram." Soon-Li's voice squawked through the intercom.

"Yes?"

"You need to see this."

"Where are you?"

"The war room."

Hager sighed, most likely at the use of the new name I had given the meeting room. I smirked in the doorway.

"I will be right there."

"Is Christian with you?"

"As a matter of fact, he is."

"He should come too."

"Very well, we will be there shortly." He clicked off the intercom.

"It looks like your reading will have to wait a little longer. Shall we go see what Mrs. Yuan has to show us?"

"Apparently," I said, using my best Hager impression.

Hager and I walked to the conference room, dropping the letters off in my quarters along the way. The whole team was there, pouring over some printouts. They all looked up when we entered. Tira's eyes were red-rimmed. The other two just seemed worn out. Tira walked up to me. I froze, waiting for another attack. Instead, she gave me a hug.

"I'm sorry," she said as she put her arms around me, squeezing me until I thought she would leave marks. "Between poor Morty, Jelena, and... well, I had no right to blame you for any of it."

The words tumbled out of her. I was taken aback and took a second to return the gesture.

"I'm sorry too... for what I said."

After a brief moment, Tira pulled back. She gave me a quick, tentative smile before she wiped a stray tear away and walked back to the table.

Hager cleared his throat. "What have you found?"

"After we... took care of Denise... we gave her room a once over. This was behind the bed."

She pulled up a picture on the main screen. It showed the wall behind Denise's headboard.

A very detailed picture was carved into the sheetrock of the wall. "What is that?" I said.

"It's a schematic," John replied.

"Of what?" Hager asked.

"We believe it's the bomb," Soon-Li said. We both looked open-mouthed at her.

"Holy shit!" I exclaimed.

"Exactly," Soon-Li replied.

Hager shook his head. I had a feeling he was close to saying the same. "How did she do this without Baldemar knowing?" Hager asked.

"We wondered the same," John said. "So, Soon-Li went back through the footage of the kitchen camera to see if there were any clues."

"And you found one, I presume?" Hager asked.

"You could say that," Tira replied. "Play it for them."

Soon-Li looked apprehensive but pulled up the video. It was dated during the time we were traveling upstate. It showed the empty kitchen area. Denise rushed in from the bedroom, grabbed a chair, and dragged it below the camera. She stood on it, and her face filled the screen.

"I don't have much time. He only leaves me alone when no one is around—at least I think so. But he seems to know when I am talking and usually breaks in. I have begun to talk to myself to throw him off, but I think he may be getting wise."

She looked around as though someone might be listening in from the corner of the empty room.

"Maybe it's all in my head, but I can't take any chances. I finished the schematic. At least I can do that much, to make up for the part I've played in this. It's hidden behind the headboard, so he can't see it. As far as I can tell, he can't read my thoughts."

She looked up, searching. "Can you, you little fuck?"

She looked back in the camera.

"But he can see what I see and hear what I hear. And he can make me feel things: pain, fear, loneliness... pleasure. He does it just to amuse himself."

Denise wasn't talking to the camera anymore.

"Sometimes, he will build me up, bring me right to the edge... then flood me with fear... or pain. I can feel his amusement from it... almost hear his laughter. Then he will start all over again."

She looked out into space, not speaking for a few seconds. Then she blinked, looked around, and finally looked back into the camera.

"I don't know much about explosives, but I have an eidetic memory and they needed my help with the nuclear aspects. The morons had the schematics on the table like it didn't matter. Assholes. I don't know when or where they will deploy the thing, but I think it's soon."

She stopped and looked around again, fear etched in her face.

"Shit! I've talked too long! I can feel him coming back. Stop them, please!"

Denise's voice was pure panic as she jumped down from the chair and hurriedly put it back in place. She started to make coffee while singing. The tune made me break out into a cold sweat. 'Somebody's watching Me' by Rockwell.

She had barely gotten into one verse when it all changed.

"No, no, NO! Leave me alone, you little shit! I didn't do anything. Go play with someone else!"

Her eyes went wide, and she gasped. "No, not now."

She turned, heading for the room where she slept, but only made it a step or two before she collapsed. Denise rolled onto her back and pulled her knees together as her eyes rolled up under half-closed lids. She began panting.

"Turn it off," I growled.

Soon-Li stopped the video, switching the display back to the picture of the schematic. No one spoke for several moments. Hager quietly slid into one of the seats. I stood leaning on the table, staring into the wood grain.

"That poor woman." Hager's voice was a near whisper.

"We can't let him get away with this. We can't let her suffering be for nothing." I spoke slowly, practically forcing the words out. No one replied.

There was nothing to say.

Reading schematics was in John and Soon-Li's wheelhouse. Between the two, they came up with a set of instructions to disarm the bomb that the rest of the team memorized. No one knew who would have to perform the actual disarming, so everyone was becoming an expert. John built a mock bomb based on the plans, and we took turns running through the steps. We spent nearly every waking hour reviewing every assumption and every possible scenario, hoping to come up with either a location or a timeline. It had been three straight days and we were no further along. My communication with Jackie at this point was reduced to the occasional text.

I walked into the kitchen for a quick break. Tira was already there, eating a salad while reading the book she had been carrying around. I made myself a sandwich with whatever I could find in the fridge and grabbed a beer. I sat down near her but left space between us. I took a bite and washed it down with the microbrew. I wasn't hungry, but I was getting weak and lightheaded so I powered through.

My mind bounced from subject to subject, but I tried not to engage Tira in conversation. I know how annoying it can be when people keep talking to you while you're reading. Watching her reminded me that I still had not taken the time to read through the rest of my mother's letters. I made a mental commitment to read one tonight before I went to sleep. For the past few days, the intense focus had tapped all my energy levels, and I passed out as soon as my head hit the pillow. As I took another bite, I noticed a piece of paper sticking out of the pages of Tira's book. By the time I finished what was in my mouth, my curiosity got the best of me. "What's the bookmark you're using?"

Tira looked up at me, then tilted the top of the book towards her as if just noticing the paper sticking out.

"I found it in the book."

"Can I see it?"

Tira looked back to the piece of paper and hesitated. She placed the fork in her bowl and wiped her fingers off. Gently, she removed the bookmark and held it out to me. The motions were not lost on me. I put down my sandwich and thoroughly cleaned my hands with a napkin before reaching out for the bookmark. Tira smiled in acknowledgment.

The paper was folded twice and expanded out to the size of a typical desk pad. Folded, it mimicked the standard dimensions of a bookmark. I doubted that anyone would look twice at it. The header said *Scratch Pad*. In the bottom corner was the cartoon of a naked man scratching his right butt cheek. On it was written:

Playlist:
Dirty Pop - NSYNC
Sex Bomb - Tom Jones
The Thanksgiving Song - Adam Sandler
Parade of the Wooden Soldiers - Harry Connick Jr.
Santa Claus is Coming to Town - Bing Crosby
Sleigh Ride - Johnny Mathis
Toy Land - Perry Como
Body Bags - 50 Cent.

"Very eclectic," I said, passing it back.

She took it and slipped it gingerly back in its place.

"What's the book about?"

"It's a romance novel." She smiled as she said it.

"It was the guard's?"

Her smile faded slightly, and she nodded. "He put it in my hands just before he died. The cover was removed. I have a feeling that the other guards would tease him about his taste in books. He kept it wrapped in a handkerchief—not sure why."

"Sweat and oil," I said as I took another bite.

Tira cocked her head at me. I held out a finger as I chewed and swallowed.

"I got a paperback out of a donation box when I was a kid. I think the store removed the front cover and sent it back to the publisher to get credit for not selling it, then donated the book for a tax write-off. Anyway, I remember two things about the book. First, it was great—though I couldn't tell you what it was about. Second, it was long. I spent weeks reading that book whenever I had the chance—on the bus, between classes, during class. I carried it everywhere." I smiled at the memory. "By the time I finished it, the first two pages were completely ruined. The sweat and oil from my skin had soaked into the pages, smudged the writing, and finally caused them to start disintegrating. May I?" I asked, indicating the book.

She saved her place with the bookmark, closed it and handed it to me. I pulled back the handkerchief and examined the book.

"He must love these books. Probably keeps them restored back at his place."

"Why do you say that?"

"Here, look. The glue was sliced cleanly with an Exacto knife, or something like it. The cover was ripped off the book I had, and the spine had a frayed edge. Anyone who takes that much time to remove something plans on returning it to its original condition."

I pushed the book back over to her and returned to my sandwich. "I didn't realize you like books that much."

"My first reaction to the library didn't give you a clue?"

"I thought that was for the wood."

"The what?"

"You know, the wood. The architectural aspects. The allure that hardwood molding and Chesterfield chairs hold for all men."

"So, you figured I was grunting internally and planning to run off to find a glass of scotch and a Cohiba?"

"Pretty much."

"Well, I've got news for you. I had already finished my scotch, and I prefer Monte Cristos."

Tira laughed out loud. We both returned to our lunches smiling.

After a few minutes of silence, Tira said, "Hey, you know what I just realized?"

"What?"

"Tomorrow is Thanksgiving."

I tried to remember what day it was. Failing, I pulled out my phone. "Things have been so crazy, I completely forgot about it."

We were silent again for a few moments.

"I'm finding it really hard to think of things I am thankful for right now," Tira said with a little quiver in her voice.

"Yeah."

I thought back to everyone I had seen killed or critically injured over the last couple of days. The confirmed threat of a dirty bomb being set off somewhere in the Five Boroughs. My friend Father Murphy lying alone in a hospital bed.

"I know what you mean."

Chapter Thirty

THE HOSPITAL CORRIDOR WAS barren at twenty minutes to midnight. The illumination was set to mimic the darkness outside while still providing the minimal lighting needed to see. Sounds were limited to air conditioning, the buzz of fluorescent lights, and the occasional electric floor cleaner being navigated by the late-night crew.

I walked quickly towards Room 348. Walking with an air of purpose prevented me from being stopped by the staff. Whatever amount of good luck I had, held up this time, though I was seriously starting to doubt its existence. I entered the room and moved into the shadowed corner, near the head of the bed. I pulled out a small device and started scanning the room with it, passing it over anything that looked like it could hide a bug. After a few minutes of work, I pocketed it. An uncomfortable-looking chair stood off to the side, and I shifted it closer to the bed.

"Hey, Father," I said in a near whisper. "Happy almost Thanksgiving." His beard was growing shaggy, and his ordinarily full face was sallow. "Looks like you are losing some weight. You'll have to tell me which diet you are on."

I smiled—not at my joke, but at the thought of my friend rolling his eyes at me.

"I'm sorry I haven't been by to visit much. Or at all, really. To say that things are crazy would be an understatement." I sighed loudly. "Mom always said that holidays were for family, Thanksgiving especially so. I remember telling her one time that I liked Christmas better because we got toys. You know what she told me?"

I smiled and shook my head at the memory.

"She said that she loved Christmas because it celebrated the birth of our savior. But Thanksgiving... that was a holiday about family. About being with loved ones and friends. And about acknowledging the good things in your life. Since you are the closest thing I have to family, I couldn't let you be alone today. Well, that and I need some advice. I'm having difficulty connecting with my abilities."

I rubbed the stubble on my face as I brooded. I hadn't had the time to shave, and it itched.

"That would be a nice way of putting it. More accurately, I have no control over them. They pop up only under extreme stress. The first time was when you got shot, but I think you planned for that to happen."

I considered my statement.

"The ability thing, not the getting shot. I don't think you're that stubborn. Oh, by the way, I found a letter from Mom. In her locker of all things. Her necklace too."

I pulled it out and absently played with the charms.

"I don't know, Father. I am not used to having faith in God. My life hasn't exactly been a Disney film. Well, maybe one of the earlier, darker ones. Not a 'grass is greener' story, like The Little Mermaid. Is Bambi too on the nose?"

I thought about it. What was really stopping me? Did I believe in God? That's a loaded question. Let's say that I'm intelligent enough to know that I don't know everything. The world is full of mysterious wonder. If I was pushed, I would have to say yes. I believe in God.

"Huh. Go figure," I said to no-one.

But there was a difference between believing and having faith. Yeah, so, there's a God. Big friggin' whoop. It doesn't mean that he is taking a hand in anything.

I talked to Father Murphy for a while. Well, I talked. He was a good listener. I looked at the clock, which read nearly one in the morning. "Hey, it's official."

I reached into my jacket pocket and pulled out a flask. The other pocket held two collapsible metal shot glasses. I filled each with his favorite, Johnny Walker Blue, then capped the flask and put it away. I raised my glass in his direction.

"Happy Thanksgiving."

I poured half of the shot into my mouth and let it sit there, rolling it around on my tongue. I breathed out slowly through my nose, letting the smoky vapors fill my olfactory senses. You don't shoot Johnny Blue. If there was an eleventh commandment, that would be it. I finally swallowed and savored the warm feeling as it ran down my throat.

"Ahhh. Now that's good scotch."

I finished my drink while blathering on about nothing.

"I better get going. We still have to figure out where the h... heck that bomb is."

I looked at the remaining shot glass, then over at Father Murphy's unconscious form.

"Well, if you're not going to drink this..."

I reached out and took hold of the metal container, my mouth already watering. The amber liquid shimmered, then sloshed as my hand jerked to a stop. I looked down at my arm. Father Murphy's hand was wrapped around my forearm. I glanced over at him, and his eyes were wide open.

"Father!" I leaped up from the chair. "I'll get the nurse."

I tried to move, but the priest held my arm in a grip of iron I didn't think possible. I stopped and looked back. Father Murphy's eyes were hard. He tried to speak but couldn't form the words. With his left hand, he mimed like he was writing something. His right hand still held fast to mine. There was a small notepad and a pen on the bedside table. I handed it over. He started to write, again left-handed.

His increased respiration and pulse made the alarms go off. A nurse bounded into the room.

"What are you doing here? What's going on?" The nurse looked from me to Father Murphy.

"He woke up!" I replied.

The nurse's face took on a no-kidding look until it dawned on her that this patient hadn't been awake for a week. As she made her way over to him, Father Murphy yanked at my hand and shoved the pad in. Then he let go, falling back into the pillows. The sudden release of the old man's grip made me fall back a step. I looked down at the pad and read the scrawled writing.

G 1:27.

I looked from the pad back to the priest, who was now being ministered to by the nurse. She had the unique ability to talk sweetly to him while simultaneously yelling at me. My brain wasn't registering any of the actual words. Father Murphy's eyes were soft now, and he was smiling.

"Is this alcohol?" The nurse accused me in a high-pitched wail as she reached for the shot glass.

"NO!" I jumped and grabbed it before she could dispose of it.

"Sir, this is a hospital, not a bar. You need to leave before I call security."

"How is he?"

"Besides having a drunk freeloader visiting him in the middle of the night, he seems to be doing fine."

"Please, he's the only family I have left."

Hearing this, she cut her speech short but continued to take vitals. "The fact that he is awake is a good sign. Now you really need to go."

"Thank you."

"You're welcome."

"You gonna be okay?" I directed my question to Father Murphy. He nodded once and made a shooing motion.

"Good to have you back." I took his hand in both of mine. His eyes widened as he looked down at his hand, which now held an oral care swab I had dipped into his scotch.

He looked at me with a question on his face.

"Holy water," I said in answer.

A smile split his face as he popped the sponge into his mouth, looking like a kid with a lollipop.

The nurse glanced up, took in the scene and yelled. "Security!"

I finally took the hint and bolted for the door, yelling behind me, "Happy Thanksgiving!"

As I left the room, I caught sight of the nurse trying to grab the oral swab from Father Murphy as he defended it for all his worth. I drained what was left in the shot glass and hoped God would forgive the slight to the eleventh commandment. Smiling, I took the stairs two at a time, leaping the last four or five before each landing.

The next morning, I spread the news that Father Murphy was out of the woods, and everyone's spirits lifted a little. We were all in the war room, digging into possible target sites and dates. At the top of the list was New Year's Eve, due to the number of people that flooded Times Square each year. There were also several food festivals.

As a much-needed break, Tira and John made brunch. We all picked at spinach and mushroom quiche, cakes, bacon, and fruit as we worked. Someone had turned on the Thanksgiving Day Parade and we would occasionally look up as Snoopy, Spiderman, or SpongeBob drifted by. There was a general feeling that we were close and would get our breakthrough any minute now.

"I still say it's got to be New Year's Eve," John said for the eighth time.

"And I still say it is too far away," Tira countered. "The longer they sit on the bomb, the greater the chance we will figure it out."

"From the way Baldemar talked, he didn't seem to think that was a problem," Soon-Li added.

"There are several more important days with more religious significance. In the past, Baldemar has preyed on our religious affiliations in order to send a greater shock wave of grief and outcry," Hager suggested.

John nodded. "Agreed, but any of those days would only affect a portion of the population. Everyone celebrates New Year's."

"Yes, but not everyone celebrates at the same time. Chinese New Year is not until February."

"Okay, but everyone in the U.S. celebrates on December 31st."

"Huh, tell that to Chinatown, in every city."

I smiled as I listened to them go around and around again. On the television, the parade announcer was busy building up dramatic tension.

"Coming up after the break, Frosty the Snowman, the Rockettes, and, later on, the big man himself! Santa Claus comes to town!"

I picked my head up.

"I'm telling you, what bigger event is there than New Year's Eve?" John went on.

Things started to fall into place. I ran through questions in my mind, and each one was answered. "The parade."

"What?" asked John.

The elation that comes with figuring out a problem hammered in my chest, then I quickly realized what this meant. "NO, NO, NO!"

"What is it, Mr. Bateleur?"

"The parade! Don't you get it? What is as big, if not bigger, than New Year's Eve? What is attended by thousands of people from across the country, as well as internationally? What holiday is celebrated by every American, no matter your heritage? What would cause the most grief and the worst ripple around the US? A dirty bomb, going off in one of our biggest cities, during the biggest nationally televised parade of the year."

"Holy shit," Soon-Li said in a flat tone.

Hager didn't even blink.

"But where?" Tira asked.

"The guard was trying to figure out how to tell someone without getting caught."

I grabbed the book that was always at Tira's side, removed the makeshift bookmark, and unfolded it onto the table.

"A list of songs?" Soon-Li asked.

"Not just a list of songs."

I grabbed a pen, underlining specific words:

Playlist:
<u>Dirty</u> Pop, NSYNC
Sex <u>Bomb</u>, Tom Jones
The <u>Thanksgiving</u> Song, Adam Sandler
<u>Parade</u> of the Wooden Soldiers, Harry Connick Jr.
<u>Santa</u> Claus is Coming to Town, Bing Crosby
<u>Sleigh</u> Ride, Johnny Mathis
<u>Toy</u> Land, Perry Como
Body <u>Bags</u>, 50 Cent.

Chapter Thirty-One

"WE HAVE AN HOUR and a half," I said.

"How do you know? It could be rigged to blow now or in twenty minutes," countered John.

"Because," Tira said, smiling at me, "one song choice was a double clue."

"Why do you say that?" asked Hager.

"How about she enlightens you as we go," I said.

We all ran for the stairs

"One, both songs referring to the bomb's location were by Bing Crosby, hinting there was something extra about them. And two, why choose 'Santa Claus Is Coming To Town?' If he was just trying to say Santa's Sleigh, there are so many Santa songs with shorter titles to choose from."

"And the third reason?" Hager asked.

John answered this time. "It causes the biggest impact. He isn't just blowing up New York City, he's blowing up the whole holiday season."

I called Jackie on the way down. It went to voicemail. I said something like, "Happy Thanksgiving. Get out of the city, fast. I'll explain later."

Not my best work, but there was a bit of a time constraint. As I got into my tactical gear, I reached into my pocket and found the paper that Father Murphy had given me.

I yelled so I could be heard by the entire team. "Anyone know what G:127 means?"

"What?" Tira asked.

We all exited our changing rooms at about the same time and

headed for the garage. I handed the note over to Tira as we walked.

"I'd have to say Bible verse if it came from Angus," she said.

"Who?" I asked.

"Angus. Father Murphy's first name." She looked over at me, eyebrows raised high up on her forehead. "How did you not know his first name?"

"I always thought it was..."

"If you say father, I will gag you for the rest of the op."

She handed the paper to Soon-Li. To my surprise, she wore a classic Chinese sword across her back, complete with a cross brace that was carved with a dragon and tied with a long red tassel.

"I agree, but Bible verses are not my area of expertise," Soon-Li said.

John took the paper and looked at it for barely a second before handing it back.

"Genesis 1:27. *So God created man in His own image. In His image He created him; male and female He created them.*"

"Okay," I said. "Not sure what that's supposed to mean."

"I'm sure you will figure it out," Tira said and gave me a little smile.

"Great. If we don't die before then."

As we entered the garage, I walked over to the cars and stood waiting for John to hand me the keys.

"Not that way," John said. "We have just over an hour and no time for traffic."

I turned and saw him pull back a large tarp, uncovering six motorcycles. My smile faded as the number of bikes hit me. I felt a pang of sadness for Jelena, still recovering inside. Trying to clear my mind of worry, I headed for one of the bikes.

"When did you have time to get one for Jelena?"

He gave a big smile. "Yup, I am that good."

Hager walked up and stood next to one of the bikes. His usual baggy, black wool coat had been replaced by a longer, form-fitting version; it had a larger collar and a long vent that ended at his lower back. The front was only buttoned to the sternum, allowing the wearer to straddle a motorcycle. I had to admit, he looked badass.

"Hager, did you want to ride with me? It might get a little hairy."

He answered by sitting on his bike and pulling on his helmet. He lifted his visor and looked at me. I could see that he was smiling by the lift in his eyes. Hager closed the visor, flipped up the large collar, and revved the engine a few times. He popped the clutch and the back tire started spinning, pushing him forward a few feet. He kicked his foot out, planted it on the floor and gunned the engine.

The bike fishtailed and pivoted around his foot—once, twice, three times. The smoke emitting from the burning rubber filled the room. Then, without pause, Hager shot forward toward the open elevator, the two halves of his jacket streaming behind him. At the last second he jerked it to a stop just inside. The back wheel lifted up and swiveled around landing inches from the back of the elevator. We stared after him in open-mouthed shock. Well, everyone except for Soon-Li who wore a satisfied smile.

We serpentined in and out of traffic, dodging cars, bicycles, people, and blockades for the parade. Hager drove like a bat out of hell up Canal Street, moving like nothing I had ever seen before. At one point, he got boxed in, so he popped a wheelie and rode over the car in front of him. Horns blared and people screamed.

"Where is the sleigh now?" Hager asked as he came down off the hood of the car.

Janice's voice came over our headsets. "It's at 70th and Central Park."

"Shit." The sound of Hager cursing nearly made me crash. "I was hoping to get to it before it left Central Park. Now we have to fight the Tainted as well as the NYPD."

"All without hurting any officers or bystanders," John added.

"Quite so. This just became much harder."

"You think the Tainted will be here?" I asked.

"Put it this way," John replied. "If you were moving a big drug stash, would you have guards?"

"Point taken."

Hager led us up Sixth Avenue, the bikes leaning at a steep angle. More horns announced annoyed drivers all around us. Ah, New York.

"Looks like you guys are on the fastest and most direct route, but it also leads you to a head-on collision with the parade," Janice said.

"Look for traffic patterns and parade detours. Guide us around them," Soon-Li said.

"Roger that, boss," Janice responded.

"What is our ETA to rendezvous?" I asked.

"Stand by."

"What's the problem?" Soon-Li asked.

"Still getting used to this tech."

"We went over this."

"Sorry that I don't have a God-given super talent. Got it. At current speed, ETA—fifteen minutes."

"Rendezvous point?" Hager asked.

"59th between Fifth and Sixth."

"That should give us time to get it done," Tira said.

The lights ahead on West Houston changed to yellow. Hager leaned left onto a side road that ran in front of the Second Battalion Fire Department. We zigged in between cars that were forced to screech to a stop as our motorcycles screamed through. We crossed the street, zipped along the Greenstreets walking path, and swung left onto Bedford. The team followed Hager as he weaved in and out of the next few streets. Then he took a hard right onto Seventh and cranked down his accelerator.

The motorcycle's vibration sunk into my abdomen as we opened onto the broader road. At points, we hit speeds that made the dotted white line look solid. Then, seconds later, we'd screech to a halt to avoid traffic, pedestrians, or a combination of both. At about 15th Street, the Tainted began to make their presence known.

A sniper on top of the Walker Tower started laying down fire, but without much success. Hager reached out to grab a light post and whipped himself into a right turn onto 16th, back toward Sixth Avenue. The rest of us struggled to keep up with his pace. The move gave us cover from the shooter, but it also put us in the parade's path—where the police were more in force.

To avoid being easy targets, we were forced to drive up four more blocks. As we crossed 17th Street, the sniper nearly picked me off with a shot that would have made Christopher Kyle proud.

"Shit!" I yelled.

"Christian, are you okay?" Hager asked.

"Yeah, but I felt that one fly by. He's getting closer."

"Maybe it's a she," Soon-Li added.

"Really? You want to highlight my sexist views right now?"

"Just saying."

"Enough, kids. There are too many of us in a row. It's giving them a chance to get lined up. I will take 18th with John and Tira. You and Soon-Li take 19th."

"Acknowledged."

The plan worked. The only casualty was a smart car that was turned into Swiss cheese by a full metal jacket round. But, as far as I was concerned, anyone driving one of those was asking for it.

"Look out!" yelled Tira.

As we crossed 30th, two black SUVs barreled down from the side street. John and I were nearly taken out but managed to avoid disaster. This apparently pissed them off. They started peppering the surrounding road with gunfire.

"I got this," said John through the headset.

He punctuated his statement by locking up his breaks, which screamed in resistance. I watched in my side mirror as John jumped off the bike and ran directly at the head SUV. At the last moment, he jumped going right through the windshield. It veered at high speed and flipped over, causing the trailing truck to crash behind it. Before I was completely out of sight, I saw John climbing out of the window. He dusted himself off.

"Cops set up a roadblock," Janice informed us. "Three blocks down." She guided us around it, which sounded a lot easier than it was.

Our path pissed off several shop owners and nearly killed a family of alley cats. Oh well, happy holidays. The alternate route allowed us to continue unhindered, but it cost us precious minutes.

"New rendezvous point?" Hager asked.

"55th."

"Noted."

We were approaching Times Square at high speed, weaving in and out of traffic. Up ahead, we could see commotion but couldn't determine the cause. As we got closer, we saw Kali walking straight up the middle of the road, knives in both hands. Traffic had come to a full stop. People were scurrying in every direction.

"Soon-Li, Tira, she's yours," Hager ordered.

"Yes, sir," Tira replied.

"With pleasure," Soon-Li added.

The two hit their accelerators. Hager and I split up, each going around the scene in opposite directions. We didn't want to give Kali a chance to pick us off as we passed. Soon-Li stood up on the seat while the bike was still in motion. As Kali came into range, she launched herself into the air so lightly that the bike never wavered. Tira locked her brakes, pulling her bike sideways to a stop, and used the momentum to throw her body into a forward somersault. While in motion, she drew two expandable batons.

The two women landed at virtually the same time, Tira coming up in an extended stance. Soon-Li touched down in front, standing ramrod straight—even a gymnast would cry out in envy. Menace radiated from Tira; even I could feel it from the back of my bike. Kali actually stopped at the force of it. Then all three sprang into action as I drove out of range.

Even with all that was going on—the danger to the city and my new friends, the risk to my own life, the devastation that was about to rain down on us all—I could only think: that was awesome!

We finally reached 54th Street, but all the roads leading to the parade were blocked. A vast number of people were milling around, trying to get a better view. We parked the bikes and ran, reaching the blockade as the sleigh passed by. We paused, trying to get a feeling for how the security at this end of the parade was set up. Several Macy's star balloons followed Santa, just in case anyone forgot who was hosting this massive event. Then came a sea of followers. I assumed they were employees and their families, selected for the honor of closing out the parade. I counted four patrol units on our side of the street and another four on the other side. "Damn, they're not kidding with security," I said.

"And that's not even counting the ESUs positioned on the occasional rooftop," Hager replied.

"The what?"

"Emergency Services Unit on Counter Terrorism."

"ISMS, in my opinion, are not good."

"Excuse me?"

"Forget it."

"Splendid. Focusing on the task at hand, the schematics indicate a remote detonator. We also know that none of the Tainted can trigger it," Hager said.

"That would be direct action, right?"

"Precisely. The Tainted must have some way to watch for a problem. They can set it off as Plan B."

We watched as the crowds started to disperse, trying to get home to their individual celebrations.

"Okay, which cameras would be constantly focused on the rear of the parade?" I asked.

"None, in fact. It's the one float that no one records until the end," Janice said through the com. "Santa can't come to town before he, well, comes to town. That happens at noon. I have been researching since you left."

"What about body cams? The police are lining this route. If they were able to tap into them, they would have a clear view the whole way," I offered.

"They are not transmitting. They record onto a memory card and are downloaded to a docking station at the end of the shift. Plus, look at the body cam's position. The view from a cop's chest would just be row after row of bystanders' backs," Hager countered.

"Okay, what about one of the employees?"

Hager looked at me, realization dawning on us. It had to be an employee. No one else would have a consistent view of the back of the sleigh. It was not a camera we were looking for, but a Converted.

"Okay, Mr. Bateleur, here is what we will do."

Before he could finish, a man grabbed Hager by the shoulder and threw him like a rag doll halfway back down 54th Street, into the windshield of a parked car. The man faced me, evil radiating through him.

Baldemar.

Chapter Thirty-Two

I STARED INTO THE eyes of the most powerful and evil thing on the planet. They were cold blue and astonishingly amused.

"Good morning, Christian, Happy Thanksgiving."

"Fuck you."

Baldemar made a tsk tsk sound and waggled his finger at me. "Hardly complimentary."

"No, you don't get to do that. You can't plant a dirty bomb in my city and then quote *The Princess Bride*. That is not happening!"

"What, were you expecting some creature that has half a face? Or how about a clown?"

"Cut that shit out."

"Listen, I like you."

"Is that supposed to make me feel better?"

"I have been watching you over the past few weeks, and you have grit."

"I'm sorry, what?"

"I think you would make a great addition to the team, but I don't think you are ready yet."

"I've got news for you. I'll never join your team."

"I will make you an offer."

"Sorry, you're not my type."

Baldemar smiled at that. "Get back on your bike and drive out of the city. You still have time to get far enough away. Live to fight another day and all that."

"Very kind of you."

"Think nothing of it."

"Assuming you'll win."

Baldemar smiled again. It made my stomach drop. Hager was quietly making his way back up the street toward us. People were still trying to figure out what was going on. The crash had drawn a small crowd, along with some police.

"So, what do you say? Quit now. Walk away. We can pick up this conversation at another time."

"Why?"

"Why, what?"

"Why are you so intent on me leaving?"

"Isn't it obvious?"

Hager blurred in, going for a tackle. Baldemar moved like lightning. One second he was facing me; the next, Hager was bent over in an armlock.

"Let him go."

"Of course, just go."

"Mr. Bateleur."

I looked down into the older man's eyes. They strained to find mine from his current position.

"Find the triggerman," he said.

"Do so, and I will be forced to beat your leader to death with his own arm."

My eyes never left Hager's. He very subtly winked.

It took all my will to not change my expression as I looked up at Baldemar and said, "Go ahead. I'm getting sick of the Sir John Gielgud act, anyway."

I backed slowly away. Baldemar's face turned dark. "Don't even..."

Hager flipped lightly out of the lock. Baldemar adjusted his grip and twisted, trying to recapture Hager, but he slithered away. They were playing cat and mouse now. While Hager had him distracted, I melted into the surrounding crowd. Cops were moving forward to intervene with the two grappling men. I tried to think of a way to warn them without giving away my position. Nothing was coming to mind, and I doubted they would listen in any case. A hand came down on my shoulder. I grabbed it and was about to spin into a grapple of my own when it pulled back.

"Whoa, whoa. Christian, right?"

I turned around to a familiar-looking face.

"Rich. Tira's brother-in-law," he said by way of explanation.

"Yeah right, sorry. Listen, things are a little crazy right now," I said, trying to dismiss him.

"Yeah, I know. This woman named Janice called. She's a piece of work."

"You have no idea."

"She said Tira told her to call, that you guys may need help. Luckily, I was doing a plain-clothes check. She told me to look for you."

I jerked my head around to face him. "Yes... Yes! Have your men keep everyone back from those two. The collateral damage from that fight could be extreme."

"Are you sure?"

"Positive."

"Okay. I don't like this plan already."

He pulled a radio out of his pocket and gave the instruction—saying that the two were putting on a show and that everyone should be kept well back. No one was to intervene.

"What else?"

"Do you have an ESU on a nearby roof?" Rich glanced at me askance.

"Yeah, why?"

I gave him the rundown of the situation: the bomb, where it was, the triggerman, and the proximity switch. He took the news rather well, meaning he didn't vomit on the spot. He only looked like he was going to.

"We need to evacuate," he said.

"We can't do that. If the triggerman senses something is wrong, he will blow it early."

"Okay, we find him, then evacuate." I shook my head.

"Why not?"

The massive stress was hitting him too fast. He wasn't thinking straight.

"Look around, Lieutenant. Do you think that is a good idea?"

Although fewer people crowded around now that the parade had passed, the sea of humanity was still clearly visible.

"No. That will cause almost as much death as the initial explosion," Rich finally admitted.

"Let's focus on the triggerman. My guess is that he is with one of the families bringing up the rear of the parade. Can you have the spotter check for someone who doesn't look like they're having as much fun as everyone else? Probably nervous. Looking around a lot."

Rich nodded and relayed the information as we started moving towards the parade.

We nearly caught up with it when the radio squawked back. "Possible target acquired. Dead center of the sleigh followers."

The police on either side immediately moved in to apprehend.

"NO!" I exclaimed.

Rich grabbed the radio and nearly screamed into it. "All units, stand down! Do not approach! I repeat, do not approach!"

"Too late," came the reply through the radio. "She's noticed the movement and is getting edgy."

"She?"

"Yeah, old lady, probably close to ninety. In a wheelchair."

"Are you sure?"

"As sure as I can be. We rechecked every face there. She's the only one that fits the profile."

"Okay."

"Lieutenant, there's something else. She looks... wrong."

"Oh shit," I said.

Rich glanced at me and spoke back into the mic. "What do you mean, wrong?"

"It's hard to explain," came the reply. "Several of the team have taken a look. We are all in agreement but cannot describe it better."

"Forget it. She's the one."

"Should we take her out while she is still in range?"

"Shoot a ninety-year-old woman in a wheelchair while she's marching in the fucking Thanksgiving Day parade? Yeah, that won't cause any backlash!"

"Yeah, we didn't think so either."

"You can't shoot her," I interrupted.

"I was just saying that," Rich countered.

"No, I'm saying that will just piss her off." Rich stared at me, dumbfounded.

"So, what do we do?"

"I'm thinking."

Chapter Thirty-Three

I WENT THROUGH A pros and cons list in my head. We knew the bomb's location. We had the schematic on how to disarm it and had identified the trigger woman. I was steps away from both. But we were also running out of time. And the trigger woman was a little old lady in a wheelchair. Oh, and she also happened to be a demon.

"Okay," I said, "I have a really stupid idea."

"Oh, that does not sound good," Rich said.

"We make her push the button."

"What!"

"Well, not to the point where she pushes it, but considers it."

"And then reaches for it," Rich finished.

"Exactly."

"Wow."

"What?"

"That is stupid."

"Yeah, it really is. But I can't think of anything else."

Rich thought for a second. "Yeah, me neither."

"The problem is, we need someone blazingly fast to grab the trigger. I can't do it with any consistency."

As if on cue, a motorcycle engine split the air over the din of the parade, and Tira pulled up. She flipped up her visor.

"Need any help?"

"As a matter of fact, we do," said Rich.

I smiled. "I love it when a plan comes together."

"Really?" Tira said.

"What? I've always wanted to say that."

We brought Tira quickly up to speed. She peered from Rich to me, then back again.

"Oh, this is a stupid plan."

"Okay, if we could all stop calling the plan stupid, we need to get to saving the world."

"Easy, Iron Man, it's only the city," Rich replied.

"He's a downer," I thumbed in the direction of Rich.

"He keeps me grounded. Where is Amram?"

"Fighting Baldemar."

Tira searched around, then located them based on the commotion they were making. She moved toward them, but I grabbed her arm.

"Let go of me! He'll die!"

"So will a crap ton more people if we don't stop that bomb." Her eyes darted back and forth. My grip stayed firm.

"We have fifteen minutes," I said quietly.

She pulled her arm free and walked back toward Rich, wiping at her eyes. Before I joined the two, I looked back toward Hager. He was battling for not just his life, but for the lives of everyone in the city. I nodded to him and moved to put my stupid plan into action.

I stumbled through the small crowd of people holding huge, star-shaped Macy's balloons, doing my best to make a scene. The cops were instructed to allow me to get to the sleigh before intervening. Little Saint Nick—as The Beach Boys liked to refer to it—sat upon a mock roof peak. The reindeer were in a simulated take-off. Dasher and Dancer were airborne. Prancer and Vixen were in mid-leap, and the rest were still grounded. The enormous sack hung precariously, reminiscent of the end of *How the Grinch Stole Christmas*.

As I staggered around, I blurted out, "Happy Thanksgiving," in a very slurred voice. I added to the scene by bumping into people. Plenty of them turned and gave me dirty looks, but no one stopped me. I had attended enough corporate functions with Jackie to understand how the whole dynamic worked. Nobody was going to take a chance stopping me when I could be related to a Senior Vice President. Tira was not supportive of revisiting my drunken maneuver; but, as John Candy said in *Splash*: "if something works for me, I stick with it."

When I reached the sleigh, I started smacking the sack with an open hand.

"Hey, I want my present now. I don't want to wait for Christmas!"

"Nope, no response. She just looks perturbed. You'll need to try harder," Tira said.

"If I try any harder and the cops don't react, she will know something's up."

"Can't be helped. We're losing time."

I growled. I started climbing the back of the sleigh, pulling at the large sack. Although it was secured, it was never intended to be scaled by a two-hundred-pound man. It shifted ominously.

"That did it. She's reaching...aw shit."

"What?"

"Spotter says she's reaching into her shirt. She's got it under her bra, for God's sake."

"Aw, shit." I said. A thought came to me. "Which side?"

"Seriously, Christian?" Tira said.

"Again, any other suggestions are welcome."

"Left."

I wasn't sure what I was going to do. I was still trying to figure it out when a hand grabbed me by the shoulder and pulled me off my perch.

"Christian, what the hell are you doing?" It was Jackie.

"Are you trying to get me fired?!" My mind shot into high gear. "Jackie! Happy Thanksgiving!"

I engulfed her in a big bear hug, which she struggled against. "Christian, what the fuck is wrong with you?"

I grabbed her around the waist with one arm and took her hand with the other. I started gliding around to the music of the band that preceded Santa's arrival.

"Seriously, Christian..."

"Jackie, shut up and listen. Do not react. There is a bomb in that bag of toys."

She inhaled sharply but, to her credit, didn't miss a step. "The woman in the wheelchair has the trigger, and I need to get close to her without alerting her."

I started guiding our dance towards the old lady. "Mrs. Brigham? You're crazy. She wouldn't hurt a fly."

"That's not Mrs. Brigham. She is a demon."

"Oh, come on, you are drunk."

"I wish."

She leaned back and stared into my eyes as we continued our dance. "You're serious."

"I need you to do something for me."

"Okay." Her voice trembled slightly. "I need you to shove me toward her."

"Now?"

"Wait for my signal."

"What's the signal?"

"I think you'll figure it out."

I maneuvered us into position as Jackie badgered me to give her more information.

"Seriously Christian, what's with the cloak and dagger crap? Just tell me what the signal is. This is serious, you moron."

I turned us into position. With a dramatic flair, I grabbed Jackie's ass. Right on cue, she shoved me. I turned while staggering and fell right into old Mrs. Brigham. I quickly found the trigger and pulled it free. A hand gripped my wrist and held it fast. Our faces were inches away from each other; the old woman stared deep past my eyes and into my soul. She grabbed the back of my head with her other hand and pulled me into a kiss. I tried to pull away, but it seemed like I was strapped in place. I felt violated, horror-stricken, and helpless. I could do nothing against the incredible strength of this creature. I almost gagged when she forced her tongue into my mouth.

She finally released my head. I pulled back as far as I could, but she continued to grip the hand that held the detonator. Her smile turned my stomach almost as much as her tongue did. The voice that came from her lips was not human. It sounded as though it resonated from vocal cords which had been sliced and burned until there was little left.

"One last kiss. Thank you and goodbye, Mr. Bateleur."

Her eyes never left mine. My wrist might as well have been locked in cement. The device was a tube with a button on top, covered by a plastic cap. The woman reached up with her other hand, stroking it down one side of my face. Then she reached over to the trigger and flipped back the lid. I panicked, trying to grab it with my free hand. She caught it halfway. Then she forced my fingers closed, extending only my index. She dragged my hands together while I struggled uselessly against her. I was like a child in her grip. I considered dropping the device out of desperation and taking the chance that it would not trigger the bomb. But her grip on my forearm was too strong, and I couldn't move a muscle.

Suddenly, I felt a pull. Then the tube was gone.

The old woman/demon studied at my empty hand, shock plainly on her face. Her expression turned to rage. Grabbing me by the shirt, Mrs. Brigham stood up and kicked the wheelchair off to the side.

She pulled me close to her face. "That was a nice kiss for a Bishop."

She threw me one-handed, and I flew backward toward the sleigh. The thought of protecting myself barely flashed across my mind. Instincts I still did not comprehend kicked in. I felt my skin shift before I rammed into the back of the sleigh. The whole float shook from the impact. I looked up to check the sack and saw Santa teetering. The jolly man looked down at me, so I waved to show him I was okay. The look I got in return could have soured the milk kids left out for him.

"Jeez," I said, while extricating myself from the remains of the float. "Bowl full of jelly, my ass."

My rag doll impression apparently caused a scene. The police rushed in to make a perimeter, pushing everyone away from danger. I heard some people complaining that they had been sitting in the same spot since five AM and were not about to leave before the parade finished. Typical New Yorkers.

I looked back at the demon. Jackie stood between us, clearly in shock.

Tira appeared in front of me. "I'll take care of her. You disarm the bomb."

I felt a momentary bout of hero complex. My whole body screamed to rush to Jackie's aid. I could imagine her rolling her eyes at my idiocy. My inadequacies grated on me. There was no way I could battle a demon. Tira held out the detonator. I took it.

"Right."

I turned to get on it when Santa Claus landed next to us. I moved to see if he was okay until I realized he was still standing. He hadn't fallen, he'd jumped. I was trying to figure out what kind of idiot jumped from the top of a ten-foot float when I got a good look at his face. Santa was a demon.

"Are you friggin' kidding me?" I asked no one.

We put distance between ourselves and the demons, giving us some room to work.

"What the hell do we do?"

"I'm thinking," Tira said.

The two of them were a sight to see. Santa Claus and a ninety-year-old, frail-looking woman, walking with more menace than a black ops team. They were just about on us when I heard the whine of a motorcycle.

"Move the girl," John said over the com.

Before I could decide on an action, Tira blurred. She appeared next to Jackie, threw her over her shoulder in a fireman's carry, and appeared back next to me.

The motorcycle screamed in and skidded to a stop. The back-end whipped around and took out the old woman, flinging her into Santa. John took off his helmet and tossed it aside. He looked at the two demons in a heap, hopped off the bike, and jogged over to us. Tira placed Jackie down next to me. "Are you okay?" I asked.

"Yes, thanks to... Tira I assume?"

"I'm John."

"How about we save the introductions until after we save the city?" I suggested.

The two demons were starting to extricate themselves from each other.

"What do you have left?" Tira asked John.

"Nothing. I got shot, which sucked up most of it."

"Okay," I said. "You're on bomb duty. We're on blocking."

"How are you going to block these things? You still can't control your powers." John pointed out.

"They kick in when I need them most, so we are just going to have to hope that they continue like that."

Tira and I placed ourselves in the path of the demon odd couple. "Christian, be careful."

I looked back at Jackie. "Seriously?"

"Shut up and try not to get killed."

I nodded. "That's better."

The dance began. I choose the Santa demon, figuring the old woman and I had too much of a past; one which would give me nightmares for years to come.

He came thundering at me. I met him halfway, putting my shoulder down and trying to do as much damage as I could using sheer momentum. When I hit him, my shoulder felt like it had just connected with a tree trunk at full speed. The plan worked, for the most part. The problem was that they weren't trying to attack us, just get past us. Santa staggered off course, and even went down to one knee, but didn't stay there long. He got back up and started toward John again.

Cradling my shoulder in pain, I tore off after him with the only move I could think of. I pulled a Kirk. Yes, it was a ridiculous idea worth mocking me for. I ran at Santa full speed, and then jumped and kicked him with both feet. Apart from landing on my hurt shoulder, the move worked astonishingly well. It used the demon's forward momentum and angled it away from John. Santa went cartwheeling, trying to regain his balance. I spared a quick glance toward Tira. She was engaged in a Jiu Jitsu match with the old lady, exchanging grapples and throws onto the cold, hard asphalt.

I clearly needed some enhancements. I reached for the calmness of the lake. It was like experiencing predawn. I could see the light from the sun, but I couldn't bask in its warmth. It was still out of reach.

"Damn." The cursing probably wasn't helping. So far, the only saving grace I had was that my demon seemed to be a little slower than the old woman. That would not help for very long. Little by little, he was getting closer to John.

I got up and ran at the big man, leaping into a flying sidekick to his head. With my heavy boots on, any ordinary man would have been rendered unconscious. Santa went down but shook it off. He stared at me, fury etched on the wrongness of his features. Deciding more was better, I took the opportunity to drive my fist into his upturned face. I might as well have been a five-year-old, for all the damage it did.

"Oh shit."

Santa got up and backhanded me with one fluid motion. I was hit with a baseball bat during an altercation once. Never mind why, let's just say it was a misunderstanding. In any case, this was worse.

As I flew backward, I finally felt my gift kick in. I landed in a heap, right by where John was working. I pulled myself to a standing position.

"How's it going, John?"

"I found it."

"What do you mean, you found it? How many dirty bombs are in there?"

"They wrapped the bomb like a present. It's like trying to find your drink in a sea of red Solo cups!"

"So, get the biggest one!"

"You are a damn genius, Gump."

John heaved a massive package out of the sack, and smaller presents fell out all around it. A couple of quick cuts and the bomb was out in the open.

The big demon was coming again. I reached into the hole my back created. I pulled free a two-by-four and hoisted it like a bat.

"Good luck," I said to John.

"You too," he replied, indicating the stud.

I ran back toward Santa. This was my newest stupid plan—keeping Santa down. The red-suited demon tried to grab me as I got close. He moved so quickly this time that he damn near did. I ducked under his arms just in time, then swung the long piece of wood at the back of his knees. He dropped to the ground in a crawling position. With a quick spin, I swept the board under him and took out his hands, laying the demon flat. From there, I focused on aiming for easy points of failure to keep him on the ground.

"I got the panel off! Oh, shit!"

"What?"

I turned to look at John.

"It looks like the schematic was incomplete. We have sixty seconds left."

"You've got..."

My encouraging words were cut off as Santa grabbed my foot and yanked it out from under me, slamming me straight down to the asphalt. I was still conscious but dizzy, struggling to get my bearings. Then suddenly, I was falling again. At least I thought I was falling. It turns out the demon had flung me into a brick wall. Pain shot through my whole body. I nearly blacked out from it. The waves of agony crashed and ebbed through me.

I forced my eyes to open and found myself all the way across the street. The scene was horrific. In the far distance, the old woman was astride Tira, pummeling her with blows. John wasn't in much better shape, being held up at arm's length by his throat. Apparently, the demon was just going to let the clock run out while watching John struggle against his grip.

Jackie dropped into my vision, blocking the carnage. She was yelling something at me, but I couldn't hear. I closed my eyes to block out my latest failure. Without the noise or the images of our imminent death, there was only calm. The lake coalesced around me. I flopped down cross-legged in the grass. My physical body was shattered. I could sense it, but the pain associated with it was distant. The dragonfly buzzed up and considered me.

"Hey," I said, though I'm not sure why I was talking to a bug. "Looks like I blew it. I tried to push past my inadequacies."

I shook my head. "I'm just not a Bishop."

It continued to hover in front of my face.

"What?"

The dragonfly was nonplussed.

"I'm untrained and unable to use my blessing against two demons. We were doomed from the start. Baldemar was right."

Then something occurred to me. If he was so sure of his plan, why

did he care if I left or not? He was adamant about it. Did it mean
that I had the ability to stop him? For the first time since all of this
began, I started to consider the possibility that I had more to offer
than just sarcasm and a razor-sharp wit. Could I really possess what
was needed to turn the tides? I was no Bishop, no demigod.

"God." I said it out loud. "What did John say again?"

I thought for a second and was able to grab onto it.

*So God created man in His own image; in His image He created him; male
and female He created them.*

"He created us in his own image, flaws and all."

I thought about what Father Murphy had said back in the diner
about the confessional. "Everyone sins, because everyone is flawed."

Was it really that simple? Faith. Not in God, not in Divine gifts, not
even in destiny. Faith in myself. Self-reliance and faith were two very
different things. That realization triggered something in me.

I felt a warmth course through me. My senses buzzed with excite-
ment like a small child on Christmas Eve.

The barrier fell. Dawn now blazed over the horizon, and the light
shone upon me. I reached for it and bathed in its warmth, letting it
fill me. My eyes closed to the blinding light. A purple halo remained
behind my lids as a reminder of its presence. My face tingled as it
soaked in the rays. I felt my ruined body healing itself. It didn't hurt.
There was no pain in this light, only joy. No struggle, just peace.

I opened my eyes again and saw my mother. She stood in front of
me as she did in the little church in upstate New York. She said nothing. Her smile did all the talking. Then she faded. The lake dissolved
and I was once again lying on the sidewalk.

Jackie was still screaming at me, and this time I could hear her.
"Christian, for Christ's sake, get the fuck up!"

I smiled. "You know, we really need to work on your manners."

When I stood up, I was given a gift that I never thought possible.
Jackie was stunned into silence.

Time slowed its march as I walked past her. I still felt some of my
bones knitting, my muscles reattaching, but this was far off in the back
of my mind. I took in the scene again. My joy and peace changed

to rage against the atrocities being committed and toward the evil creatures trying to bring it about.

I moved for the first time with full awareness of what I was doing, entirely in charge of my body. In a blur, I stood in front of the demon that held John. I no longer saw a man; I saw the evil that was inside him. I lifted it by its own throat and reveled in the surprised look it gave me. It dropped my friend back onto his feet. The demon struggled in my grip. Its attempts were as feeble as John's had been. It looked down at me and met my eyes. His soul opened up to me then. It was as plain to me as watching a movie. It laid everything bare. From childhood through to adulthood, I saw his choices, his ups and downs. The chances to do the right thing, and the choice to do the opposite instead. I watched as he scammed the elderly out of their pensions and stole pain killers from hospitals. During desperate times, he robbed liquor stores and left a trail of bodies. The corruption ran deep. This one had a black heart.

I lifted him up higher, standing on the balls of my feet. I focused my rage into a beam of power and aimed it at his chest. With one swift movement, I slammed him into the street. A blinding light burst from him, and he stopped moving.

Stepping up to John, who still struggled to catch his breath, I put a hand on his shoulder. His breathing returned to normal and his eyes shot open regarding me with disbelief.

"Can you stop it?" I asked, nodding towards the bomb.

The timer was dipping below twenty seconds. John tore his eyes away from mine as he reconnected with reality.

"Yeah, I just figured it out before he grabbed me."

His pliers were on the ground. I picked them up and handed them over. Then I turned toward the old woman. It had stopped the attack though was still hunched over, arm positioned for another strike. Tira was about to lose consciousness. The demon rose to her feet, staring me down as though planing all the things it would do. The demon woman blurred toward me, its inhuman movements were jittery as it carved a path for me, her clawed fingers leaving deep gouges in the pavement.

The demon collided with me, and I caught it by the throat in mid-leap. It writhed there, all appendages flailing, trying desperately to reach me. I watched her calmly and smiled. The smile seemed to make it stop. It just stared at me, seething with hatred. I peered deep into the beast—past the flesh, past the demon, down into the soul of the tortured woman who gave herself to evil. Unlike the other, I could sense a possibility for redemption. A spark of hope, and empathy that was not fully extinguished. In there I found her name.

"Isabel," I said quietly.

Her eyes changed and her body calmed, though I could still feel the demon within her writhing.

"You are forgiven."

The creature within her screamed as if thrown into a bonfire; it was a blood-curdling scream that seemed to vibrate around us. The ground shook, causing golden leaves to fall to the ground. Her body went into convulsions, dancing as though from a high voltage current. I laid my hand on her head. The demon screamed louder. I pushed my blessing into her, forcing back the darkness until it exploded out of her in a shock wave.

Isabel's body went still. I changed my grip, cradling the old woman's limp form. She was so thin, I barely felt her in my arms. She looked up at me and smiled as a tear ran down the side of her face. Then she closed her eyes and passed on to the next world.

I carried her body to her wheelchair, removed the blanket that had covered her legs, and spread it out on the ground. I laid her down on it and covered her. Then I looked up to see John staring at me.

"Bomb?" I asked.

It took a minute for him to answer. "Uh, disarmed."

I nodded then went over to check on Tira. She had run out of blessing. She was bleeding with several obvious broken bones. Her face was starting to swell. She looked up at me and tried to talk, but I stopped her. I took her hands, and, for the third time that day, I did the impossible. I healed another person with my gift.

Chapter Thirty-Four

I SAT HEAVILY DOWN next to Tira, exhausted. She regained full consciousness and sat up. John came up to us, still wide-eyed. Jackie came across the street, a bright smile stretching across her face.

"How are you guys feeling?" I asked.

"Not great but much better," Tira answered. "I didn't think I had any blessing left, but I must have. I was so out of it."

"You didn't. I saw you as I was being held up in the air by my throat," John said.

"Well, then how did I heal?"

"You don't remember?" he asked.

"I saw Christian take my hands, then..." She shook her head as the realization dawned on her.

John nodded.

"That's not possible."

John shrugged. "That's how I understood it too."

"Can we talk about this later?" I interrupted. "We need to check on Soon-Li and Hager."

Tira gasped and her eyes went wide.

I got to my feet. "We need to find them, now."

"We are right here, and we are fine, Mr. Bateleur."

We looked up to see both Hager and Soon-Li walking toward us. Hager looked to be limping slightly. Tira leaped up and ran to them, taking Soon-Li in a big hug.

"I can't believe you beat Tai-Fan."

"WHAT?" Hager and John said in unison.

I wasn't following, but I was used to that by now.

"Ha!" Soon-Li laughed. "I tricked my way out and got very lucky."

"You two actually saw Tai-Fan?" John asked.

"How can that be? No one has seen him in a millennium," Hager said, looking over at Soon-Li.

She nodded. "He showed up shortly after we engaged with Kali, who took the opportunity to get away."

Tira wiped a tear away. "Soon-Li ordered me to help with the bomb. I thought for sure she was sacrificing herself."

"Dear Lord." Hager mused.

"It's been a day for the impossible," said John.

"What did you guys deal with?" Soon-Li asked.

"Two demons," Tira said.

"Two?! How did you manage that?"

"Not us," John said, nodding at me.

"What happened with Baldemar?" I asked, trying to change the subject.

"Took off after that flash of light," Soon-Li said. "I got there just in time to witness it."

"What was that?" Hager asked.

"Let's talk about it later," I said. "Right now, we should get out of here."

Jackie insisted on acting as my crutch. I was out of juice and bone tired, so I didn't argue.

The police began to flood in. Rich organized for the bomb and the two bodies to be moved into a truck before the civilians could see. A cover story would be put together, probably one that linked it all to drugs and mobsters. Video footage was sure to get out, but Soon-Li's technical resources would take care of that too.

The vice president in charge of the parade ran up, trying to find out why it wasn't moving. The police let him through the barricades, and Rich did his best to calm him down. That is until he saw his Santa Claus was gone.

"Great, where are we going to get a Santa Claus?"

"Try every street corner for the next month," Rich replied. "Those are not good enough. This marks the official start of the holiday season. Hundreds of kids are waiting for him to show up! Thousands more on TV. I won't be the first exec to not finish the parade!"

An idea popped into my head.

"Do you have an extra suit?"

The executive turned to look at me. "Of course we have a back-up. Why?"

I looked over at Hager.

It took him a second to realize why. When he did, his eyebrows disappeared under his hat.

"Oh, no you don't."

The exec seemed to have just realized Hager's existence and caught on faster.

"Yes, he'll do."

"No!"

"You have to."

"I most certainly do not."

"Why not?"

"Well for one thing, I'm Jewish."

"Great, so am I. So was Jesus as I recall. Danny!"

The exec looked around, and his younger Mini-Me version appeared out of thin air.

"Yes, Mr. Stanwick?"

"Good, there you are. Get the spare suit, would you Danny?"

"On it."

Danny disappeared again and was replaced by a flock of other senior executives.

"We need to make him Santa in five minutes."

Crew members spoke into radios, and makeup artists appeared out of nowhere seconds later. Instructions were given, and people started disrobing Hager.

"Now wait a minute!" Hager yelled.

All motion stopped. He stared daggers at me.

"Mr. Hager," I said softly, causing Amram's eyebrow to once again disappear. "Think of the children. It's only for a few more blocks."

Amram's mouth turned into a thin line. "Oh, very well."

The makeup crew moved forward again, and he held up a hand. "I am quite capable."

"I'm sure you are, Santa," one of them said. "But the suit is complicated, and we have no time."

"Then how about a little privacy at least?"

"Fine. People form a circle!"

A well-muscled black man stepped into the circle to assist. I could no longer see, but I heard Amram's exclamations and could not contain my laughter.

"I hear you laughing out there, Mr. Bateleur."

"Quiet, sugar, and get this shirt off. Dear Lord above, this old man is ripped. Get the padding!"

Jackie, Tira, Soon-Li, John, Rich, and I watched Santa come to town from the VIP seating area. Despite his complaints, Mr. Hager made a great Santa. He wore a smile on his face that Soon-Li said had been acutely missing for the past twenty years. He waved to the children and threw out lollipops. As expected, Jackie got along famously with the team within minutes. Tira was already pumping my friend for embarrassing stories about me, and Jackie had plenty. This was not going to be good.

Jackie turned to me at one point and asked, "What's wrong?"

"Nothing."

"Cut that shit out. You know we don't play that game."

"This is a little bigger than the normal 'my girlfriend is dumping me' issue."

"Yeah, okay?"

"I feel like we lost."

"What do you mean?"

"All the people who died along the way. All the people who suffered from the Tainted's plan. We didn't stop any of them. They all got away. Now we have to start all over again."

"Wow. Way to look at the ass crack of a sunrise."

I turned to look at her.

"Christian, you stopped a dirty bomb from exploding in the middle of the city. We still haven't healed from the last time this city was attacked. Let me ask you something. Who do you think they would have blamed this tragedy on?"

I looked at her in mild shock. "To be honest, I was so busy trying to focus on solving this problem, I hadn't even thought of that."

"Well, frankly Christian, that is unacceptable. The hole that September 11 left in New Yorkers' lives was life changing. Not acknowledging it is an insult to the memories of those that lost their lives that day, and the days that followed."

I only nodded. There was nothing to say.

"My point is, this one incident would have been the catalyst for a larger problem that could have gone on for decades."

I looked over and met Jackie's glare. "Bottom line."

"Pull your head out of your ass and see this for what it is: a win."

She took a pull from her Corona as if to put a period on it. She was right of course. As the parade wrapped up, only one thought plagued me: *where the hell did she get that beer from?*

A few days later, Father Murphy came home from the hospital and stayed as a guest of the Covenant while he fully recovered. I explained how his Bible passage had helped, skipping the whole confrontation with the two demons.

"Took you long enough," he replied.

A few nights later, I sat reading a book in the library, an untouched glass of brandy on the side table. Mr. Hager came in and sat in a high-backed chair next to me.

"Might I have a word, Mr. Bateleur?" I looked up at him.

"Only if you call me by my first name."

"Of course, if you will do the same."

I nodded. "What can I do for you?"

"You have been very tight-lipped concerning the incident."

"Not much to say."

"I disagree. From what John tells me, you dispatched two demons single-handedly."

"I got lucky."

"You did no such thing. You have finally connected with your gift."

"Partially."

"Explain."

I stood up and paced, trying to sort out my jumbled mass of thoughts.

"I did breach a barrier. With it, some abilities were unlocked."

"Some?"

I nodded.

Hager sighed. "If you are going to make me pull every answer from you, this is going to be a very long conversation."

I sat back down.

"I can blur, somewhat. I won't be setting any speed records, and I definitely won't be stopping time again in the near future. I can heal, though I'm not sure to what capacity, or the surrounding circumstances. I have enhanced strength to some limited degree."

"The pothole you left on Sixth Avenue seems to belie that statement."

"That wasn't me, that was the drowning."

"I beg your pardon?"

I looked up, the question plain on my face.

"You said it was the drowning."

"Yeah, so?"

"I assume you mean the exorcism. Why did you call it that?"

"I wouldn't say it was an exorcism."

"You removed an evil spirit from a human vessel. What else would you call it?"

I thought for a second, then shrugged.

"So why a drowning?"

"It's just what popped in my head. Why?"

Hager looked around the room, then finally rested his gaze on me. "You're assuming that no one has ever done it before."

"Someone has? Who?"

Hager looked at his hands. "Jesus."

I stared at him, dumbfounded. "Are you f..."

I didn't stop in deference to Hager's dislike of harsh expletives. I honestly couldn't form the words.

"Do you know the parable?"

I shook my head. I can't say if I was highlighting my lack of knowledge or asking him not to tell me.

"Jesus came by boat to Gerasenes. Immediately upon stepping onto the shore, he was set upon by a man whose spirit was unclean. He ordered the demon out of the man—Legion was its name, for it claimed to be many. It begged Jesus not to cast them away, but instead to let them inhabit a nearby herd of swine. Jesus gave Legion permission to enter the herd; then the swine rushed down the steep bank and into the sea."

Hager made direct eye contact with me before finishing the story. "Where they drowned."

I stood up again and continued my pacing. I glanced back at him. "There's more, isn't there?"

He nodded.

"When they picked up the Santa demon, the hole was full of water."

"That doesn't prove anything, I probably hit a water main."

"That was what Rich's team thought too, except for two important points."

I looked at him, waiting.

"There are no pipes on that side of the road."

He seemed to hesitate, so I pushed. "And the second?"

"It was sea water."

I struggled to connect the dots, but my mind was all over the place. "What does this mean?"

"I don't know. But it is significant."

I let out a long sigh.

"You said you only partially connected with your gift," he continued. "How do you know?"

I shrugged. "It's just a feeling."

"Please explain."

I thought for a moment, trying for the first time to put what I was feeling into words.

"It's like a half-remembered song."

I looked over at him for a sign of understanding but saw that I needed to elaborate.

"Have you ever heard a line, or a few notes put together, and you think: wait that's a song." I paced faster. I looked inward to find that feeling, rolling it around my tongue, getting a taste for it.

"You keep trying to grasp at it. Start from where you think the song begins. Work the parts you know, trying to pull the rest of the song out. But you never quite get it. The song is just out of reach, though you know it's there."

I stopped and looked back at Hager, hoping to find comprehension. What I found instead was astonishment.

"This is what you are feeling now?" he asked tentatively.

"No, that's what I've felt for the past few weeks. Starting at the wedding."

"And now?"

"On Thanksgiving, I made a fatal flaw. As a result, I was lying in the street with my body broken. In the calm before death, with the lives of everyone in the city hanging in the balance, I remembered the first verse."

"Just the first?" I nodded.

"And one other thing. I remember that it is a very long song."

Hager stood up and walked over to me. He placed a hand on my shoulder. It seemed like he was about to say something but didn't. What could he really say to that? He turned and headed for the door.

"Amram?"

He stopped and turned back. "I'm leaving."

I didn't know when I decided this. But, having said the words, it felt right.

"I understand. Though I am disappointed, just as the rest of the Covenant will be. Where will you go?"

"I'm not sure. Travel. Visit the other Covenants. Try to make sense of this whole thing. I would appreciate it if you did not share these details with the other Covenants. At least not yet."

"I will keep it quiet for now, but I will not be able to do so for too long. The meaning behind this may not be completely clear, but it is momentous. It needs to be shared."

I nodded. It was as I expected.

It looked again like he was going to say more but decided against it. "Good luck, Christian."

I looked up at him, swallowing a small lump in my throat. "It's just Chris."

Unworthy Preview

Chapter One

The rain hammered on the roof echoing through the spacious Range Rover Velar. I thought back to the asshole sales agent that had guaranteed me that outside noise would never penetrate the double insulated interior.

"Bullshit," I responded to the blatant lie I was told two months before. I stared out the windshield at the warehouse and shook my head. This was ridiculous.

"What's wrong now, grumpy?"

I looked over at Jelena Torres in the passenger seat. She was short compared to me with long black hair, pronounced eyebrows and full lips.

"I feel stupid."

"More than usual?" Her accent gave her sarcasm a sharp edge. "Look at this." I waved my hand at the windshield.

"What's the matter? Big bad Bishop is afraid of getting a little wet?"

Yup, that's me, Chris Bateleur, Bishop. I'm not sure I really liked the title. After a childhood of playing Dungeons & Dragons, a person with supernatural powers derived from religious connections was a cleric. Period. I'm pushing for a name change.

"The whole scenario. We are sitting in a car, watching a warehouse on the docks in a rainstorm. If I had a sports jacket with rolled-up sleeves, and your hair was teased up to the moon, we would be every eighties cop show."

"What's with your eighties obsession?"

"It's not an obsession, it just happens to be the best decade for movies and music."

"Whatever, old man."

"We are almost the same age."

"Then why are you so crotchety?"

"I'm not…" I took a deep breath, trying to calm myself. "Remind me again why I let you tag along?"

Jelena made an annoyed sound. "Because you need someone to watch your back and keep you out of trouble. Plus, you were going close to Disney and I've been promising Enric a trip." She lifted the book from the armrest between us. "And explain this."

"What? You have a problem with poetry?"

"It's in French, and it's like a thousand years old."

"It's only 16th century."

"Yeah, only." She waggled the book. "Why the hell are you reading this?"

"It was one of Jackie's favorites."

Jelena crossed her arms. "You know she's gay, right?"

"I'm aware."

"Which means she's not having sex with you."

I frowned at her. "I'm not trying to have sex with her."

"The way she looks, everyone is trying to have sex with her. Hell, I'm trying to."

"I'm not." No, seriously, I'm not. Well, not anymore.

"Okay sure. Then why the book?" She held it up as if it were empirical evidence.

"Research. The author had many of the same symptoms as Denise. Also, some poems have similarities with what we know about the Tainted. She was a fan of the poems before all this and made the connection afterwards. I'm trying to see if anything in there makes sense."

"And?"

I adjusted myself in the seat. "I'm hopeful. There is a section in here that hints of a way to kill one of the Tainted."

"I thought that was impossible."

"Not impossible. Just never done before."

Jelena tossed the book in my lap. "Same thing." She pulled up the hood of her parka and took her sniper rifle case from the back seat. She grabbed the door handle, paused and looked back.

"Let me tag along," she said, as if it were the stupidest thing she had ever heard. "Like I gave you a choice." She opened the door. "I'll tell you when I'm in position."

She slammed it closed again, and I cringed.

"It's a new car, you know!" It was my first new car ever. Not counting my work van. An Econovan. One side painted with a tropical scene, the other a frozen tundra. The Miser Brothers were engaged in a pictorial battle on the hood and rear doors. A Luxury car it was not, but thinking about it made me smile. Then I remembered someone else was driving it.

I left Miser Brothers Heating and Cooling behind with the rest of my old life. I hadn't seen Jackie, my childhood best friend, in over a month. She came for a visit shortly after I got settled in Miami. She dragged me along to club after club as if this was her second home. My ears were still ringing from that weekend.

I checked the time on the heads-up display then turned on my coms unit. Killing the ignition, I put my hood up, and got out. "I'm going in."

"I'm not set yet."

"I'll be fine."

The drug dealer I harassed, a guy by the name of Skinny, pointed me toward this warehouse. I assumed the name was ironic based on his keg sized belly. He said this was where the shipments were coming in. If there was a Converted involved, they would be here.

I walked nonchalantly towards the entrance gate, the rain sounding twice as loud slapping against my waterproof hood. The security booth was outside where the guard on duty could check people in before allowing them access to the property. I could have snuck in, but I really didn't feel like playing a muddy version of hide-and-go seek. Instead, I walked up to the booth. The guard opened a little square in the Plexiglas door. Apparently, he wasn't thrilled about the weather, either.

"Yeah?" He was a big guy. Not big as in round, big as in, I pick things up and put them down. The one thing this monster couldn't put down were his arms, which were the size of legs jutting out at an angle. His tone suggested he was not expecting to use the phrase 'sure go right in' anytime soon.

"Hey Arnold, I'm here for the drugs."

"What? What drugs? Ain't no drugs here."

He was obviously not waiting for his big break in acting. "Oh, good they are here. Can you buzz me in?"

I pointed in case he forgot where the button was. He looked down, confused. For a second, I thought he might comply with my request. He came back to himself before fully succumbing to my charms.

"Do I need to come out there?"

"I rather you didn't, Lou. I don't feel like dragging your wet, gargantuan body back into the cramped booth after I knock you on your ass."

It took him a second to figure out that I was insulting him. His face contorted into what I imaged he considered his mad face, but it came across more constipated. The Hulk opened the door to his tiny house, and I reached for my gift. Its soft glow lit the horizon of my mind. Power flowed through me. I became acutely aware of my surroundings, as though someone switched the lights on in a dark room.

The guard took one step out of the booth. I took one step towards him, lashing out with both fists and a lick of power. I struck him in the chest with the fast staccato rhythm of a drumroll. The so closely timed strikes caused his heart to skip a beat and his breath to leave him. His boots hydroplaned on the wet asphalt, and he fell backward into the booth. I leaned in to look at him. The guard, stared at me with wide eyes. He clutched at his chest as he struggled to inhale.

"See, wasn't that easier?"

He looked around the booth for his dignity. "No, that's alright. I've got it."

I grabbed his legs and shifted him into the cramped space. Then I flipped him over. Still struggling to inhale, he gave little resistance as I zip tied his hands in back of him. For good measure, I put on a second one and contemplated my work. I grinned madly as I added another. Then I leaned down next to his head and spoke with a Boston accent.

"He can't with three on him. Not with three."

I added two to his feet and then hog-tied him. I took his radio with me, since that's what they did in the movies and closed the door on him. A decent start to my first solo mission.

The gate was still closed. I didn't know if there was a motion sensor in the warehouse, but I didn't want to take the chance. Plus, it was only like ten feet with barbed wire and not really preventing my entrance. I used some of my gift for an enhanced jump and launched myself over the fence. I misjudged the amount of power needed and sailed a little too high. I landed hard and slipped just like my buddy in the security booth.

"I really need to practice more."

I only hoped that Jelena didn't see it. She would never let me live it down. The ex-Army Ranger, superhero klutz.

"Nice move." I could hear Jelena's laughter over the com.

Oh well. At least I remembered to reinforce my back before I landed on the pavement. No need to waste my reserves on healing. I dusted off my pride and made my way to the warehouse.

It wasn't large compared to many of the others that filled every space around one of Miami's many industrial complexes. In fact, it was its size that made it so inconspicuous. Wedged in between the massive on-line giant, the top selling electronics retailer, and an iron supplier that shipped out more raw materials in one day than I had seen in my entire life.

This short, square, tan building with a low-pitched roof was ringed by a high fence. It could accommodate four tractor trailers, nothing compared to the monolithic buildings its neighbors put up. Those could handle ten times the volume. This one had several skylights but few windows. I saw cameras in strategic locations. Safe to assume they had motion sensors. Even doorbells did these days. They were easy to avoid when I could blur past them. I headed straight for the front door.

In hindsight, this may not have been the best plan. But in my defense, I had just recently come into superhuman powers that I had been wanting to play with. I mean, come on, what kid at heart didn't want to play Superman? Plus, it was night. How many guys could be hanging around in there? I snapped the door handle off, using more pressure than the man of steel would use in the old black and white series. He always made it look like they were made from rock candy. This one might have been made from stale taffy. Maybe not as elegant, but I was in.

I walked into a small reception area with a few rickety chairs, a table, and an empty water cooler. The door on the far side led to a hallway with a row of tiny offices. Each had just enough furniture to not call it empty. In the first office, a window looked in on the reception area. A shotgun leaned up against the folding table just under the window.

"Not very welcoming."

I made my way down the hall to the door that I assumed led into the main warehouse. In the old days, I would have used tech to verify the number of combatants, room layout, egresses, and choke points. Now I just used my gift to enhance my senses. Sound and smells that were muted became amplified. I could make out the sounds of a small group of people in the warehouse. The smells made me wish I knew how to enhance one sense at a time.

"Overwatch, can you see anything in the warehouse?" I asked.

"Negative. There are no windows. Thermals show a group of people but it's hard to distinguish how many, or if they're armed. I suggest backing out until we have more intel."

I considered this but I was getting impatient with our lack of progress. If the stash here was half of what Skinny implied, it would be a big step to cutting off the distribution.

The problem with vanquishing a couple of demons single handedly, it made you cocky.

"I'm gonna take a peek."

"Not a good idea."

I stepped up to the door, putting a light touch on the knob. I tried it and found it unlocked. "It's all good. I'm just gonna sneak around the warehouse and find the drugs before anyone notices me. No sweat." I pushed the door open, and a loud buzzing sounded in the warehouse.

The cat was already out of the bag so I continued in trying to look like I was supposed to be there.

Seven men and a woman stood together in front of two trucks. There was a raised office accessible by a stairway, lit from within though seemingly empty. Otherwise, the warehouse was empty.

All the men carried various assault rifles, or submachine guns, which, thanks to my noisy entrance, were all trained on me. The woman carried no weapon but gave off a more dangerous aura than the men. She looked me up and down and said, "Who the fuck are you?" It wasn't what she said that gave me a little shiver, but the way she said it. She said it lovingly like an entomologist finding a new species of caterpillar. She looked to be Japanese but that was mostly a guess.

"Did you guys not order the stripper?" I casually approached the group of people and tried another excuse. "Would you believe this is a case of a wrong address?"

One goon lifted his rifle, but the woman put a hand on the barrel and lowered it. She leaned forward and whispered in his ear. My senses were in high gear now that I had walked into the middle of a shit storm.

"Only a complete idiot would burst in there without backup." I tried to push Jelena's berating to the background so I could focus on the woman in front of me.

"Right now, he just walked in on people holding guns. If he is a cop and you shoot him, we all become accessories." She cooed the words as she caressed the steel of the rifle.

The man nodded, but she wasn't done yet.

"If you move again without my permission, I will feed you to Krissi."

The goon went three shades paler and the woman smiled ear to ear. I only knew two women with that name and they were both from seventies sitcoms. Neither one filled me with dread. Now if she'd said Alice...

The chastised guard stepped back, and the woman whom I so shrewdly identified as the one in charge approached me like a snake hypnotizing its prey. She performed the catwalk strut so quickly towards me I was amazed she didn't trip. Stopping well into my personal space she scratched a fingernail down my pectoral muscle. "Can I help you?" She looked up at me past long eyelashes.

If the stance was supposed to throw me off, it worked. Almost.

Luckily for me, my sarcasm takes on a life of its own.

"Yeah, I'm looking for the rave. This woman at the bar told me it was here, but now I'm thinking that she was just blowing me off."

"There is obviously," she fanned her fingers out to indicate the surroundings, "no rave here."

I gave the aw-shucks motion with my fist. "I knew it. Only phone numbers on TV start with 555."

"I am sorry for your inconvenience, mister?"

"Tully, Louis Tully."

She hesitated only a second, then continued with her marketing script.

"Mr. Tully," she practically whispered. "I'm afraid we are very busy and I am going to have to ask you to leave."

"You're saying you don't know Krissi?"

All eyes focused on me, some registering shock, others fear. The woman in front of me narrowed hers.

I held my hand up about shoulder height. "Short woman, purple hair, multiple piercings." Everyone relaxed. "And a tattoo on the back of her neck." The playful scratches she had been performing on my chest developed into an annoyed tapping. I estimated my host was at the end of her patience. Time to kick it up a notch. "I think it was a Bishop."

Her eyebrows twitched, letting me know I was in the right place.

But otherwise, the rest of her remained calm. "You know, the chess piece."

No response, at least not to me. She cocked her head as though she was listening to something else. Then she stepped back away from me.

I tried to reengage her. "I'm sorry I didn't catch your name."

Again, no response. No witty banter. No threats. What ever happened to playing to the tropes? She just stood there, staring at me. It was making me kind of uncomfortable. While she was saying nothing, everyone else's body language was giving me all kinds of intel. One guy even chambered a round. Amateur. I didn't think I could hold the staring contest for much longer without saying something cliche.

The door opened to the office and another woman emerged. She was also Japanese, or just really into their Kimonos. The entire outfit was various shades of red. Even her skin tone had a pronounced red tint as though she had bathed in blood. Her hair was divided and twisted into five horns making it appear as if she was wearing a disturbing looking crown. She just stood there at the railing looking down at me. The other woman looked at the newcomer then back at me narrowing her eyes as again though just given information she didn't like.

"Chris, you have incoming. Get out of there. I say again, evac." Jelena said.

I perked up my enhanced hearing again and caught the sounds of pre-breach activity.

I took in the overall scenario, smiled and said, "saved by the bang."

I tried to keep it in, I really did. The breaching charge became a period to my sentence, and a flood of officers poured into the warehouse from different entrances.

"DEA! Everyone on the ground!"

Pandemonium ensued; rifles being waved around, and goons being thrown down on their stomachs. The unnamed woman and I never moved. She never even twitched again. I just smiled down at her. Until we were both dragged to the floor. When everyone had been secured, everything quieted. Footsteps reverberated on the concrete floor echoing around the open space like gun shots.

They came to a stop in front of my face, which was currently pinned to the dirty floor. She started tapping her foot.

I tried to say, "at least someone knows how to play their role," though I'm not sure how much of it got past my smushed face. The owner of the shoes crouched down in front of me and I strained my peripheral vision to get a look. If I wasn't physically restrained, I would have done a double take. Hazel-green eyes stared back at me, framed by wavy black hair. She wore jeans, a gray sports jacket and a white V-neck tee shirt. "Hey there, John Wayne."

I tried to reply, but was, again, prevented. "I just wanted to congratulate you."

Nodding was apparently not an option either.

"You got here just in time for the bust." She did a slow clap, then brushed the hair out of my face. "No, no. Don't speak. We'll talk real soon." She stood up. "Get CSU in here."

I was cuffed and as they lifted me to my feet, giving me the opportunity to take a final look around. The woman in red was gone.

Buy Unworthy to continue the adventure!

Get Exclusive Content From
W. J. Grupe Jr.

If you have enjoyed this book, I would really appreciate if you would leave a rating and a review.

Are you curious about the challenges on the parade route leading to the final battle?

Learn the circumstances around how John's gift was drained. Experience the battle between Soon-Li, Tira, and Kali, and learn how Soon-Li survived a fight with the legendary Tai-Fan.

Get the John McCaw novella and learn how he came to join the New York City Covenant of Bishops.

All are available exclusively on my website:

www.WJGrupeJr.com.

Acknowledgements

This book started in the deep recesses of my brain,
not a good place to begin with,
but before completing its journey needed a host of input.
The first of those is my family. Marie, Kris and Will were my
first sounding boards, and my biggest supporters.
My wife and daughter came up with the title,
my son designed the publishing logo
and everyone helped with the cover.
Thanks to my extended family who constantly encouraged me
along the way, and never once asked me to shut up already about
the damn book.
Thanks to Lawrence Mangine for his help with the military
elements,
my beta readers Marguerite, Jen, and Brian for their insights.
Special thanks to:
my editor Liv Mammone that kept this from being a male chau-
vinist version of a cheep Cinemax late-night movie;
my proofreader Marissa Ciampi who kept the final version
readable;
the gang at The Best Seller Experiment who kept me on task for
fear of a great bollocking;
Mark Stay who acted as my Obi-wan, got me to rewrite the
entire thing in first person, and provided the kick-ass blurb;
and finally
to Sam and Matt, who's inspiring wedding ceremony was the
catalyst for this entire endeavor.

www.ingramcontent.com/pod-product-compliance
Lightning Source LLC
Chambersburg PA
CBHW060526260626
47161CB00003B/774